Lady Franklin
of Russell Square

Lady Franklin of Russell Square

A NOVEL BY
ERIKA BEHRISCH ELCE

Stonehouse Publishing
www.stonehousepublishing.ca
Alberta, Canada

Stonehouse Publishing Inc. is an independent
publishing house, incorporated in 2014.

Cover design and layout by Anne Brown.
Printed in Canada

Stonehouse Publishing would like to thank and acknowledge
the support of the Alberta Government funding for the arts,
through the Alberta Media Fund.

Government

National Library of Canada Cataloguing in Publication Data
Erika Behrisch Elce
Lady Franklin of Russell Square
Novel
IBSN 978-1-988754-07-9

For Jane Beauchamp, aunt and friend

Note on the text

This book is a work of fiction. Though the trajectory of events follows the historical path of the search for Sir John Franklin's missing ships, I have picked and chosen the parts of it that helped me tell the fictional story I wanted to tell. American intervention and the details of some British expeditions are intentionally missing from the plot. I drew extensively on information in *The Times*, the daily paper that followed the search, and on original Admiralty records. For the ease of telling the fictional story, some *Times* articles have been edited and their spelling has been silently corrected. All other material is pure invention.

All *Times* articles are included with permission.

Research contributing to this book was supported by the Social Sciences and Humanities Research Council of Canada.

Editor's Note on the Text

The following collection of documents was discovered in the attic of 21 Bedford Place in 1919, when the building and its neighbour were being joined and renovated. The original discoverer was a charwoman employed during the conversion of Bedford Place from private residence to a portion of the Penn Club, an incarnation it currently enjoys. The documents were glued or written directly into a scrapbook which was found in a wooden packing crate nailed shut with an address slip glued over the side. On the slip was written "For Burning" in what historians recognize as Sophia Cracroft's hand. For the duration of the search for Sir John Franklin, and until the end of Lady Franklin's life, Miss Cracroft was Lady Franklin's constant companion and occasional amanuensis, living with her full time after the marriage of Lady Franklin's step-daughter, Eleanor, in 1849. Though Miss Cracroft and Lady Franklin did not live in Bedford Place after 1849, it had been the home of her childhood and was inhabited by her sister Mary's family, the Simpkinsons, and so the box may have been left there for storage when Lady Franklin resumed her travels after 1857, in order to keep the material private. The box's discovery was recorded in the February, 1920 Club Board minutes, but its storage and whereabouts over the intervening 96 years remained a mystery until 2013, when the Club Executive considered renovating once again in order to accommodate an elevator shaft through the former coal room. In 2014, the box was opened and its contents discovered.

One scrapbook comprises the collection, in octavo format with a stiff card cover, hand-sewn spine, and no back (in order to accommodate additional pages), with documents pasted or written on both sides: occasional newspaper clippings from *The Times* are interspersed between hand-written letters and notes. The scrapbook was given no title. It appears to be Lady Franklin's hand-written correspondence to her absent husband, Sir John Franklin. All the letters appear to be written in Lady Franklin's hand and are from the active years of search for her husband: 1847-1857, after which she recommenced travelling, this time with Miss Cracroft by her side. Each year was given a title page with the year written in large numerals at the top. Likely, none of these letters was ever sent: the transcripts in the scrapbook are the only known copies extant. What is especially remarkable about the collection is that it exists at all: as historians of Sir John and Lady Franklin know, Lady Franklin either redacted or destroyed much of her personal writing, especially during the period of the search. That this collection escaped the flames is probably due at least in part to Miss Cracroft's legendary ingenuity. Since its recent rediscovery, the book has been sold by the Penn Club and purchased by a private Canadian collector. With the kind permission of the scrapbook's owners, the documents are published here in their entirety. For ease of comprehension, spelling errors have been silently corrected, but all punctuation remains original.

Oh my love, how can I be the one to tell you that
you are finally, really, irrevocably dead?

1847

23 May 1847

My dearest love,

Where are you now? If our standing in society were accorded to us for the miles we crossed, I think at this point I would outrank you—much to the consternation of your masters at the Admiralty, I'm sure! Young Eleanor and I are back in London—Bedford Place, no less—from a trip Thomas Cook would have made a fortune from: in no particular order, we've been hither and thither, getting ourselves royally lost in Paris's most beautifully distracting arrondissements and museums, warming ourselves in the Tuscan sun, pushing through the rowdy crowds of Philadelphia and New York. Wherever we went, my love, but especially in America, your name was universally known and your expedition praised—it is a terribly brave thing you are doing, and everyone—myself not least!—admires you dreadfully for it. We had barely to sign the hotel register when people would insist on talking polar this and polar that. You make us proud! Shy Eleanor could hardly hide her blushes, but they were from pride as much as anything. I insisted that they prettified her, but she refused to hear me speak of it.

The voyage back across the Atlantic was not even fretful for a minute—the *Britannia* herself carried us home in not much more than two weeks—and when Ireland swam out to greet us and the ship's sails snapped in the sunshine, I must admit I snickered more than once to think of you slipping around the helm of your frozen *Erebus*, going nowhere, and that not even quickly. I am sure you are longing for a warm—rather than frozen—breeze on your face, and that seductive roll of a moving deck beneath your feet. I tell you it was as beautiful to me during our latest ocean crossing as it always is for you, and in the middle of the Atlantic I raised my sherry glass and called your name to the wind, in hopes of sending you a little zephyr, to let you know I love you. Of course I included your official title, with the name of your ship, so there would be no mistake, but I had to guess at your coordinates. If you don't feel that English kiss on your cheek within the next week, that silly little breeze has got itself lost and wasted my affections on some unsuspecting (but incredibly lucky) whaler. Tant pis! I will save the rest of my kisses for your return, if the Admiralty briss-brass will let me through the guard of honour they are already preparing for you. I know you must see them and see them and see them, and there will be that endless round of dinners and talks, &c. &c., and of course you have every right to them, but my love I am just as hungry for your return as everyone else, and I am decidedly more selfish! When you come home, you come home to *me*.

It has been three weeks since Eleanor and I arrived and settled ourselves in Bedford Place, in the rooms that good sister Mary and her Frank always give us up on the third floor—the same rooms of my girlhood and our own early married days, in between our adventures. I'm happy to be home amongst all the familiar smells and sounds, and toast and tea, but I'll tell you what I really long for. Before I sat down to write this letter, I took our wolf-skin blanket out of the chest where it has lain dormant since your—and our own—departure; I haven't seen it since 1845, and its smell and texture brought back so many wonderful memories of our time underneath it. Remember? I am a schoolgirl, your Desdemona, when it covers me, and you are my adventurous Moor. When I close my eyes and think of your return, what I most long for are my cold feet against your warm thighs, and that endless spinning story that pulls out the weeks and months and years of our mutual absence and knits them together with our breath under the blanket. You will tell me of your life among men and heroes, ice bears and Esquimaux, and I will tremble to hear it.

France and Italy were much the same and still worth the effort, but America waggled its gilded fingers and beckoned to both me and Eleanor, with all its clanking, shiny progress and youthful vigour. In between its grand metropolises (metropoli?) it was, truly, "beautiful with spacious skies," but the cities were surprisingly dirty and cramped for such young places. Manners, too, tend to the uncouth: perhaps it's a "frontier" affectation, but I suspect the people rather enjoy forming their round drawling vowels, and view slapping each other familiarly in the street as an especially "American" gesture of amity, both men and women alike. In spite of our enthusiastic reception in Boston (where we visited the wharf of the Tea Party—dreadful!), New York, and Philadelphia, Eleanor behaved as if she were personally menaced by the gaudy colours of the women's dresses, and hunted by the clop-clop-clop of the men's thick boots. Eleanor is a different girl to what you knew two short years ago. I am sorry to say that your daughter's head turns in several directions, and not just because of the clop-clop! She seems often overwhelmed by crowds, noises, and strangers, and tends to seek out solitude—a difficult proposition in the world's most populous and cultured places—and, perhaps, with one such as me guiding her around. She has been a good little travelling companion, though, and writes to you diligently in her small, girlish script. She won't let me read her notes, and keeps them all in a leather pouch to give you when you arrive. We all expect this to be in the coming months. Don't disappoint! She also writes to her Gell, still lumbering his way towards an English curacy in Van Diemen's Land, and I don't see those letters, either. I'm sure she misses him—it's a long engagement, and they both may be growing tired, though she seems steadfast enough. Her dedication to her monthly letter to you is admirable—she has quite a collection now—and she keeps her spirits up in every expectation of seeing you soon.

Since we've been back at Bedford Place, I have caught her gazing out of the window, and I know it's for listening and watching for the Admiralty cab that would signify your arrival. I don't think she likes staying here among my family and my past; even though you and I were here frequently together, there's not enough of you or her mother here for her taste. I can't really blame her: my girlhood was so very different from hers, and what she sees here I suspect reminds her of all that she is not. She does not willingly fill the fourth place at the bridge table, as you did, so Mary, Frank and I are left playing loo and the like, for spare hairpins. We will shift before long; I will let you know our address as soon as we settle on a new place— or I will let the Admiralty know, for they will be the ones escorting you home. For now, though, the comfort of my old girlhood room, and its proximity to my beloved Russell Square, keeps me here and grateful for the respite. Father is delightful, but with his teeth even longer, his silences are becoming more pronounced. We often read together in the evening, and I find his expostulative snorts just as comforting as ever. Even with all her children throwing themselves about and her husband, Frank, snapping his papers at her, Mary still pours a lovely cup of tea and remains a gracious hostess and an accommodating sister. The two Franks, the Elder and the Younger, we tolerate. Eleanor is always conciliatory. She learned that from you, and gets along well with the Simpkinson children.

You will be pleased to know that in the first week after our return I successfully bullied Eleanor into at least one turn in dear old Russell Square. She suffered the ritual: I could tell by a twitch in her eye, though, that my usual performance in front of the Duke of Bedford's statue embarrassed her. From our past—sometimes lengthy, as I hope you fondly remember—sojourns at Bedford Place, Eleanor knew the words to speak in turn to the Duke, but she mumbled and fretted – a little girl no longer:

O Duke! O Duke! The North wind blasts!
It blasts from North to South! (Eleanor here with arms crossed)

But with your blessing we may pass—
A blessing from your mouth! (words hardly discernible,
mouth mostly closed)
The garden awaits, beyond your plough,
The flowers awake, so cheery! (hands wringing, looking
with horror at the passing omnibus)
We wait upon your blessing now!
Without it, life is dreary! (hands covering face, ears pink)

Do you remember how she used to love the poem? And to beg to re-cite it together, no matter the weather, or crowds? How, arms flung wide, she could hardly be constrained to wait for her line? Well, those days are gone. Mary, too, is busy these days, but I have half a mind to drag her out again, my original co-conspirator; but perhaps discretion is the better part of valour, and I will abandon everyone altogether and simply go out on my own. Pah! I know what you will say, and you are right: I shall leave them to it, abandon Eleanor to her window-gazing, send Mary off to her visiting, and stride forth to salute the Duke myself, reciting Mary's (Eleanor's, your own) lines quietly to myself in counterpoint to my own, proud, sonorific recitation. Imagine, if you will, the majestic scene! The proud Duke on his granite plinth, wrought hand on his giant plough (ahem!), a meek (?) lone woman—sometimes in the rain—saluting and curt-seying beyond the gates, searching closely for a change in the iron man's expression, and then sauntering into the garden with an en-thusiastic wave of thanks. I admit it must look slightly (okay, per-haps a bit more than slightly) ridiculous to passersby, but my dear, worrying about public opinion has never been my strong suit. Even alone, I assure you I do the salute regardless of any milling crowd, and each time, as you yourself admitted the first time I introduced you to the Good Duke all those years ago, I sense his welcome—a calming of his iron brow, a softening in the gesture of his ageless hand. The amount of sherry and port with which my father had plied you in 1825 had nothing to do with your willingness to see the Duke's welcome, absolutely nothing. And besides Mary herself, no-one recited the lines with more earnest intent than you, my love. Shall we do it again, once more? I can see from the lines around the Duke's mouth that he himself is wondering where you are. I tell him you'll be back soon, but he is less convinced now than when you were pushing around the Mediterranean in the *Rainbow*—perhaps because then you beat me home. I sense, too, that he is worried about me: besides you, no man knows me better than the Good Duke. I assure him I am fine, right as rain. He knows, though, that I await your return. I hope you know this, too.

And with that, I leave you with a poem, as I know you have been missing my extemporized rhyming, along with my several other talents.

> *I took a ship across the sea*
> *To meet my lover fair,*
> *But heaving to beneath the lee,*
> *I found he wasn't there!*
> *He'd gone up north, who can tell where,*
> *To see what he could see;*
> *But when he's done his business there,*
> *He'll sail right home to me.*

Your Jane

P.S. Is the monkey still among the living? Has he made a good crew member? Have you taught him to read?

Times *29 May 1847* p8
THE NORTH POLAR EXPEDITION

Some weeks ago a paragraph concerning this expedition, from a Portsmouth journal, made the tour of the newspapers, and was noticed in the *Literary Gazette*. It was to the effect that Dr. Richardson had undertaken to conduct another expedition in search of that under Sir John Franklin and Captain Crozier, and to carry provision and succour to relieve any distress or danger which might have occurred to our brave navigators. As this statement seemed to imply an immediate alarm for their safety, we have deemed it our duty to make the best inquiry into the subject for the sake of satisfying the public mind, and have now the satisfaction to make known the result. It is true that Dr. Richardson, the old companion and sharer in the toils and perils of Arctic discovery, nobly offered to the Admiralty the service of which we have spoken, and that Lord Auckland, feeling the deepest interest in the subject, lost no time in giving it the earliest attention of the board. It was judiciously suggested, by competent and experienced persons who were consulted, that supplies of provisions should be forthwith sent, under the direction of the Hudson's Bay Company, and conveyed through their agency to the northern shores of America, by the Mackenzie and Coppermine rivers, so as to meet and furnish the expedition if it arrived in that region. This has been done, and the stores are in the course of transit to the destined points. It has also been determined that, should nothing be heard from Sir John Franklin in the meantime, Dr. Richardson shall set out next spring upon a similar errand, and so follow up the proceedings already in progress. But we ought to observe, that though these humane and salutary precautions have been adopted no apprehensions are or need yet for a long time be entertained respecting the fate of the expedition. In the first place it was fully provisioned to last till the autumn of 1848, and if, in the prospect of detention by elementary causes, reduced to shorter rations, to the end of that year. It has therefore, wherever it may be at this moment, 18 months' provision in store. In the interim we have two alternatives in view. Within the next few months we may have accounts from Sir J. Franklin overland through the Russian territories; or before the period when Dr. Richardson would start, we might hail the return of the enterprising commander himself and his gallant companions, having achieved a successful termination to their arduous voyage. God grant it may be so; but at all events we repeat that there is not any ground for national alarm, as far as the present consideration is involved. We certainly agree that the measures so promptly adopted by Lord Auckland do honour to his foresight and feelings; and we are sure it would only require a hint from some proper quarter, whose opinion and authority would carry weight, to induce his lordship to take a further step in the event of such intelligence as we have alluded to not being received. We think that his lordship should be prepared with two vessels, to pursue as far as possible the track laid down for the expedition, and carry out every aid that its probable condition might render necessary; for it ought to be remembered that no sufficient overland supplies could be carried to above 160 men, and especially by parties who must themselves encounter great hardships and privations in the attempt to find them. We, however, confide the whole case to the same alacrity and discretion which has already distinguished the Admiralty's proceedings.

3 June 1847

My dearest love,

There is a push-me-pull-me in the papers these days: are we worried? Are we not? The local rags report "great fears," hoping I am sure to boost sales in the short term; *The Times* responds with caution and calm. I offer a ditty in praise of cool heads:

Those who know naught know—no!—not where you keep—
Those who know, ought to know; soundly we sleep.

I keep careful counsel with *The Times* each morning, as per usual, and trust that calmer, intelligent minds (such as mine and Eleanor's) will prevail. You said on leaving Woolwich that we should not expect to hear from you before October, 1847, and so I write these lines just as a record that I fully intend to hold you to account. October it is. In the interim, I write also to apologize to you that we *have* been at least a *little* worried while you've been gone, but, really, this is to be expected. It is nothing out of the ordinary for a wife and daughter to worry for an absent husband and father—not lost, but gone almost, almost too long. It will all seem so terribly pedestrian to you, I'm sure. I've said enough on the matter, and will let it rest. For now.

Your old companion in adversity and adventure, Sir John Richardson, has been to the Admiralty about you. You may already know this from the American papers, if you are reading them wherever you are. I have more private news: he has also been to see me. "Nothing to worry about," he assures me, and yet his own visit belies that statement even as he says it. He has been agitating in official and unofficial circles (i.e., round my tea table in Bedford Place) for action on your behalf. He has volunteered to lead a trek up the mainland, using the caches and forts of the Hudson's Bay Company for shelter and support. He is willing to do this, but, like me, is concerned that if he finds you and all 135 (125? I can't remember how many went out, and who came home early) of your men, he'll have no way of practically helping, with such a small retinue of his own and hardly any provisions. I have discussed the matter of your absence and possible route, and Richardson's trek with the First Lord, Lord Auckland, who actually called at Bedford Place (!!). You should have seen how the Franks goggled as I led him to the third floor parlour, which I am using as our sitting room. Having spoken my mind to Lord Auckland, I was equally gratified to read that my opinions were echoed in the *Literary Gazette* (!!!), that to take Richardson only and a few men to help 135 who may be stuck and getting low on provisions is not to ensure success. Instead, or rather in addition, I suggested that the Admiralty might provide two ships loaded with food, for ships only can provide what's needed: provisions, and space for you and your men, should you need to come home without the poor *Erebus* and *Terror*. It would also keep the H.B.C.'s hands off of you and yours; they have never done you any favours, and likely will be sure to skim their requisite 20 per cent from what Richardson hopes to carry with him. Lord Auckland makes no guarantees, but having heard my case, he has promised to consider it. Two ships after two ships, and trusting to the "alacrity and discretion" of the Admiralty, we hold our collective breaths.

Ever your Jane

10 June 1847

My dearest love,

After careful reflection, I have decided not to write you a travel diary, which I know you generally detest and would read only out of a dual sense of obligation and husbandly resignation. In looking over my diary from America, I am even a little embarrassed by it: it is a stupid, petty little project I can't even bear to open anymore. It will be burned by and by, once the memories start to fade. Now, it is you who captures my attention: I simply can't bear the thought of writing about how the roast beef tastes, or who wore what, or you reading such a ghastly account of our silly experiences while you have been braving the passage. Instead, now that I am settled in London and have what really is far too much time on my hands, I find my inclination is to write you letters, and though I know you won't receive them until you are with me again, I have started using them as a record of my life in anticipation of your triumphant return, which the whole world and especially your wife and daughter anticipate will be shortly, so be quick about it. I now, before you as my witness, pledge to keep each note in order, so you can read them as if the days were passing as they did; and when you are here, I will tuck that wolf-skin blanket under your feet and bring you tea whenever you require it, and you will, when you are done, do the same for me.

Your Jane

P.S. I absolutely trust I will see you soon, my love.

Times *Monday 14 June 1847* p6
SIR JOHN FRANKLIN'S POLAR EXPEDITION

We understand that Dr. King, the medical officer, and for a considerable period the commanding officer, of the overland expedition in search of Sir John Ross, in 1833-4-5, has addressed a letter to Earl Grey, as the principal Secretary of State for the Colonies, volunteering his services in search of Sir John Franklin, who sailed in the spring of 1845, in search of a northwest passage, and has not since been heard of. The plan proposed by Sir John Richardson, and accepted by the Admiralty, does not meet with his approbation, and he has therefore sought of Earl Grey an appointment in search of Sir John Franklin, under the board of which his lordship is the head,—the board under which Dr. King acted in search of Sir John Ross. Dr. King maintains that to save Sir John Franklin's party, comprising 126 men, it would be futile to attempt to convey provision overland to him; and he adduces in support of his opinion that the expedition upon which he was engaged for the relief of Sir John Ross failed in their attempt from the poverty of the country over which they travelled, although in that case it was only contemplated to relieve 23 men. Over that same provisionless country an overland party in search of Sir John Franklin must necessarily pass. Dr. King proposes to the Government to send out one or more vessels laden with provisions next spring to the western land of North Somerset, where he maintains, for several reasons, Sir John Franklin will be found; and at the same time to call upon the Hudson's Bay Fur Company to store up provisions in their trading houses on the Great Slave Lake and the Mackenzie River. He then proposes, in company with any officer the Government may appoint, to be the messenger of such news to Sir John Franklin, and at the same time to take with him Indian guides for the conveyance of that veteran officer and his party, either to the provision stores on the Mackenzie River or the Great Slave Lake, or to the provision vessels, as may appear most desirable. He maintains that he is the only person who has all the requisites for such a journey,—youth, health, great physical strength, and an intimate acquaintance with the country and the Indians. He has placed a heavy responsibility on Earl Grey, for he does not hesitate to state that it is the only plan which can afford that relief to Sir John Franklin which he has a right to expect from the Government. Sir John Franklin, he asserts, should not have sailed in the face of the facts he laid before the late Government; for, to use his own words, it was altogether "impracticable, as the expedition would have to 'take the ice,'—as the pushing through an ice-blocked sea is termed,—in utter ignorance of the extent of its labours, and certainly with no better prospect before it than that which befell Sir J. Ross's party, whose escape from a perilous position of four years' duration was admitted by all to have been almost miraculous." (Letter to Lord Stanley, February 20, 1845.) As it now stands, therefore, it is imperative on the Government to use every means to save the lost party from the death of starvation, or, what is dreadful to contemplate, the necessity of feeding upon each other. Dr. King proclaims aloud against the Government for using secrecy in their scientific pursuits; for it is a fact, that beyond the walls of the Admiralty, not only the route that Sir John Franklin has taken is unknown, but also the means that board are adopting to relieve him. Such a course, he observes, is scarcely worthy the honourable service in which the explorers are engaged.

16 June 1847

My dearest love,

A terrible article has appeared in the paper, with slanderous, impugning remarks hardly fit to print, by that vile soothsayer, Dr. Richard King. I will not upset you with the details, but they prey on every shadowy fear known to women whose husbands disappear into the wilds in search of grander things than daily grub. Actually, I will upset you with the details, as you will know best how to refute them. They portend nothing short of death!

He published a report that was as depressing a sequel as one could wish—instead of the Admiralty sending you to form the nucleus of an iceberg, which he kindly predicted before your departure, he now anticipates your death en masse, with *cannibalism* (!!) thrown in for good measure. He says no to Richardson, no to the Admiralty, no to you, and a resounding *yes* only to himself: according to him, he is the only person who can save you, with "youth, health, great physical strength, and an intimate acquaintance with the country and the Indians," according to the article in *The Times*. I snorted at his resumé, that, in his list of physical attributes (funny, he failed to mention his chin!) he should be advertising what is likely a scandalous intimacy with various members of the native tribes. What on earth would this prove beyond his inability to find an English wife? The man is monstrous, and his ideas about what even the best of humanity becomes in the first breath of danger are anarchic in the extreme. What of leadership? What of authority? If King were in charge, how on earth would the empire ever have been won? The man simply begs for a slap.

Yes: to counteract Dr. King's awful Cassandra prophecies, I have had your friends round to Bedford Place to discuss what might be done. Parry, James Ross, and Richardson are here nearly every day; so regularly do they visit that I can distinguish the sound of each man's particular boot heel on the step before he rings the bell. Mary is kind enough to let them stay as long as they like, and gets us all fed silently up in the library with our maps and books—even the pianoforte falls silent to let us get on with our work, though her daughters have little else to do to fill their days. In a way, I feel like I'm being courted: the gentlemen give me the occasional sidelong glance—Sir James Ross still has those swoony lashes you used to tease him about, in spite of getting a little grey at the temples— and our shoulders brush as we pore over maps together—but of course, it is love for *you* that brings us all together. Indeed, *you* are the damsel being wooed here, the topic of discussion, the big prize for which we all strive. Eleanor simply reads and waits for decisions to be made.

Richardson, who is himself hazed by King's burning arrogance, adjures me to ignore that fatalistic serpent, King, who calls himself a doctor but who spews doom, gloom, and catastrophe as loudly as a Methodist. Still, what he says touches a nerve in the centre of my heart, and I worry—not that you could possibly ever become the monster he imagines, but that there is some truth to the danger you may be in. If only I could hear from you, I could dispel these vile thoughts, and knock King to the corner where he belongs. Richardson blinks at me when I chew my nails and reminds me to repeat the mantra he has taught me, and which we say together to ease the tension: "Sir John knows what he's about." I know it sounds silly and girlish, but it actually does slacken the tightrope on which I tread over this terrible abyss. I see Ross and Parry shift uncomfortably when I say it to myself, but Richardson locks his eyes to mine and I cross that tightrope to the other side, at least for a few moments, to stand beside him and move forward with our plans.

Oh yes: our plans! Richardson hopes to come to you next Spring, with approval from the Admiralty and the support of the Hudson's Bay Company. I spoke to Lord Auckland myself concerning the trip, and he was keen to let the Board have at it—he even visited me again here at Bedford Place, fragile as he was. He is good at the helm; you would do well to keep close to him, as he has science and exploration in the palm of his hand, and wants to advance his good career officers. With your seniority and experience, you could do much under his administration, were you so inclined. But I digress: Richardson will come to you next Spring, full stop. I had wanted to be with him, and then wanted to be in Montreal, but have been convinced to remain here. As Richardson says, I have Eleanor with me, and (though this is what he doesn't say), we both see that she needs fairly active supervision to avoid backsliding into sloth, and at the very least to stop the rooms from bursting at the walls with samplers and watercolours of imagined landscapes. You will have a hard time, my love, deciding *which* bucolic paradise to display from week to week, and you will no longer fit into your favourite reading chair from the sheer volume of antimacassars that have been tatted on your behalf. Never mind! You are used to inconvenience, and I daresay the discomfort of a slight slouch due to excessive lace in front of a roaring fire and a nice cup of tea is nothing compared to frozen ground and hard tack. What with all the creature comforts we have waiting for you, you might even find yourself reminiscing about frozen sheets and the snores of your men before too long.

I've got the chess set all ready, my love. Come home and be amazed at my prowess.

Your Jane

30 June 1847

My dearest love,

Happy summer! London, if you must know, continues to smell like a privy. I imagine that your nose is tickled much the same by the collective halitus of your men, with little possibility of opening a window in your ship. Still, you all eat the same food and you know each other by name, which must build some sympathy into your gaseous exchanges. Here, the smell of thousands of strangers living their lives in close quarters puts us at a disadvantage to each new passerby: we've never laid eyes on each other, but we seem to know the contents of everyone's respective chamber pot. I wonder any of us can reside in town for any length of time. The summer is the worst, even though so much of the town seems to empty out. It's the Thames, that looks like it revels in all of London's refuse floating on and near its surface, erupting in dark boils now and again as the tide mixes with the river.

Eleanor and I stay inside most of the day, where it is slightly cooler—not much sunlight penetrates into Bedford Place even on the brightest days. We spend much time poring over the papers, and are keeping all the references to you from *The Times*. We scan the pages each day for your name, or the names of your ships. It has become a pleasant morning ritual, your two favourite ladies reading together in the light, with our tea and toast. Mary joined us for a time, but as Frank kept calling her away on unknown errands, our pace proved too slow for her. With thoughts of you between us, the paper gives me and Eleanor a connection that even you must admit we all too seldom have. America was much better for us than grey old London.

When E. and I were in our trunks, it was your niece, Sophy Cracroft, who kept the home fires burning, and she has saved the clippings for us of all the papers she could get her hands on in the country, and now we're doing double shifts at the table, searching out current articles as well as rifling through the archives Sophy has collected on our behalf and sent to us in London. We haven't seen her since we returned, but she keeps us apprised of all the world-shattering news from deepest Guernsey in a regular stream of correspondence. Dinners with curates! Fig drying! Trala! From her letters, it seems Sophy's salad days were most decidedly with us in Van Diemen's Land—so in spite of all the troubles we encountered there, at least someone has good memories of the place. I suppose Eleanor's heart is there, too, though Mr. Gell will be returning to England soon enough. As much as Sophy hints at her desire to come to London, there simply is no room for her at Bedford Place, and Eleanor and I keep ourselves perfectly busy as a pair. I'm not sure when we shall see her again.

One clipping from 1845 elicited quite an American hoot from young Eleanor: did you know that when you left England the last time, there was more than one of you? Eleanor held a small article aloft about the poor transport vessel the *Sir John Franklin*, aground in heavy weather at the Mole. The brave little ship does get around, my dear: from Riga to Bristol, and then reports of it from Odessa— just as beyond the limits of the habitable world as you are yourself! To tell the truth, I am not entirely surprised if the universe may have confused you, the barrel-chested man, for that bluff-bowed tub. I hope sincerely that, though the *Sir John Franklin* was detained by strong easterly gales, you yourself experienced smooth sailing and favourable speed. It ran aground—I sincerely hope that you did not! I refuse to treat this as an ill omen (Richard King be damned!), but rather have decided to view it as proof that your path is blessed with good fortune. I feel for the transport, but your shipping twin must accept the heavy burden of fate.

Your Jane

1 August 1847

My dearest love,

Here I am supposed to say thank you for your latest letter, but instead I offer a gentle reminder that I am still waiting. Are you thinking of me? Daily we expect news of you from the west, Esquimalt or Victoria—why is there none? There is nothing in the papers, nor any news from Whitehall. I imagine you are ready for those weeks of recuperation: juleps, fresh cotton, fine linens for the table, new books. Your own library aboard the *Erebus* must be thumbed half to death—perhaps you've even been forced into opening *The Vicar of Wakefield*! How I laughed when I saw that awful novel was still part of the ship's collection. You should have put it right next to the Bible—haha! I imagine you've found some way of getting rid of it by now. I tease, but these are gentle returns to common humanity after all that heroism, no? Are you tired of the legend you are making?

Each afternoon, I sit at tea in Bedford Place and can almost feel you with me; I miss those moments of easy silence between us before the world intruded once more and we went "zigzagging" (as they say in France) off like dragonflies to our various destinations. Lately I have been pulling out our old map of London—do you remember the one? We drew the lines of our travels between your postings, after the happy *Rainbow* and before those forgettable years in Van Diemen's Land, the routes in and out of the City almost soaked through with ink, the Admiralty offices a ruined hole in the fabric, as much as Russell Square, but with those dainty tendrils trailing elegantly off into the countryside, too… I did the same with the map of America Eleanor and I shared, but she wasn't so interested in seeing where she'd been; her fascination was with what was right in front of her. I can appreciate this—she is young and relies on the present—but there is nothing quite so wonderful as to watch your trail unfold like a dark stream across the page, the space literally covered with your passage over it. Actually, there are perhaps two things just as wonderful: to give those places names, and to look forward to where you have yet to go. And you are doing all three, my love! How proud you must be. How proud I already am of you! I cannot wait to see the map you have drawn, to trace your movements through those blank spaces with my finger, all the way around the Horn and straight back to me.

I have started a new map of London—this time it is my own, to accompany these letters.[1] So far I have attended a musical concert in Piccadilly and one *conversazione* in Hampstead, and of course gone several times to Russell Square, the space of which is already weakening under the weight of ink I've applied to it. No matter: I know that lovely shape by heart, and in the crystallized incursions of blue and black ink that expand beyond its borders on the map,

---

[1] Editorial note: This map was not with the collection, and has never been found.

I can still make out my little buds of campion, fighting valiantly against obliteration. I think they are waiting for you, too, as their blooms are lasting longer than usual this season. I think they've even had two blooming sessions, a London miracle.

Yesterday, a sunny day, there were three pigeons on the Duke: one on each shoulder and the largest on his head. I don't need to tell you directly what was happening up there, but the Duke looked ashamed of those impromptu epaulettes and that rather imperfect peer's wig. You should have seen his expression: his mature resignation, his dignified acceptance of his avian burden! He gazed haplessly, stoically above my head, wondering how it had all come to this. "Well," I consoled him, "it's a lesson for the ages." I attempted to shoo them away, but short of throwing a pebble at them, which would have brought a Bobby, they were immovable, so I left them to their triumph, knowing the good Duke would eventually clean himself off, and in a war of attrition, he would emerge triumphant. I gave him what I hope he accepted as a sympathetic wave.

We had some peaches delivered this week, from the Keables, our wonderful old friends from Mortimer—they arrived in a crate loaded with clean straw and ice, ice, ice! They were perfectly firm, and not a bruise on one of them—better than any strawberry—and so cold! You would think peaches were a polar fruit! Eleanor and I, and even Mary, somehow between engagements, each grabbed one and herded ourselves out into the patchy little back garden in Bedford Place that was never cared for by us when we were growing up, where we sat ourselves against the wall, crouching in that one triangle of sun that pushes its way between the buildings in the middle of the afternoon. It was hot and breezeless, a perfectly still moment, and the scent of the peaches pushed the odour of coal and horses, shoeblacking and slops out of our heads for a few precious moments. And without a thought to the work ahead of us on our cuffs or collars, we set to on those peaches, bursting them with our teeth, ripping the skins like carnivores, letting the juice run down our chins. Oh! That tart sweetness was as painful as a first kiss. I watched Eleanor; she had her eyes closed. Mary and I made faces at each other, the peach juice dribbling out the corners of our mouths. We were working ourselves up to a froth of silent hilarity when Eleanor let escape the most profound sigh, her eyes still closed, and murmured,

"How I wish Papa were here!"

Not that you have ever, my love, been a check on my behaviour (and for that I adore you), but Mary and I quickly collected ourselves and attempted to eat the rest of our peaches in dignified silence. "We wish he were here too, Eleanor," I consoled her. Mary snorted—"yes," she said, "for *he* would have known how to eat this peach!" At that, everything devolved back to its original merriment, and even melancholy Eleanor joined in, and you were right there among us, peach juice on your own chin, and your face the funniest and stickiest of all. We couldn't save one for you, but we ate the peach that should have been yours with gusto, taking turns telling lovely stories about you as we shared it between us, bite for bite.

I think if we hear nothing of you and yours by October of this year, I will trace a line on my map from Bedford Place to the Admiralty offices, where I have not been since your grand departure or our return from our own New World adventures. I am loath to go there, suggestive as that visit will be of worry or doubt, of which I am doing my best to feel none. I just want to make sure they are keeping nothing from me—you know those secretive gentlemen in their shored up offices—ever willing to extend a hand in public, but not so eager to offer help behind closed doors. I apologize, my love—they are your employers, and for them I am grateful—they've given us a life we have loved and done well by, but as this is *my* letter, you are forced to sit and read it, and there it is; that's how I feel. Humbug! They have until the end of October next, and then I make my first foray into their territory. Heaven help them if they get in my way, haha! Until then, though, I play.

Your rather sticky Jane

Times *Thursday 9 September 1847* p7
NAVAL INTELLIGENCE

The month of October, 1847, is near at hand, the period named by Captain Sir John Franklin when intelligence might be expected relative to the officers and crews of the Erebus and Terror steam screw propeller vessels, employed in the Arctic expedition; and captains of vessels may now expect to meet with some of the hermetically sealed tin tubes, containing accounts of the vessels written in six different languages, which were to be thrown overboard at certain periods, in the hope that some of them might be picked up by vessels navigating the North Seas.

10 September 1847

My dearest love,

Your friends, as I promised you already, are doing much more than merely thinking of you, and well before you admonished them to; Sir John Richardson is now officially in the planning phase of his trip. An article in *The Times* of a few weeks ago was the cause of deep general alarm—it announced that Richardson was going to "carry provision and succour to relieve any distress or danger which might have occurred to our brave navigators," but this has received a hasty correction: no danger is as yet suspected. As planned, supplies are being sent through the Hudson's Bay Company—may they find a clerk intelligent enough to handle them properly—and Richardson will meet them there. This is the culmination of only a few polite enquiries—Lord Auckland still seems amenable to receiving encouragement from this direction (ahem), and has promised to give the matter the Board's earliest attention.

I have promised Richardson to wait patiently upon my tuffet while he goes off to find you. I promised the same to you, I know. But I can't help but feel that the best place for me to be—where I can do the *most good*—is ultimately by your side, helping you stand if need be, celebrating your many triumphs, and perhaps, helping you mourn your losses. I hope they have been few. I cannot wait patiently, comfortable tuffet or no. Eleanor picks up her embroidery when she feels tense but says little—sometimes I can hear the needle squeaking through the muslin, she pinches it so tightly, but I don't have a taste for those diversions. So instead, I look at the maps, I read your instructions, I pester Richardson for permission to go, and I consider what might be done.

Lord Auckland intends sending out an exploratory ship under Sir James Ross, but I have my suspicions as to Ross's true purpose for accepting the post. I know he was the first choice for the expedition you are on—I've heard the rumours that what stopped him from accepting that one was his sense of obligation to his wife, while the reason you accepted it was the same sense towards yours. The contrast makes me a little ill. I can't hide my hopes for you, but I will never let them say I don't love you, or have never loved you. That you sailed aboard the *Erebus* is proof of how much I do.

Your ever restless Jane

3 November 1847

My dearest love,

Well, the deadline I have given you—indeed, the one you gave yourself—has come and gone, and still no word from you: none of those silly little tin tubes, and nothing more definite, either. I will tell you then what I have done: I have seen Captain Hamilton at Whitehall. I know you will shake your head at my silly woman's worry, but I could not help myself—if I let your silence slide into nothingness, what will I be? Only a wife without a husband, and there are enough of those in the Navy already, thank you very much. If you are not here with me, then someone should know where you are.

The day I went was overcast, the clouds a perfect accompaniment to the grey of the stuff dress I chose for the visit. I projected a sombre earnestness, if I may say so, but I think was not completely successful in hiding my growing anxiety for you. Captain Hamilton was, as always, such a youngster—hurriedly shuffling papers on his desk as I was ushered in, glancing wildly around as if I were his own mother catching him looking at French postcards. We are not so different in age, he and I, but a conversation with me always pushes him to his limit. We've only ever had one or two chance encounters, but you remember that it's ever thus: *yes, madam, no, madam, three bags full, madam!* And now I have extra gravitas by association: I've called it the "Franklin Factor"! Well, it was the same this morning: shuffling pages, sitting up straighter, eyes casting about for an escape route. I blocked the door, and was glad I'd chosen my grey dress, which is understated but accommodates my largest petticoat. Ha!

I won't bore you with the details, but we mutually suffered through a dignified and not very useful conversation before I asked for news. He said he had none! Instead, taking me to the map table over by the window in the anteroom, he showed me your intended route through the Eastern pack—a story I have heard and traced myself countless times before (though infinitely more lovingly). I almost felt he had overstepped personal decorum when his finger traced the same line mine has so many times. I asked about news from the Northwest or Hudson's Bay Company and received a shrug and a point to Norway House. Esquimalt—point. Victoria— point. Montreal—point. Kamtschatka—point. Valparaiso—point. I suggested to him that I had come to his office for reasons other than a geography lesson, at which he held his palms to the ceiling in a gesture of surrender. "Yes, madam."

"Captain Hamilton!" I raised my eyebrows at him and hovered my own hand over the map as his own retreated, "are you telling me that not one person in your limitless and noble institution has heard one official word concerning the whereabouts of my husband?"

The truant schoolboy: "Yes, madam."

"May I ask what you propose to do about it?" I couldn't help it; I felt my hand twitch, a grasping motion over the blank polar space.

This was the question of the moment, and the good Captain actually rose to the challenge—it turns out those nervously shuffled papers were not French postcards, but letters from your old comrades: Sir James Ross, Sir John Richardson, Sir Edward Parry; and from some of your others: Sir George Back, Sir John Ross—all the ones you left behind in 1845, some of whom make up the table at Bedford Place. All had been asked for their opinion as to your whereabouts, though Richardson and Parry never mentioned it to me. It wasn't exactly news, but it was a good indication that more than Eleanor, Richardson and I were thinking of you: men who can do something about it are on your trail, too. Though we don't yet have you actually with us, knowing that the Admiralty has started to stoke its vast administrative engine on your behalf is a balm on my nerves, for now I know there will be news. They send men up the Niger, up the Chaddu, down the Amazon, and to the Great Barrier Reef. A few hundred miles of blank space, with two ships, will hardly be a challenge. I can almost smell you, you are so close.

Your Jane

Times *Saturday 27 November 1847* p8
THE ARCTIC EXPEDITIONS
(From the *Athenaeum*)

We were the first to announce, a few weeks ago, that Government purposed taking immediate steps to send out expeditions in search of Sir John Franklin and his party, and have since been earnest in pressing, on the plea of the public anxiety, that nothing might be omitted or postponed which the real circumstances of the case demanded. We are now enabled to present our readers with the following particulars, which proceed from the highest official authority. Three expeditions will be sent to the Arctic regions; one will be despatched in the course of a few days to Behring's Straits; the second will sail early in the ensuing spring to Baffin's Bay, and will be under the command of Sir James Ross; and the third will consist of an overland expedition to be placed under the direction of Sir John Richardson.

The boats, with their crews of 20 men, belonging to the last named expedition, went out to Hudson's Bay during the late summer, and intelligence of their safe arrival at York Factory and departure for the interior has reached this country. They were to winter at Cumberland-house, or at Saskatchewan River, and as soon as the navigation opens in the spring are to resume their voyage to the Mackenzie River. Sir John Richardson and another officer will leave England, in March next, for Canada; and by travelling in light canoes by the usual route of the fur-traders to the north-west, they hope to overtake the boats in July and with them to reach the Arctic Sea in the beginning of August—with an ample supply of nutritious and solid food. The intention of this party is to track the coast to the eastward of the Mackenzie River—to communicate with the various tribes of Esquimaux, in expectation of gleaning some tidings of the discovery ships—to examine Wollaston Land, and trace, as far as practicable, any inlets that may lead to the north—to erect land-marks on various headlands, with written communications buried underneath—and when the season closes, to repair to winter quarters at Great Bear Lake, by the Copper Mine River. The boat parties to be sent out from the vessel which is to winter within Behring's Straits, together with parties over the ice in the spring, will, it is hoped, fully explore the sea to the westward of the Mackenzie—and, as one of Sir James Ross's ships is to be stationed in Lancaster Sound, at the north end of North Somerset, parties sent out thence, both to the northward and southward, will explore that neighbourhood. Another of Sir James' ships will push on to Banks Land, and in like manner send out exploring parties in every direction; the one sent southwards having the prospect of intersecting Sir John Richardson's route, and—if thought expedient—of communicating with him by the Copper Mine River.

The search of the coast and of Wollaston and Victoria Land will be resumed by Sir John Richardson in the summer of 1849, if necessary.

Notwithstanding that the Admiralty have judged it prudent to make the preparations for these extensive researches, we are gratified at being informed that most of the officers, who, from having acquaintance with the navigation of the Arctic Seas and the intentions of Sir John Franklin, are qualified to judge in the matter, continue to hope that Sir John Franklin has succeeded in passing Behring's Straits. Had his vessels been nipped in the ice, or stopped in Lancaster Sound, he would, we are assured, have returned to England about this time; and as he has not done so they consider it probable that he had succeeded in getting so well to the westward that first year that he has been enabled to clear Behring's Straits this October, in which case they look for tidings, either through Russia or by the Isthmus of Panama, in February next. He had provisions enough, it seems, to enable him to winter this season in the Arctic Sea, if he had penetrated so far to the west as to render the prospect of his passing Behring's Straits next summer such as to make his stay a third winter expedient.

---

30 November 1847

My dearest love,

Well, husband, here is news indeed! There are to be no fewer than *three* expeditions sent out to find you over the coming months: our own Richardson, as promised, overland with the H.B.C., Sir James Ross in two ships through Baffin's Bay in the east, and a third over from the west, through Behring's Straits. Richardson leaves next

March, and is already preparing. He comes by to tell me how long he walks each day, and how much he carries on his back. King is nowhere on the horizon, but he lurks like a goblin in my thoughts. Your own October deadline has passed my love, and I am doing my best to tread lightly on my fears for you. You are not a man to break a promise—you, too, must have felt October pass by with a heavy heart, knowing as you do how many would have marked that date as one set in stone.

She says little about it, but I know that Eleanor longs to marry her Gell, who is supportive as well as patient. I am doing my best to hold that tide back, but love and youth wait for no-one. Come as soon as you can; your daughter is quite grown, and you must come home to fill your role as aging patriarch. You will be the grandest of grandpapas, but the whole process waits on you to give your daughter away.

Your Jane

P.S. In Russell Square today, I composed a poem. It was exceptional, but I have forgotten how it goes. It was about a man in uniform; can you guess whom?

18 December 1847

My dearest love,

I am going frequently to Russell Square these days—not in spite of, but because of the weather. Hard frost already! *The Times* is calling this season the coldest in years—I wonder if you can tell the difference where you are, haha! Surely you are not still taking hourly readings in the sun and the shade. Thinking of it, you haven't any sun right now, have you? In Russell Square, I have delicious solitude, and spread mutiny and dissent wherever possible among the beds. Don't tell anyone! The seed pods of the little poppies brave the wind, and if I can stand still for a few moments without freezing, I can hear the seeds shaking in their cups. I've been cracking them off and shaking the seeds into my gloved hands, and sprinkling them among the other beds as I walk. The rose campion, whose heads look like frilly maids' parasols that are closed for the season, get the same treatment. I can't wait to see where their bright red and pink heads will appear next summer: among the grey lamb's ears, snooty coreopsis, staid Russian sage, and shrinking cinquefoil, expect fuchsia chaos, haha! Imagining the eruptions of blooms in spring fills me with hope that all good things I wish for in this life will eventually come to pass. You yourself are my favourite hardy (crusty) seed in a little ship of hope; you, too, will survive the hard frost of winter and the buffetings of chance, and like the little black kernels lost amongst the gravel of Russell Square, you may also seem infinitesimal in that vast polar expanse, but come spring, as *The Times* and good Richardson tell me, you will, like the campion, make yourself known, and be all the more loved for the hardship you have endured.

The irreproachable Sir James Ross is deep in preparation for the upcoming search expedition, commanding two ships, and they will push their way to the mouth of Wellington Strait. Of course I am glad for the expedition to be planned and nearly underway, but I hope I am the only one who notices the irony in this situation. He was the Admiralty's first choice in 1845, and here he is, stepping forward like the dashing young hero to pull you out of a mess he never would have got into himself—or at least I am sure that is what he thinks. It is what they all think; I can see it in their eyes. The Lords at Whitehall (through the nervous obsequiousness of good Capt Hamilton) have given me the courtesy to tell me privately what they have decided—mostly because I arrive on their doorstep and refuse to leave until they give me something, but with Ross at the helm of the rescue voyage, I am sure I have caught a whiff of re-proach in the air, as if your disappearance into the white emptiness is somehow connected to me. Sir James Ross himself never looked more puffed; I can barely see his pleased face past his expanded chest. He just loves playing the hero, and now his wife's protests come to nothing, now that he has a mission to really get him into the history books. A dashing polar hero rescuing a portly one, and two wives—one considerably younger and more pleasant—twisting their handkerchiefs back home while the world holds its breath. It doesn't get much better than that: it's practically worthy of Dickens, except as of yet there is no death. Please, husband, don't let there be one. I couldn't bear to live a Dickens plot!

Well, so here we are, with James Ross fulfilling his destiny and putting yet another old hero in his scrapbook beside his doddy uncle. Yes, his poor uncle, your crusty old compatriot Sir John, clamours in vain for a ship and a crew, holding to his promise to you to seek you out. We all thought his *sturm und drang* simply too fatalistic, didn't we? I remember your kindly brush-off in 1845 when he pledged himself to find you in the ice. Well—we're not laughing now. He has been pushing since early 1847, before even any of us, myself and Eleanor included, were even worried, and now we all fear he's right. Unlike his nephew, though, he has the grace not to look triumphant in the face of our anxiety. He gave me his arm the last time we met in Whitehall, and I clung to it as if I could hardly stand. In his uniform, he reminded me of you, and he smiled at me with genuine affection. At that moment, I loved him right back, in spite of the smell of whiskey. As per my promise to you, I said nothing to him about it.

We all miss you here, and need your baritone to help with the carols.

Your Jane, singing, as ever, off-key

1848

Times *01 Jan 1848* p5
THE ARCTIC EXPEDITIONS

H.M.S. Plover, which, as we have before stated, is intended to go to the relief of Sir John Franklin and his brave companions, has completed all the necessary preparations, and will sail this day (Saturday), as was originally proposed, from Sheerness. She has been admirably prepared in every respect for this service through the zeal and energy of the dockyard authorities of that place. She will touch at Plymouth on her way down Channel, and we give this final notice to those who may have friends in Sir John Franklyn's expedition, to whom they may wish to have letters conveyed, that they must send them under cover to Lieutenant Moore, of H.M.S Plover, Plymouth, so as to get there before Saturday next.

—Literary Gazette

8 January 1848

My dearest love, and secret husband, Captain "Franklyn,"

This quick note just to say that I have given a letter to Lieutenant Moore of the "Plover," who this very day takes his small supply ship to the west in search of you. Rest assured I have spelled your name correctly!! I have said all I could in my letter, and put in a dried sprig of last fall's late rose campion for good measure—one that Eleanor and I found still in its prime the last time I was able to drag her the few steps to Russell Square—October, I think it was. It was a late bloomer, but aren't all the best ones that way? Isn't that what you have always said to me? Consider it a promise of more springs, summers, and falls to come. It comprises, too, part of a collage we are making of the Russell Square gardens, so please do bring it back with you; it will stay as a gap in the paper until you are here to re-place it. I have written all this to you in the letter Lieutenant Moore will give you, of course, but want to remind you of its importance.

I am off to do something. I am not actually sure what, but feel the need for activity. Brooding doesn't suit. As always, Russell Square beckons, as does poetry:

> *The modest garden of my youth*
> *Now lies a-blanketed in snow,*
> *Yet when I most need truth and ruth,*
> *It's my best place to go.*

> *Small Russell Square is always there*
> *When in my woman's heart I'm low;*
> *Beneath my Duke I take a chair*
> *And let the breezes blow.*

Your Jane

1 February 1848

My dearest love,

1847 has now gone, and I did my very utmost until the year was up, just as you bade me, to imagine for you only triumph. I admit I was not entirely successful, but that nasty Dr. King has a knack for slicing through one's equilibrium. His predictions of starvation and failure still shadow my mood. He's a bastard. I was reminded in a letter by Sophy of an earlier article in *The Athenaeum*, admonishing the worriers that our gallant Franklin, "previous to leaving

Woolwich, desired his officers and crews to inform their friends that they could not expect to hear from them after they entered the ice until the month of October, 1847,—when he trusted they would be successful, and vessels would meet them after accomplishing the objects of their voyage of discovery." She pointed out, too, that this may be the time when you are just getting free—it's still early days yet. I concede the point, but now feel the stirrings of connubial insubordination. I have daily expected a letter from you with a postmark Valparaiso or Esquimalt, to know that in spite of certain difficulties—a broken mast? a case of scurvy? a crushed hull?—you and your men have landed on an inhabited coast, are refitting and resting, and are preparing for the final stormy run back to England. Of course I will allow you as much time as you need to recover, and dare not begrudge you a rest, wherever you might choose to take it, but your silence turns a part of me hollow, red, and raw. I have fulfilled my duty, as you asked me to, in silence. Now it is my turn to speak.

To this end, I have begun my own campaign on your behalf, doing what I know best. I can't abide picking up a pen and writing a single word that does not somehow advance my efforts to find you, a single word that does not somehow bring you closer to me. I can't keep any kind of diary now, even for myself—everything I would write in it would be either tragedy or farce, and neither is palatable to reflection. This morning I finally did burn my American diaries, in the hopes that the energy released by those memories would strengthen my resolve to do what I must do now. To Richardson and Ross I say "godspeed"; to the men who have so far not moved one hateful slippered foot in your direction, I will make myself a burden: if they do not take responsibility for you, they will take responsibility for me, or they will answer for it. And I, how will I help? Not with my own slippered feet, that is assured: no ship will take me, and I know this because I have asked. No: but I will write for you, and urge your case wherever I can. I am still writing *to* you—you are a key witness to my efforts, and these words in this book, which I sew together myself with my incapable but loving hand, page by page, will be our story. The men going north right now look both for you and the tale you can tell. They may well find you, and if that's so, my life will end happily. But if not, you still live in these secret pages, this explorer's diary that will never endure the clinical eye of a Barrow or a Murray, but will be our own language, our own story, our own words. My own husband.

Your first lieutenant on land,
Jane

Times *20 March 1848* p3
ARCTIC EXPEDITIONS

We have noticed, from time to time, the active and judicious measures which have been adopted by the Admiralty, with a view to render assistance to Sir John Franklin's expedition, which sailed in the spring of 1845, for the purpose of exploring the north-west passage into the Pacific, and of obtaining a series of magnetic observations, required to complete the set which had been obtained from every other part of the globe. In June last Mr. Bell, one of the most active and intelligent of the chief traders of the Hudson's Bay Company, proceeded in their ships to York factory, in temporary command of the four boats belonging to the Arctic searching expedition, accompanied by 15 picked men of the sappers and miners, and five seamen, forming part of an expedition to be fitted out under the command of Sir John Richardson, who (accompanied by Mr. Rae) is now on the eve of departure to join the boats, for the purpose of proceeding to the shores of the Arctic Sea. Mr. Bell's party were ordered to advance in the spring of this year to Fort Simpson, on the Mackenzie River, to be there joined by Sir John Richardson, having wintered, probably, at Cumberland-house, which was the furthest point the party expected to attain before the closing of the navigation. The boats were amply stored with provisions, winter clothing, &c. and a fifth boat, similarly stored, will be furnished by the Hudson's Bay Company, who have displayed the most laudable desire throughout to render every assistance in their power to carry out the intentions of the Admiralty. Sir James Ross, whose whole life may be said to have been passed in the Arctic and Antarctic Seas, is now actively employed in fitting out the Enterprise and Investigator, the latter under command of Captain Bird, an experienced officer on the Polar voyages. They will sail early in May to Baffin's Bay, and through Lancaster Sound to the westward, sending out their boats and steam launches to different points of the coast, and examining the Wellington Channel, through which it is not improbable the Erebus and Terror may have proceeded, with a view of making the passage to the northward of the Parry group. Commander Moore, also an experienced officer in the navigation of the icy seas, of Her Majesty's ship Plover, who is now on his way round the Horn, by Behring's Straits, where he will be joined by Captain Kellett, of Her Majesty's ship

Herald, has been ordered to proceed to the eastward in his boats, along the northern shores of America, as far as the Mackenzie River. It may confidently be hoped, under Divine Providence, that these admirable arrangements may be crowned with success, should Sir John Franklin's expedition have got into difficulty. A reward of upwards of 100 guineas has also been offered to any of the whale ships which may bring information of the expedition, the actual amount of the reward depending upon the authenticity and value of the information conveyed. They have also been invited to look out for any of the copper cylinders which Sir John Franklin was directed to throw overboard daily on reaching 65 deg.

north. Although these precautions are most proper and creditable to the authorities, we do not ourselves feel any unnecessary anxiety as to the fate of the ships. That they may have been hampered, as others have been, is very probable, and is almost a necessary contingency in the navigations of an icy sea, but we place great hope in the *materiel* as well as *personnel* of the expedition, for ships better adapted for the service, better equipped in all respects, or better officered and manned, never left the shores of England on any of those arduous voyages of discovery which have helped to raise the character of the British seaman in the eyes of every enlightened nation in the world.

---

23 March 1848

My dearest love,

I have determined, with Sophy, to travel to Hull to visit the whalers myself. Sophy is desperate to escape even for a few days from Guernsey, and frankly I feel the same about London. I am leaving Eleanor with the young Simpkinsons, where she much prefers to be, and will be joined by Sophy on the road north. Bedford Place is becoming a haven to Eleanor, especially the room that her two cousins share. She is rarely out of it these days, except to climb into the carriage or to emerge for breakfast. Sophy, who did come in January for a shortish stay (she slept in my anteroom on the divan) has been somewhat subdued of late herself, perhaps wondering what connections might be in danger of being severed had she accepted Captain Crozier's proposal. We don't speak of such things, but you—and possibly Capt. C.—seemed often between us as we visited. The trip will do her good, as it will do me: it takes us both away from the pressures of home for a time. You may tease me, an old woman, visiting the whalers in my black stuff dress and quilted bonnet, seeking those rough men out for conversation. Rough they may be, but no less moral or merciful in the cause of humanity: they are as British as the rest of us, too, and must share the anxiety of their nation when a hero goes missing. You can't deny, my husband, that you now hold that title: you are a hero, a champion of progress, a Prometheus of the frozen wastes! So I dress the part and speak the words and, simply, request their help. It doesn't hurt to have a broadsheet that Sophy will help me distribute, advertising the reward I am offering of Two thousand pounds to be given to the party who will find you and offer you relief. The Admiralty has generously offered 100 guineas for the same. Please draw your own conclusions. I have the perfect title for *The Times* article that might announce the news:

Lady Franklin Launches Broadside!

Though I doubt the gentlemen at Whitehall would see the humour in it, or sense the bite. I would leave the adjudication of this reward to you, but Sir Francis Beaufort, Sir Edward Parry, and the Whale ship owner Mr. Thomas Ward, from Hull, have generously agreed to act as referees. I am certainly no Elizabeth, but I am off to deliver my speech to the troops. May the odds be not nearly so long, and luck be as bright on our side. They are our loving people and loyal subjects.

Your Jane

Times *28 March 1848* p5

THE ARCTIC EXPEDITION

Lady Franklin has offered a reward of 2,000*l*. with a view of inducing any whaling ship which resorts to Davis's Straits or Baffin's Bay, to make search for the expedition under the command of Sir John Franklin, respecting whom the greatest anxiety has for some time past been manifested, no tidings having reached England with regard to the progress of the expedition or the safety of those who compose it. Her ladyship's notice stipulates that search shall be made in those parts which are not in the scope of the expedition sent out by Government; and that the 2,000*l*. is to be divided as follows: 1,000l. between the owners, captain, officers, and crew of any ship which shall depart from the usual fishing grounds for the purpose of exploring Prince Regent's Inlet, Admiralty Inlet, Jones's Sound, or Smith's Sound, provided such ship, finding the expedition under Sir John Franklin in distress, shall make up to and afford it relief; and 1,000*l*. to be divided amongst the officers, owners, and crew of any ship which shall at an early period of the whaling season make extra exertions for the above object, and, in the event of discovering the expedition, should such assistance be required, bring Sir John Franklin and his party to England. Her ladyship intimates that, in order that there may be no misunderstanding about the rewards, the matter shall be referred to the following gentlemen, whose decision shall be final, those gentlemen having kindly consented to act as referees in the matter: —Admiral Beaufort, Captain Sir William Edward Parry, and Mr. Ward.

---

15 April 1848

My dearest love,

We are home from Scotland with a carpet bag full of jumpers and single malt, which I will share with you if you insist, but you'd better be home soon if you expect any to be left. The whalers were just as they should be: rough and polite, gargantuan bodies holding tender women's hearts. They saw their own wives and daughters in me and Sophy, who looked the part to perfection. We heard some rather shocking sea shanties, but know that this portends nothing.

Sophy is back in Guernsey; we actually had a pleasant time together. She is a good conversationalist, willing to listen and respond with an enthusiasm which Eleanor somewhat lacks. It was good to see her.

Jane

1 May 1848

My dearest love,

I've never been one to doubt myself, but your continued absence is making me feel neglected. I! the woman whom you've let roam on the longest leash possible, now wants it pulled considerably tighter. Trust me, I am aware of the irony of my position, though I wouldn't mind if you were here to point it out to me. Many probably long to call me a hypocrite. But tell me, as I am beginning to wonder: what exactly is it that you want up north? What precisely are you missing at home? I suppose the more accurate question in my current line of thinking, is whom? It can't help but rankle that I have lost out to an iceberg, that you would rather sidle up to her cold, sharp sides than my own, I hope more welcoming, arms. Was I mistaken in the kind of lover I took you for? I am not too old or too distant to ask. I know you were affectionate with your Miss Porden—don't be embarrassed; she as much as told me so in our carriage rides, and you could tell just by looking at her, really. And we, my dear, never exactly stood on ceremony with each other. But no matter the heat that you and I may have generated on those sunny afternoons, even in the blasting seasons of Corfu and Hobart, there was always that frozen corner, wasn't there? The frigid woman in blue, beckoning you with her ghastly fingers. She must have been standing behind me all the time. It explains that look you used to get as you gazed past my shoulder in your final moments. It was me you were with, but not me you saw in your moments of truth. I used to think it was your Eleanor, actually, but now I know it was her, the Blue Woman. I feel a little embarrassed for myself.

Do you remember that rainy afternoon in Bedford Place, after you'd been asked by that conniving opportunist Sir John Barrow to write your opinions on trying the passage one more time? In his blind sense of purpose he hadn't even asked you if you'd wanted to go—he merely wanted your opinion on the feasibility of such a scheme, with a plan to send younger, stronger men—never considered how such a request would devour your old sailor's heart. Or maybe he did—maybe he knew that you would sit up taller and imagine yourself at the helm, clear your throat and put your name in the hat—maybe he knew he could catch you without even trying. If that's true, I am even more than a little embarrassed for myself—I would rather lose to an iceberg than to doddering Sir John Barrow.

I knew what Barrow's letter was about the second it arrived, you know: the telltale broad arrow on the envelope, Barrow's distinctive arrogant hand—even the colour of the paper looked like polar ice. I didn't have to read it to know I hated what it contained. You don't know this—I'll tell you now—I read your answer. You left it on the desk and took a turn in the library—you must have been excited by the idea of it, to get up and walk away from a letter like that. As you fluffed your coat tails and puffed your chest downstairs, I picked it up and learned your secret. I knew then that I had one chance to win you over. And when you came back and sat by the window with me, watching the rain streak down the glass—do you remember? I stood behind you, hands on your shoulders, breathing in your ear with all the feminine virtues this dowdy old adventuress could muster—you took my hands like you always do, and we started our usual routine:

> *You are leaving me again, aren't you?* (my arms twining around your neck)
> *Only because you're already gone.* (you catching my hands in yours)
> *Where to this time?* (a slight pinch on the wattle)
> *Where to this time?* (your head nestling against my bosom)
> *I promise to come back!* (me twisting forward to look you lovingly in the eye)…

Well—you were *supposed* to say, "I promise to be here," and look at me right back, but you said nothing. Nothing! And I knew you were thinking about *there* or *her*—it's funny how *there* contains *her*, and *her* is always already *there*—as if there really *is* someone waiting for you the minute you get onto the ice. And so I tried my next trick—do you remember? a last ditch, Dickensian appeal to pathos: "I suppose you don't want this old shoe anymore..."—and what did I get? Not the assurance I usually got from you, my love, that this old shoe was worth keeping around, still worth putting on now and again—no. It hurts to write it, but I remember your silence, even if you don't. It nearly broke me, to see all that desire in your eyes to leave, but when you could not play our game, I knew you had to go. Even at that moment, before you'd even been considered for captain, I knew you were already gone. Come to think of it, *her* is in the middle of *here*, too. You were never mine. Now I am even more embarrassed.

Men will condemn me for letting you go—they will blame me, a woman who should have kept her portly, kind, *59-year-old husband* at home. I have done no less than your first bride Eleanor did all those years ago, but this time I fear that you will not come back, and that will be my legacy.

Maybe you have never truly been mine, but no matter where you are, I will always be,

Your Jane

8 June 1848

My dearest love,

It is summer here, and the Russell Square garden beyond the Duke is all vibrant decision and fecund will: poppies! rose campion! Not pulled up in a frenzy of order and control, as I considered inevitable, but left to flourish wherever their renegade seeds have found purchase! This is news indeed. A new bank of roses surrounds the fountain, and the new gardener, a Mr. Rowe I see from the sign on his shed door, is retraining the lime-tree bower, the one that was so tragically blighted before we left for Van Diemen's Land. Much has changed, but not enough that you would not recognize it; some, like the lime-tree bower, has been returned, and wonderfully so. The benches are in the same places, and I visit the original bank of campion whenever I can, as well as the fledgling new colonies struggling forth. All that tiny assertive fuchsia unrepentant in the middle of granite-grey London—it gives me strength to bear the world in your absence! It is popping up in the most unusual places this season—hiding under the dogwood hedgerow, peeping from among the pinks, and puts each of its companions to shame. I suspect Mr. Rowe of aiding and abetting its incursions into the other beds as much as I have, but who am I to complain? It is a conspiracy I welcome. I have not seen the man yet, but suspect that he will be someone after our own hearts.

I'm not sure how long we will stay with Mary at Bedford Place: the Simpkinsons are active entertainers and the house is full of young people, and it's a world I would not have Eleanor exposed to overmuch, and we will not have Sophy with us, who turns strident with so much company and for whom there simply is no room. Even now in her letters, Sophy sounds despondent, and already reminiscent of our few days in Northern Scotland in March. Guernsey must feel like being buried alive. I suspect, also, that she is still mooning over who knows which absent hero. I hope you are not still dealing with the other side of that broken heart—poor Captain Crozier! He looked truly hopeless as the *Terror* was rowed out of the Thames; we could almost hear his heartstrings snap as the distance grew, and we all knew he was looking for her in the crowd, but Sophy kept her head steadfastly averted, even as her cheeks burned. If only he had the flaring nostrils and stormy hair of the fragrant James Ross, things might have gone differently. But I am convinced there is not a man alive who would fulfill all of Sophy's criteria—she is a demanding ship, and wants a captain, but will not be boarded. Nothing can please her. But me, well, that's another story. Come home and I will show you how well pleased I can be indeed.

I miss you, my good man.

Your Jane

P.S. Eleanor and I go to Mortimer next Friday week. We will stay at Mortimer Hill with the Keables, and gorge ourselves silly on wild strawberries which grow even between the flagstones in the courtyard. Of those particular ones we will steer clear, of course, but there won't be a berry left from the hollyhocks at the front to the ha-ha. It would be oh-so-lovely if Eleanor and that eldest boy of theirs, Joseph, would marry, don't you think? To have them formally as family would make me so happy. Sadie is too kind to press it, but I am sure she feels the same.

18 July 1848

My dearest love,

Ah my sweet—even in the midst of all this anxiety, there are moments of wonderful, unexpected ribaldry. I must tell you of an episode yesterday of inadvertent humour—Sir John Ross, Sir Edward Parry and Sir Francis Beaufort were all in my sitting room together, with the most carefully crafted sombre faces you can imagine. I, too, was doing my best. Over a pot of my own bèrgamot tea and a bowl of fresh strawberries brought back from the Keables at Mortimer (so tiny and packed with flavour!), we were talking rescue plans, and possible routes, the progress of Ross and Richardson—nothing very joyous. I suppose they could sense I was getting fidgety—all this talk makes me just want to *do* something besides chew on my hands—but they interpreted it as losing heart, for Sir John leant forward, rubbing his chest with his left hand and looked pointedly at me, as if this comment were meant to inspire me: "Remember, gentlemen, how Sir John survived the first time he was trapped by an Arctic winter; he is the man who ate his boots." Ross leant back in his seat with a conclusive raise to his shaggy eyebrows, and nodded his head. Being the target of his attentions during this comment, I felt my colour rise and wondered, however briefly, if you could possibly have told him our little names for each other! But no, I decided—you were much too much of a gentleman for that, so I asked, with a catch in my breath, to leave the room for a moment. Instantly the room shuffled and clanked into action, the gentlemen rising from their seats, hands extended in concern for my welfare. I waved away their aid and took myself into the second chamber, not to the window, but to the corner, where my eyes could focus only on the shadow on the wall. I had to keep them open, the memory of you was so strong, and I was in danger of laughing at this highly inopportune moment. The Man Who Ate His Boots—yes, that's what they call you, but isn't it also what *I* call you, too! And what have I been? *My dear, I do believe I'm starving. What I need is something... comfortable to eat.—My good captain, there must be an old slipper around here somewhere.....* (!!!)

They thought I had retired out of grief, and I have allowed them this error. Oh, if only they knew the real reason! But even my girlish giggles were tinged with sadness, my darling, because, even though the interim years between your first Arctic journey and your last were filled with many joys, the bookends themselves are almost too tragic to bear. The too close analogy to your survival in 1821 and the horror that may await you now does nearly stop my heart, even when the occasional naughty idea of you gets it beating again. As always, you make me a mess of conflicting emotions. If you would only come home, you could devour me, again and again, and we would both live.

Your loving slipper,
Jane

Times *12 October 1848* p7
SIR JOHN FRANKLIN'S EXPEDITION

It is only a week since we afforded our readers the last probable glimpse of the exploring party who have gone out in search of a solution to the mystery that hangs over the fate of Sir John Franklin, previously to their issuing again from the mysterious ground on which that solution is to be sought; and now, for the first time since the missing adventurers were lost sight of, at the threshold of that same ground, an indication of their whereabouts has suddenly turned up. A letter just received by the Admiralty from Chief Factor Macpherson, dated March 1, 1848, says—"There is a report from Peel's River that the Esquimaux saw two large boats (query ships?) to the east of the Mackenzie River, full of white men; and they (the Esquimaux) showed knives, files, &c., to the Peel's River Indians, which they had received from these white men. Could these have been Franklin or Rae?" Mr. Hargrave, of York Factory, to whom Mr. Macpherson's letter is addressed, says, in communicating this intelligence to the Admiralty, "It could not have been Rae in his last expedition, as his boats did not go beyond Committee Bay." Mr. Hargrave adds, that "But little credence can be given to Esquimaux reports." We do not see, however, any good reason for rejecting a rumour so welcome, and we gladly give it publicity. Presuming that the boats or ships seen were those of Franklin's expedition, their position, even east of the Mackenzie, is good as regards success, and better still as respects safety, since they must have been very near the coast. It has been ascertained that open water exists, during the summer season, from the Mackenzie River to Behring's Straits; and we, therefore, dare venture to hope that the expedition may have effected the long desired north-west passage this summer, and the gallant party may be even at this moment approaching our shores. The anxiety respecting the lost party had grown finally to be very great, and the public will cling eagerly to the hope so suddenly presented. A very short time must test its value.

—*Athenaeum*

---

1 November 1848

My dearest love,

I have heard from Sir John Richardson concerning the "Esquimaux reports" as published in *The Times*. He cautions me to hold out no hope of their veracity, in spite of their positive nature. The two ships could not have been Rae's—he had no ships—and there is no one else yet there fitting that description; who else could it be but you? He says "no," though, over all my protestations. His confidence in the negative has its foundation in what he knows of you: the sounds of guns firing could not have been your men, as you would never have wasted so much ammunition; you would never have stayed so long near the Mackenzie River without communicating with the Hudson's Bay Company. The tales are nothing but lies, as he says, products of "the desire of the Indians to excite the curiosity of the questioner in the hope that they may obtain something thereby." I have never met an Esquimaux person, man, woman or child, but think, under all their layers of seal skin and train oil, they cannot be so different from us. Why would they lie? Would the women of their little communities not be equally desperate for news of their absent men, and therefore as true as their word? Who would tell such a tale? I suspect the women are even somewhat more liberated than we are, even when we look at their flat hair and simple clothing and consider ourselves so much more civilized. I squeeze myself into a chemise, drawers, a corset, stockings, two petticoats, a camisole, vest, and dress every morning, and what do they have? They have limitation in their choice of fabric, true, but absolute (and enviable) freedom of movement; they are outside, moving, working, laughing and eating; we breathe from the top of our chests and perch on chairs, and titter. And what do you do? Hold to the taffrail, polish your buttons, write in your big book covered with broad arrows? If you are doing that now, and if the stories are true, you must come back, come back into history and tell your own tales. There are too many that you haven't yet told, and we all are waiting to hear them from your own lips.

Your Jane

17 December 1848

My dearest love,

Once again I prepare the festivities for Christmas without you—another December almost gone. Eleanor has all the Simpkinsons gathered around the pianoforte for carols; it sounds pleasant echoing through the stairs. She is actually quite good at pounding out a tune for a crowd, though she wouldn't like to hear it so expressed. I'm not one for such events, so enjoy them from afar. There's too much to read and write in my study to pay the season too much mind, though if you were here, I'm sure I would make more of an effort. My singing remains indifferent.

Sir John Richardson likely thinks he's being helpful in his letters, and generally discounting rumours is a good thing, but allowing a little hope to linger over Christmas would also have been a kindness. He has told me more than once to put no stock in the Esquimaux reports. With Richardson gone, there is no one around to assure me, and so I sit and worry far too much. If he is fatigued after a few months, you must be at the end of your tether, though you are no doubt made of sterner stuff. I wonder where he is, and where you are. Perhaps you are together. That would be a suitable gift for the season, don't you think? There is certainly nothing else worth considering.

Ever your Jane

You are there, and I am here:
And so it goes, from year to year;
It is you I hold most dear—
It's all I have.

I am here, and you are there:
My solitude's too deep to bear;
A fading look, a lock of hair—
It's all I have.

1849

Times *31 January 1849* p4
THE ARCTIC EXPEDITION

Since the appearance of the paragraph in The Times announcing the Herald's fruitless search for Sir John Franklin's expedition, news has been received at the Admiralty from Captain Kellett, of the Herald, confirming the report of his not having fallen in with the Plover, which ship was bound in search of the missing expedition, and so far the Herald had failed in her desired object; but it was hardly under any circumstances to have been expected that the Herald with her instructions could herself have fallen in with Sir John Franklin's expedition.

2 February 1849

My dearest love,

In *The Times* you are everywhere—one can hardly open the paper without your name falling out of it—and yet in the Arctic, in a little patch of blank space, you are nowhere to be seen. Captain Kellett found nothing, failed to meet even his intended accompaniment, and was not, apparently, even expected to learn tidings of you, let alone to have anchored alongside you. One wonders who is writing the sailing instructions. What is the point of it all? It makes me suspicious of other ambitions at play.

Still, we wives have other options, and we are not forced into the arena to battle with lions, icebergs, or what have you in quite the same way. Remember that look that you enjoyed so much? The one under my lashes, from the side? Well, we will see what such a look can accomplish when rendered in British pounds sterling.

Your sidelong Jane

Times 15 *February 1849* p6
THE ARCTIC EXPEDITION

We understand that Lady Franklin, with all the fervour of a devoted wife, is at present engaged in a pious pilgrimage to the ports whence the whale ships are likely to proceed to Davis's Straits, with a view to plead her anxieties and distresses, and to animate the daring and generous commanders of these ships in her cause. Lady Franklin has already visited Hull, and there, we believe, that her ladyship was received with much enthusiasm, and that the strongest desire was manifested by the masters and others connected with the whale ships, not only to carry out any instructions or wishes that may be conveyed to them from Government, but are also themselves disposed to undertake certain measures in connexion with the usual objects of their voyage for affording succour or gaining information respecting the missing ships. That this generous spirit will spread we cannot doubt; and whether it be at Leith, Kirkaldy, or Montrose, or the more northern ports of Aberdeen and Peterhead, the appearance of Lady Franklin, and the mention of her most touching case, cannot fail to excite the same generous ardour, and we may confidently anticipate such practical results as, under Providence, may tend to dispel the dark cloud that has already nearly weighed her down, and which presses heavily on the mind of every thinking individual in the kingdom. As the whale ships generally sail towards the close of the present month for their usual fishing ground in Baffin's Bay, the friends and relations of the parties serving on board the Erebus, Terror, Enterprise, and Investigator, will do well to avail themselves of this opportunity of communicating with them.

---

17 February 1849

My dearest love,

I am in Scotland with Sophy again, and am on another mission of mercy, or as *The Times* lisps, on a "pious pilgrimage." I am your devoted wife! On a pious pilgrimage! This is all true, but it's still quite astonishing to be written about in these hallowed terms. What is *not* true is my fragility in the matter: I am certainly not "nearly weighed down" with care—your goddess, when she walks, treads on the ground, and I am as strong as ever and will be so as long as you need me to be. Truthfully I'm not sure how I feel about all those rather epic adjectives; it does put pressure on one to behave in a more subdued fashion, to be called "pious" and "devoted," even if one is so, naturally. I've been denied the right to join Richardson's expedition in the spring, and cannot organize another on my own to take me in the time I have left this season, so have devised this more suitable (or conventional) project for my energies and station in life as your wife. I have zeal and intent, and I have now matched it with more funds—more money to be spent in finding you, to be distributed to whalers in the Orkneys, those who know the north better than anyone. This time, it is Three Thousand Pounds! It is a lot of money for hard working men, and hopefully sufficient incentive to goad them to action. £2000 apparently was not, though it represented considerably more than the Admiralty's miserly 100 guineas. They must come up with more if they are to have any credibility.

The coach ride to the whalers was the hardest portion of the journey. I've taken Sophy with me again this time; Eleanor is too busy with the Simpkinsons, and with Mr. Gell, who is now in London and almost constantly by her side no matter where she is—even to the back privy, I suspect, if it were still there. Yes, he is back from VDL, and has found a modest curacy in the London borough of Marylebone. I've not yet been to see his church, or his flock, but no doubt he does a creditable job. He is a hard worker, I'll give him that, as well as a devoted, if bland, suitor.

Sophy is a fine companion on such a journey: sitting all those hours with her by my side, the both of us watching the landscape grind too slowly past the window as we wait to take our first steps on Orkney soil. This time our trunks hold only two dresses each—we have started conserving our funds, for what I fear will be lean times ahead. You'll be surprised to learn that I opted not to bring my iron bedstead—I assumed that *somewhere* in Scotland there must be at least *one* decent place for both of us to sleep (more on that later). The most important cargo is, of course, the broadsheets at the bottom of the trunk, 300 of them printed for distribution to the Orkney whalemen—a lonely enough spot but a bustling metropolis compared to where you are, I'm sure. The landscape got considerably bleaker as we moved north; the air was fresh, but as it whistled through the carriage it was biting. Like Mr. Johnson, I find Scotland more squalid than anything, with the inns offering only cold comfort and little flavour in the food. The char our innkeeper served for supper last night was delicious, if a little small—we were famished! Sitting for hours, remaining upright in a public coach in spite of all the ruts in the road, took more stamina than I expected. I've done some of my fingernails an injustice, and some of Sophy's stitches are uneven, but she perseveres with her cross-stitch no matter the state of the light or the roads. Her face is almost fierce with concentration. I prefer to look out of the window. I've travelled by camel, and over Van Diemen's Land, rambled over France and Italy with impunity and climbed Mt. Olympus itself—what's wrong with me now? Perhaps it's my anticipation of the destination that tires me out.

Last night there was no spare sofa or mattress to be had, so S. and I slept in one bed. It was actually a comfort to sleep with Sophy by my side last night—though to tell her this would be to lose the last vestige of my independence. Her long hair lay between us on the pillow, and I could hear her breathe—what a different sleeping companion she is from you, you fuzzy dragon, who always made so much warmth that I had to open the window even in winter. Her white nightgown glowed against the moonlight—Scotland has no curtains, not anywhere—and I could see her shoulders move as she breathed. I remember listening to you breathe, too, my love, and remember touching your shoulder, with the whisper of dark hair on the bone, on one of the last nights we were in London together. Do you remember? Perhaps not—you slept soundly that night. I did not. The candle had guttered, and the breeze blew through the open window. It smelled like ice—I don't know how, but there was a distinct arctic chill to our bedroom, even with you smouldering away beside me. Then, I took it as a good omen, that gentle breeze: that as you lay sleeping beside me, the spirit from the far north was coming to draw you forward, to borrow you just for a short time and bring you back wrapped cozily in fame and fortune. Last night, as I lay awake listening to Sophy breathe, I began to fear I was mistaken, that the smell was instead the vanguard of a gathering army of ice, the Arctic marshalling its forces together, to make sure that, once you stole into that hallowed sea, you would never return, like Ulysses waylaid by gods after Troy's triumph. But Ulysses came home! I fear now, too, that it was the wind from your grave that passed over both of us that night. But I sound morbid, and these thoughts are to no purpose.

Here in Scotland I am on the first step of my own journey to find you: my intention is to meet with the whalers who are preparing their ships for this season's whaling expeditions—good, hard, brave men all—and to convince them once more, if at all possible, to extend their purpose one more time in the Arctic to look for you, and to offer succour to you if you can be found. What do I offer? I offer pay of yours I have already drawn, and Father has offered some, and from my own savings: all together, as I said, Three Thousand Pounds. The first two thousand from last year went unclaimed, so we will up the ante and see what happens. Some of your kind friends—Sir Francis Beaufort, Sir Edward Parry—have again volunteered to act as adjudicators of the reward, such as it is. I asked the Admiralty for assistance; they have kept the 100 guineas they offered last year for anyone with information and have attached themselves to my appeal (!!), but there is noise about the possibility of £20,000 being held out by HM Government for the same. Now, *there* is incentive—but it has yet to materialize, so I print my scanty broadsheets, and distribute them around, and wait and hope and write. If the Admiralty continue to dawdle, well, so be it: the whalers will get three thousand pounds, one hundred guineas, and I applaud them if they do. Why should rewards for grand discoveries be open only to those in the Admiralty's employ? And what on earth have they done for us lately?

Yours aye,
Jane

25 February 1849

My dearest love,

The broadsheets were delivered today; Sophy and I were met with doffed hats and lowered eyes, and like a horrid bluestocking I marched right up to the whalers and used all of my voice and eyelashes that I could, giving my presence there an air of jocularity—if the search for the Northwest Passage is a contest, why then cannot the search for you, its first discoverer, be as well? I, as well as the rest of the nation, am sure that pure curiosity rather than any trouble is what delays you—in my lighter moments I consider the broadsheets, and this trip, to be nothing more than a distraction while we wait for your expected return; a tempest in a teapot. If nothing else, it will make your return all the more fantastic—my own ancient mariner! Sophy and I will return to London after a short stay in the Highlands, where she has never been before and is willing to ramble a bit. Who knows—we may even bump into her Majesty out for a stroll!

Yours ach,
Jane

Times *24 March 1849* p8
THE ARCTIC EXPEDITION

The following paper was laid before the House of Commons last night:

ADMIRALTY, *March 23, 1849*

The Lords Commissioners of the Admiralty are under the necessity of laying a supplementary estimate for the relief of the Arctic Expeditions under Sir John Franklin and Sir James Ross upon the table of the House.

Their Lordships, having been apprised by the last letters received from Sir James Ross that it was his intention to direct the Investigator to land all the supplies that she could spare at Whaler Point, and to proceed to England, if no tidings of the expedition under Sir J. Franklin were received by the whale ships now about to sail, leaving the Enterprise to prosecute the search alone, have consulted the highest naval authorities as to the probable consequences of this step.

They find it to be the unanimous opinion of those most conversant with the Polar Seas that such a separation of the ships under Sir James Ross would be most perilous to the ship remaining in the ice, and would probably neutralise the entire object of the expedition, if Sir John Franklin's party were to be discovered at a time when the Enterprise had nearly exhausted her own stores. They have, therefore, determined upon sending out a fresh supply of provisions for both ships by the North Star, which is now fitting for this purpose at Sheerness, with orders to proceed across Baffin's Bay, and as much farther as practicable in the direction of Lancaster Sound and Barrow Straits, looking out for the Investigator, or her boats.

In the event of the Investigator not being fallen in with, the commander of the North Star will be directed to land the supplies at such points on the south side of Lancaster Sound, or other places indicated by Sir James Ross, as may be accessible to the North Star, in sufficient time to secure his return across Baffin's Bay before the winter sets in.

The expense of fitting the North Star for the ice will be 6,086*l*., and the wages of the crew, stores, and provisions on board 6,602*l*., making 12,688*l*. in all, which constitute the supplementary estimate now submitted to the House. But, in addition to this, Her Majesty's Government has determined to offer a reward of 20,000*l*. to be given to such private ship, or distributed amongst such private ships, of any country, as may, in the judgment of the Board of Admiralty, have rendered efficient assistance to Sir John Franklin, his ships, or their crews, and may have contributed directly to extricate them from the ice.

H.G. Ward

---

29 March 1849

My dearest love,

Broadsheets are one thing; a ship is quite another! I dropped Sophy back in Guernsey once more, and continued on to London, but felt as I arrived entirely dissatisfied with sitting back and waiting. So:

I am resolved to move forward on the purchase of a ship, a fortified whaler manned with experienced Navy men who can do the job of pushing through the ice to you. Don't try to stop me. I have already asked the Admiralty for a loan to finance the expedition: the reimbursement will come from my own funds. I will not touch the Porden money you left me, but will sell my East India stocks. Don't say no; you don't have a say in the matter. It is only left to seek counsel from my resident experts: the brave Sirs, Parry, Beaufort, and Ross. The request is well within reason: £5000 and the loan of two ships—all of which will be paid off with the £20,000 reward the Admiralty itself promises to the men who find you and bring you home. I think the Admiralty may well be approachable, too, for experts and materiel that might be lying fallow, rotting away on half-pay when they could be making heroes of themselves in the far north. All depends upon you, my love. What is money in exchange for love? Think of me and be warm.

Your Jane

10 April 1849

My dearest love,

Beaufort hints that I will not get a ship from Whitehall. He has asked me to give you up. Parry says the same. Please tell me what I should do. Your food has officially run out.

Your Jane

25 April 1849

My dearest love,

Your old friend Beaufort be damned. His despair has only doubled my resolve.

I feel compelled to confess that you are not the only one receiving my letters. Indeed, you are perhaps the only one NOT receiving them! I feel like an automaton, my pen starting to move automatically each time a sheet of paper is put before me; I write so many I hardly know to whom. These days I write to the press, to the young up-and-comer Benjamin Disraeli (son to old Isaac D'Israeli, though you'd never know it by the way he dropped his apostrophe and the outrageous cut of his trousers), to the President of the United States, a Mr. Zachary Taylor. Do you know that they have a new president? One who is, evidently, interested in your whereabouts, as he carried my letter in his pocket all the way to Congress, took it out, and read it aloud amid much back slapping. Nothing has yet come of it, mind you, but a great wave of sympathy for you and your men arrived from Washington, reported here in the presses and praised by Disraeli in the House of Commons. Don't worry, my dear, I am still just as loyal to you as ever—I am your Penelope! Everything I write is of course only about you and in your behalf, but I am casting my glances over several gentlemen of good standing who may be able to help me. Not the usual polar heroes, who arrive with their gold braid and epaulettes and brave, sombre words, but who have little motivation to find you themselves (or, perhaps more to the point, whose wives don't allow them to go!). So, I go elsewhere: to the Royal Geographical Society, to *The Times*, to the House of Commons. You will call me conniving and canny, but what care I for such names, trala? I blame you as the cause of my wandering eye and get on with it.

I'm the wife of a great polar hero
Who sailed off to find latitude zero!

Since, I've heard hair nor hide—
This I cannot abide—
And his absence is starting to wear-o!

These are heady days, my dear, with your name on everyone's lips, and I thrill to hear it, every time. Just yesterday Sophy (who has come to town for some social advice; there is some struggle with another cousin) and I were in our old spot in Russell Square, sitting in the sun with a bag of chestnuts we simply couldn't resist, when two young men walked by talking of you! I was certainly glad that Eleanor wasn't with us; she would have been aghast at the attention she would have felt was directed at her. As it was, Sophy and I sat very still, suddenly intent on watching the birds play in the fountain, not even chewing. The men actually stopped in their walk within hearing distance, and we heard the heated discussion: blasting the ice, using dynamite to clear a passage through the eastern Arctic, making clear water where perhaps there has never been any before; balloons made of silk, filled with chemical flame to carry messages and even a man into the polar sky, to search above the hummocks for masts, tents, men; message collars for foxes! I resisted the urge to laugh out loud: these ideas are dreams, mere fancies of idle men who are blind to the challenges (not to say impossibilities) before them, whose ambitions see distance, dark, and death as no barrier, but opportunities to be grasped. I nearly laughed until I realized, of course, that those dreams are not unlike our own; they are, my love, almost as fanciful as the search for the Passage itself, which, I suspect now, crowns all as the most useless, quixotic, and deadly of all dreams hatched by this ridiculous little island. And there you are, in the centre of everyone's dreams but mine. For me, you are at the centre of my worst nightmare.

Your embattled Jane

1 May 1849

My dearest love,

Hope moves on apace!

In terms of advocacy, you may not believe it, but I have actually been more successful than Sir John Ross, who clamours and leaves a vapour of whiskey wherever he goes. I've been writing to the Lords with recommendations for good people with good vision: we need more men on your side, my love, not so many looking to get in touch with their own glory. I am still trying to get a ship of my own, and may purchase one if it's suitable, but I am also filling others' ships with men of my own choosing regardless. A Mr. William Penny, a rough but capable whaler who had pledged his season to you like a young knight errant last year, is to head an Admiralty expedition! I almost gave him a ribbon from my bonnet, he was so gallant in his pledge. I met him personally when I went to the Orkneys in 1848 to offer my reward (if you can't remember the first £2000 I offered in your behalf, it's because you aren't reading my letters, you ingrate), and we have kept up a steady correspondence since. I recommended him, and another deserving fellow, a brother to your young naturalist, Goodsir, to the Admiralty to fill another expedition now in early preparation. How is poor Goodsir's skin these days? Hiding his blemishes under those eighteenth-century chops in 1845 made him look even younger than he was. I hoped that the cold salt air would clear his face and make a man of him. His brother, Robert, also a doctor (same tragic condition, alas, though mostly outgrown it), is joining the quest.

Why, you might well ask, am I supporting the applications of outsiders? Well, my dear, you should know by now I will always fight for the underdog. I still hold close to my heart the afternoon you called me your arctic tern, flying against the wind just because she could. You'll be pleased to know I still am. But that's not the only reason why I'm pushing their cause. Mainly it's because I believe that these men are perhaps the only ones who have *you* at the centre of their designs. All the Admiralty heroes have their sights set further than your ships, I suspect. It pains me to say it, but if, as the odious Richard King has written, you have formed the nucleus of an iceberg, I suspect that all the James Rosses of the world would be content to sail right on past you if it meant some greater glory, if they could squeeze their own ships through the last remaining 6 inches of open water and make the passage. Jesus Christ on a stick, John, where are you? If for no other reason, just come home to keep them from that ugly glory.

Your Jane

20 May 1849

My dearest love,

All is a shambles! In few words, the Admiralty, officially, says "no" to the loan of men, money, and materiel; a whaling ship simply cannot (or will not) be purchased and manned or directed by a woman, and I must needs be content with sending my list of "suggestions" along with a whaler intent on its normal route to the whaling grounds. It is filled with big, hardy, capable, stoic men with hands rough from hauling rope and flensing flesh, who know little of naval protocol or politesse, who will consort with the Esquimaux and stop at nothing for a season's profit, and whom I cannot entirely trust to seek you out where *I suggest*. This staying at home and waiting is a slow torture I never knew possible. I wish I had never come home, for all I do is fidget and worry. The best part of my woman's life is to be a wife, but what sort of wife can I be when I have no husband by my side? So here we are again. I make a terrible woman. If our positions were reversed, and *I were the man* and you the woman, would you come to find *me*? Sometimes I wish it were so, just to have the relief from the pressure that builds up here in front of our little hearth.

Eleanor cautioned against it, but in my disappointment I have given money (£500) to Robert Ward, the kind whaling ship owner from Hull who has been an adjudicator of my rewards, to give to his ship the *Truelove* in order to secure the captain's commitment to push West as far as he might go in one short season. No doubt you are beyond their reach, but £500 is cheap at the price if I feel I'm doing you some good. To do nothing is both to fall into grief and to neglect my duty.

I will not say more about other obstacles that may have been strewn across my path. Eleanor and her omnipresent suitor, Gell, have their own views, which I refuse to even open for your consideration. Suffice it to say that my answer is, and ever will be, "no" to anyone who chooses furniture expenditures over family.

Your Jane

24 May 1849

My dearest love,

The Admiralty is a ship of fools, and I am, even more, taking matters into my own hands. Those stodgy old patriarchs with their dusty sideburns and wobbling wattles pore over the same maps and read the same documents repeatedly, looking for some meaning in their own words that got caught between the lines—but I have simply tossed convention to the wind and am looking elsewhere for help. Do you know where? I will tell you: to America! I have written to Mr. Zachary Taylor, the President of the United States. Yes! And what's more: I have received a reply! Here is what he says: "All that the Executive Government of the United States, in the exercise of its constitutional powers can effect to meet this requisition on American enterprise, skill and bravery, will be promptly undertaken."

Promptly! Undertaken! what more could anyone reasonably ask for? These are two words I have never received from your dear olds in Whitehall, and mark my word, it will be the Americans who sniff you out. They are young and brash, and say "howdy" and wear their hats far too high on their heads, but they are brave and worthy of such a nation-building quest. I am buoyed by hope, and giddy with optimism. I am in awe of that splendid American efficiency we all hear so much about these days—President Taylor has taken my appeal (again) to Congress, and is drumming up support in his own government for a search expedition. What else to say but hooray! You may not be home in time for Eleanor's wedding (in mere weeks—I held her off as long as I could), but if you're here by the end of the summer it will still be a dual celebration.

Your bride Jane

Times *06 June 1849* p6
THE UNITED STATES

It is reported that the President has decided on sending two vessels of war to seek after and relieve the Arctic expedition under Sir John Franklin, or at all events to ascertain their fate; this measure will be very popular.

---

6 June 1849

My dearest love,

President Taylor has pledged two ships! The American Navy will man and plan, and as they are that much closer to the scene, being already on the far side of the world, they will take less time to get to where they need to. We expect news—good news—shortly. Hold on, my love! You will soon encounter Americans on your lee side! Slap them heartily on the back, and let them slap you, and all will be right with the world.

Your Jane

25 June 1849

My dearest love,

I write to tell you that there are no more Eleanor Franklins in the world. Do not be downhearted about it—your young Eleanor continues living—but no longer under our collective wing. No: this month, she at long last married her Gell, and that's an end on it. Of course she was beautiful in her way, with her simple gown and homely looks, but loving and being loved has made her glow, and the day was the culmination of her dream that has been six years in coming. I've settled £500 per annum from our pooled funds on the young couple; the rest I retain for my (and our) use. It goes to the search for you and little else.

The Gell has removed her from Bedford Place, and by the look on their faces, it could hardly happen quickly enough. Eleanor happily sobbed her farewells to the Simpkinsons in Mary's arms, but had hardly such emotion for me—which was just as well, as during her departure I retreated to read in my sitting room upstairs and wouldn't have borne the attention well. I was actually descending the stairs when they arrived at the front door, but when the triumphant husband himself saw me on the landing, he didn't know where to look, and bustled her out, post haste. Oh my love, I fear for the future of your family, me and them together. Without you we are all falling to nothing.

Don't chastise me, but I feel in my heart that Gell is an adversary now, not a friend, and certainly not a family member. He wheedles and needles Eleanor to accept his mode of thinking, which is decidedly neglectful of her family's proud exploring past, if I can be so opaque in my meaning. I see Eleanor as torn between the two men she loves most: you, her proud Papa, and her ambitious new husband, who has adopted the rather hateful habit of speaking for her, even when she has the privilege of being spoken to directly. You and I both know that Eleanor has always been of the retiring persuasion, but I fear for the loss of my influence on her to make decisions from her own heart and head. It confirms my suspicion that marriage is not for the faint of heart nor the weak of mind!

But what breaks my heart especially is that she perceives, somehow, that her husband represents her future *to the exclusion* of her past, and her past seems to be caught up not only in her strained relationship with me, but in her feelings for you, my love. You are her father, but you are gone; *I* am the one obstacle in her path to her new life. In their estimation, I keep the money she and Gell feel is rightfully theirs, though *you* expressly gave me leave to use it in your absence. Some of it, of course, is *my* money, too, from Father, but it all becomes one to them, and I am keeping the both of them from their future by *hoarding* (not *husbanding*) it. I keep you in the centre of all we say and do, and the argument implicit in their juvenile enthusiasm for starting a family is that *you* are no longer that centre, no more the gentle patriarch to whom we all turned our faces as to the sun. If you return to dandle your new grandchildren on your knee, then all the better; but regardless of where you are or when you return, those grandchildren will arrive as regularly as the trains in Euston Station. I can no longer tell if I will even be welcome at their door.

There was some preliminary talk of my going along with them once they returned to London, but ultimately it has been decided that I will not. In no uncertain terms I have been made aware that I have spent too long under their feet, and am asked by looks and manner, if not actual words, to decline the invitation. It is all as it should be, I suppose: the constant tatting and jellying would interrupt the actual work that needs doing, and there is no place to conduct the business of rescuing you in the little place they've chosen in Upper Seymour-street. I can already half hear the Gell's rumbling "ahem!" when he feels my conversation has gone on too long, and doubt that Sir John Richardson or Sir Edward Parry would accept such an admonition from a junior clergyman. Still, the antimacassars Eleanor left behind for you, and the pages of her favourite sheet music still on the lid of the pianoforte remind me that something more besides her physical proximity has been lost—a lingering remnant of that little girl, who tried so hard to please everyone. I can still see the shadow of her looking out of our sitting room window, looking through the rain for a carriage that would not come. It is up to me now, more than ever, to continue the vigil.

Still your Jane

1 July 1849

My dearest love,

A despondent turn around Russell Square was taken by your wife this morning. It rained. The Duke had little of solace to offer. Mr. Rowe was nowhere to be seen. Our little sitting room has no more rustle than what I myself put into it, and it's far too little after the energy needed to rescue a husband and plan a wedding breakfast over the past few months, and to make one last effort to save a relationship between an aging stepmother and a young woman in love. There was no succour out of doors, nor any inside. I am caught in myself.

I could have been a better mother to Eleanor, perhaps. I have failed both of you.

Your Jane

3 July 1849

My dearest love,

The loss of Eleanor has wrought some changes upon your household: I will once again have Sophy for company. Now that Eleanor is gone forever from Bedford Place, Mary has been perfectly willing for me to bring Sophy to London, and she has even given her Eleanor's old bedroom. The more ungracious part of me suspects that Mary wants Sophy at least in part as a buffer between me and her little Simpkinsons, but I will not peer too closely into the mouth of that gift horse. The fact remains that, alone, I cannot keep up with all the paperwork—the letter writing, the map reading, the instructions—to do with your rescue, and my own writing hand feels the loss of Eleanor's acutely. Sophy's round script will more than suffice, and her dedication to the copying and safeguarding of documents is, as we know from VDL, admirable. I know you would approve!

One slight worry is her abject position; she is neither quite family to our Simpkinson household, nor peer to the younger generation. They will tolerate her, I know, but she is no Eleanor, who got along with everyone. Sophy, too, as I know from her rather chatty letters, is more preoccupied than ever with newspaper gossip and those ghastly yellow-backed books, pulp trash suffused with unrequited love, murder, and sentiment. I really am concerned that this type of reading is bad for her health, as, when we were in Scotland, she noticeably reddened as she read, occasionally seeming to clutch at her bodice in actual pain, with an impatient gesture as she turned the page, as if the room were too hot. This latest one is *The Tenant of Wildfell Hall* or something other—some made up place with made up names, and violence seeping through its pages. Dreadful!

Frank the elder has stayed away from the breakfast room of late, and this is always an ominous sign, along with Mary appearing rather flustered when she encounters me on the stairs, as if she has a secret about me she simply cannot tell. Mary always talks incessantly when Frank is grouchy, and I suspect this particular turn of grumpiness has to do with me, rather than the soggy paper Mary blames on these damp mornings. I admit it's not an ideal arrangement here at Bedford Place: the Simpkinson daughters are doubled up whereas before they had their own rooms, but Sophy and I will absolutely *require* the sitting room as well as bedrooms (and mine with the anteroom) in order to involve ourselves with the search, and there's simply no other way around it. Father keeps his own space, as he should, and if the Simpkinsons are going to keep in the family home, well, so shall I. I'm there much less than everyone else already, and the rooms are now being used to their utmost—the house has never been so useful. I am determined to brazen it out. For me, you will have one address to attend to when you return, my love, and from Bedford Place and Bedford Place only we will embark proudly for the Gells' residence together.

Your determined Jane

Times *03 July 1849* p8
THE UNITED STATES

The expedition for seeking after Sir John Franklin has been abandoned or postponed. The reasons alleged are—the impossibility at this late season of the year of getting any suitable ships ready of those which belong to the navy, and the want of authority on the part of the Secretary to the Navy to purchase new vessels without an appropriation by Congress. In the meanwhile the Secretaries of State and the Navy have issued circulars to the commanders of vessels of war, whalers, and other navigators in the North Pacific, urging their earnest co-operation in prosecuting the search.

---

25 July 1849

My dearest love,

I have not written because I have had little to say, believe it or not. It is the middle of the London summer, and I feel as frozen in as you. I am sorry, but you have to keep waiting: there has been a slight hiccough in the American plans to rescue you from your predicament. American efficiency has won the day, but it has done us no favours. Official news from Washington is that "uncontrollable causes" have led to the abandonment of President Taylor's plans. In two months, almost to the day, they went from absolute commitment to complete rejection. It turns out that, in spite of all the assurances in the papers, that the American Congress did *not* have the money or organization to outfit an expedition to go in search of you, though good President Taylor was so eloquent and kind... and the season has come and gone. It was too late to start from scratch, the Americans have none of the materiel just lying there ready to go as we do, and, quite simply, nothing went out.

To my horror, my letter to him appeared here in London, in *The Times*, and though kind things were said about it I was completely aghast. I think young Disraeli leaked my letter to *The Times* and I find it difficult to trust him. He has given us some time in Parliament, but no money has yet come of it. I keep on asking. I am reeling from disappointment. Perhaps our own Admiralty is not so bad after all. Perhaps having a prince consort on our side, and not simply a "people's Congress," will make our own government step up to their responsibility to their citizens.

Your Jane

31 July 1849

My dearest love,

Sophy and I have outstayed our welcome at Bedford Place. That is ungrateful of me: that we have outgrown our allotted space here is a more precise statement. Mary has been very kind and accommodating as always, but the worn look that gathers around her eyes each morning when she brings me my tea and sees me unrolling one map or another is an unmistakable rebuke that I am overstepping even her generous boundaries. She hasn't looked directly at me in days, trying to avoid showing me a feeling that she doesn't know she exudes from her whole being. So, Sophy and I have secured some very proper rooms, and you'll never guess where: at Spring Gardens—you'll know the street when you see it, the little one right behind the Admiralty. It was the one we would wander along occasionally when you were early for an appointment, it being our preference to pay attention to the back as well as the front of things—always the thorough explorers, right? Well, soon I will have our favourite view before me on a daily basis, and I will get to know the sentries stationed at the back door as well as the front.

I told Mary at breakfast today that Sophy and I would be leaving in a week. I think it was the first time I'd seen regret and relief joined in someone's face. Her hands were on the table at the time, and Frank gave her right one what looked to me like a congratulatory pat upon hearing the news, which annoyed me, but it can't be helped. He *has* been heroically patient: living with one's in-laws, particularly with those who don't necessarily follow *les règles de la maison*, must be wearing. It is through Mary's bedroom intervention, I am sure, that we have been welcome here as long as we have been. Father has said nothing at all, in his characteristic style. I know he would like us to stay, but also feels the crowding as all the young people move around the house at all hours. I took his snapping of his paper as his final comment on the negotiation: transaction concluded.

Mary made all the right noises, of course —no, we must stay, it's just silly to find rooms when there's all of Bedford Place to knock around in, &c. &c.—but I stood firm on the point that our meetings with various professionals and experts required independent space, and more of it, and on that point she couldn't disagree. Sophy remained silent, but as she carved a plum into tiny slices I saw her lips retreat into her mouth and her grip on the plum tighten to the point at which juice flowed over her fingers. Hopefully even once we move she will continue to keep silent, no matter the cost to her gums or the damage to the fruit plate; I couldn't bear to hear anything said against Mary and Bedford Place, and Sophy can have the most acid tongue. Mary has done her best to keep us, but our life is simply not hers, and to stay would be to crush her under the terrible weight of hospitality. That has never been a particular Griffin talent.

So: here is our new address, so you know exactly where to find us when you come home: 4 Spring Gardens. Disembark at dawn and come early to Whitehall, my love, so you can take a few moments to wander round the back. When you get halfway down the street, with the archways on your right, look up and to the left. We will both be there, bonnets on, expecting you, waiting to join you on your stroll.

Your Jane, démenagée

6 *August 1849*

My dearest love,

You will not credit it, but I assure you it is true: the new gardener in Russell Square speaks to the birds. I took my usual turn round the garden—(though to say "usual" is to pretend that all is the same since we shifted ourselves to Spring Gardens, and it is decidedly not so)—and was trying to place an especially unusual birdsong… and noticed that the sound was emanating from the mouth of Mr. Rowe. Truth be told, he was the last one I saw in the gaggle of song-birds twittering and fluttering about in the bower; I was first struck by the number of little songsters clearly enjoying themselves among the leaves, and *then* I noticed him at the centre of them all, holding court. London is no place for a songbird, and yet there they were, revelling in all their colours and octaves in the centre of little Russell Square, chatting to Mr. Rowe as if at a garden party! Whistling, my secret ambition as you know, continues to fail me, but my initial jealousy at his prowess gave way at his sheer virtuosity; I admit I sat down just to listen, and may have been open-mouthed in wonder. When he caught me looking at him, he went silent, though I saw him deliver a wink to his feathered companions that accompanied his final trill. If I did not believe that it was impossible, I would say the birds actually turned to look at me before chirping their farewells to Mr. Rowe and quitting the bower en masse. Mr. Rowe returned to his trimming. What do you think he said to them about me? I can't help but wonder. The silly old Duke of Bedford, who sees all, is keeping mum. Harumph!

Thomas now arrives each Monday morning outside our door to take me and Sophy through the town on our errands, and my first stop is always Russell Square. I no longer have unfettered access to the park, but will honour the ritual whenever time and health permit. As always, Thomas keeps his own counsel, but our years of knowing one another makes his presence a comfort, especially under the new regime. I am unsure when I will see Mary or Father again. Luckily for Thomas, he sits on the front box, and so was exempt from suffering through my blowing and blustery attempts to make any sound come out of my mouth on the way home.

Life with Sophy is alright; she is back to her role as amanuensis, which we both fall into easily. Her tea is more than adequate to the task, and her company, though not always delightful, is pleasant enough. She doesn't play the pianoforte, and prefers maps and instructions to needlework, which I appreciate. Her novel reading is less to my taste, but the older generation can't control everything in the young—even *I* am forced to recognize that. To each his own. Unfortunately, Sophy can whistle.

Your blustery Jane

18 August 1849

My dearest love,

I have always been content to be invisible; I've even preferred it, but I am realizing that *anonymity* also has certain advantages: writing a letter to *The Times* on Thursday last, in response to some stupid comment made in an editorial about Admiralty fiscal responsibility, I omitted my name purely with the expectation that Sophy would transcribe it before posting it. Instead, she either gave me a "nom de plume," or just popped it directly in an envelope, apparently, for *The Times* printed it verbatim and with "AN OBSERVER" ominously appended at the bottom, and it has caused a tempest over the course of the week, with supporters—some identified, some as anonymous as I was—writing in to agree with my statements about the direction of the search and the general apathy of the Admiralty. Of course I didn't mean to send an anonymous note, but its effect has been inspiring. Well! It was "some pumpkins," an expression I heard more than once in America, which means here that you are not as forgotten as the doomsday editorialists at *The Times* seem to think.

What a different feeling I got just a few months ago when I saw my name in print in the same paper when I hadn't intended it to be; the helpful but misguided friend, Mr. Disraeli, sent forward a letter of mine written in confidence to him, to an unknown party, who then delivered it unbidden to *The Times*. It caused a sensation, too, and since then I have assiduously avoided even the suggestion of publicity in my own behalf. It was a fairly innocuous letter, but a powerful lesson concerning how people see me: had I not signed *that* letter, I have no doubt it would have made it straight to the dust heap, saying nothing as it did. As it was, however, for expressing "the sentiments of many of our gallant countrymen," it was "justly rewarded" by publication. It is an experiment I may well try again.

Your anonymous, loving well-wisher

31 August 1849

My dearest love,

Today you will admire two things in particular about me: my ability to occupy myself in the face of delay, and my sleuthing! In spite of your own trusting tendencies, I have run Mr. Rowe to ground; the Russell Square fox is trapped by his very own garden! To tell the truth, it is rather a sad story, but has been a worthy distraction from the pain and sheer boredom of waiting for news from you. Waiting on the Admiralty is like willing a rock to give birth, like expecting a poem from a dog. Well! Mr. Benjamin Rowe, Gardener of the Russell Square Horticultural Interest, is late (or rather early) of Oxford, where he was a botanical lecturer at one of the small colleges, and a tutor in botany. He even wrote a book on the subject: *A Year in an English Country Garden*, which I have managed to procure from one of the second-hand booksellers near the British Museum. Here is my trail, which I know you would appreciate, being yourself a steadfast hunter of geographical esoterica:

I found him in an old postal directory, which I had been idly flipping through when waiting for assistance in a stationery shop. I suppose it might not have been him, but I now know for certain that it was. There he was, "author, botanist and botanical lecturer," listed on May Street in Oxford. With that, I simply went to the British Library for a copy of the latest Jackson's compendium of printed books, and found the title of his little book. And it *is* a little book, but very charming. It takes one through the seasons of, I think, his own modest plot, saying nothing of his accomplishments in the grand beds of Oxford, but letting the flowers themselves speak through his descriptions of their first tender shoots and their early explorations of the world above ground, to the optimistic vigour of their buds and sensual aggression of their summer stamens and blossoms, to the gradual drying of the stalk, its withering retreat back to the roots in the fall, and the noble dormancy of winter. If his prose elicited one predominant feeling in me, it was love: his own love for his plants, for his garden, was true in every word. I have already told you the magic he has worked on the lime tree bower in Russell Square, but Mr. Rowe's book revealed an affection that goes far beyond professional capability; it is part of him, like the north is part of you.

And here is where true pity begins, for the book had been published 12 years before—and what had happened to him in the intervening years? The book's cover page also mentioned other authors, the names of three women, all of family Rowe. Where are they now? How might he go from living as a sequestered, botanical tutor in Oxford to a stooping gardener in a small (but beautiful) London park? I can tell you: through sheer grief. Back at the British Library, this time in one of the newspaper reading rooms, I discovered his tragedy: the tidy address on May Street, on the afternoon of April 7, 1845, burned right away. It took with it his wife and two daughters. Mr. Rowe had been absent at the university at the time, but, according to the paper, returned to May Street to find the bodies of his family laid together on the street; they had been pulled through the front windows by passersby who attempted to revive them, but to no avail. They had been seen in the window of the drawing room, their dresses not alight, but the room so filled with smoke it was only a matter of minutes before the walls themselves burst into flames. The bricks on the outside were, the paper said, hot to the touch. The reason for the fire remained unknown; the rest of May Street survived. Mr. Rowe's family were the only victims.

I've no idea what brought him from Oxford to London, but I see now why he loves the Russell Square flowers: they are the same perennials of his old plot in Oxford, right down to the shared bed of cinquefoil and campion. In spite of myself I have felt a little jealous of the closeness he has developed with the plants of Russell Square, but knowing what I do now, I cannot begrudge him their love. He deserves it for all he has suffered.

Tell me you're safe.

Your Jane

Times *05 September 1849* p8
SIR JOHN FRANKLIN

Sir George Simpson returned on Monday last from his annual tour of inspection through the Hudson's Bay Territories and North-Western settlements of this continent. We learn with regret from him that no clue had been obtained to the whereabouts or the fate of Sir John Franklin and his gallant companions. Sir John Richardson, indeed, is on his way back from the frozen regions, and may be expected in Montreal early in September. His exploring party will, however, continue their search under the orders of Dr. Rae, of the Hudson's Bay Company, Sir John's second in command, throughout the summer. Although it would be almost criminal to abandon hope in such an enterprise, it is impossible to conceal from oneself the unwelcome truth, that the chances of a successful issue become fearfully diminished by the lapse of time.

—Montreal Gazette, *Aug. 16*

5 September 1849

My dearest love,

News from the Hudson's Bay Company, and catastrophic predictions from *The Times*. I don't know why I continue to read that paper. It is poison. "Although it would be almost criminal to abandon hope in such an enterprise, it is impossible to conceal from oneself the unwelcome truth, that the chances of a successful issue become fearfully diminished by the lapse of time." What are they trying to accomplish with statements like that? They shame themselves.

Your despondent Jane

Times *05 October 1849* p5
NEWS OF SIR JOHN FRANKLIN

This afternoon a telegraphic announcement was made by the Admiralty to the Commander-in-Chief here that they had received news of the discovery of Sir John Franklin and Sir James Ross in Prince Regent's Inlet, all safe and well. Such highly gratifying intelligence was speedily disseminated throughout the port, and the joy was universal.

5 October 1849

My dearest love,

Oh I knew it,—I've put far too many pages in this book, and now will have to write to you all day every day in order to fill it up before you return. And what shall I say? That you must hurry to be home in time to welcome Eleanor back from her travels, that your chair is pulled up to the sitting room window in Spring Gardens just where you like it, that we are all so, so glad that you are coming home. I take back everything I said about the Admiralty and Sir James Ross, who has done just what was needed and is bringing you back. And it was the *Truelove*, the whaler that worked in our behalf, who brought the news—how fitting! Bravo! In fact, now that I think on it, I have *no* time to write to you, you silly man; I have to prepare for your homecoming! You are not a grandpapa yet, but I've no doubt you will be soon, and everything will just be perfect again the minute you step through that door. Oh happy day, my love. This is the best, just the absolute best. Finally, *The Times* has something good to say: "the joy was universal." Oh indeed! "All safe and well"! Oh my love, what good news. I want to spend the day clapping my hands and humming with abandon.

Your ecstatic Jane

Times *23 October 1849* p5
SIR JOHN FRANKLIN'S EXPEDITION

A letter from St. Marie River, dated September 24, announces the arrival, on his way to England, of Sir John Richardson from an unsuccessful search after Sir John Franklin's expedition. The letter mentions that after reaching the Arctic Ocean, he travelled 500 miles along the coast; and also that Sir John speaks confidently of the existence of a northern passage, the practicability of it, however, being exceedingly doubtful, the summers lasting only from 30 to 60 days.

---

23 October 1849

My dearest love,

Something has gone terribly wrong, my love: how can one go from "all safe and well" to "unsuccessful search" in a mere three weeks? On 5 October—I have the article in front of me now—we have reports that you are safe and well with Sir James Ross, and today comes the news that Sir John Richardson is returning empty-handed, with no news, and worse, no you. Perhaps there is a missed communication somewhere, that perhaps Sir George Simpson inadvertently neglected to share the good news that he must know with Richardson before he left H.B.C. territory? All Richardson talks of is a stupid, open polar passage to the north—but you are not there, you are with Ross, right? All this speculation is for nothing, right? I can only trust in the letters that come in, and they pointed first to your safety, not to your continued danger. More than anything, I want Richardson to be wrong. You are not lost!

I wait.
Your Jane

Times *07 November 1849* p5
**THE RETURN OF
SIR JAMES ROSS**

Captain Sir James Ross arrived at the Admiralty yesterday, and had interviews with the Board. The gallant officer appeared rather the worse for his perilous voyage, but was animated with his characteristic energy. We understand that it is his confident opinion that neither Sir John Franklin nor any of his brave companions are eastward of any navigable point in the Arctic regions, and if there be any chance of their existence it is on the supposition that he proceeded in a westerly direction, and in such case we can only expect to hear from the missing adventurers by the Mackenzie detachment, or by Her Majesty's ship Plover, Commander Moore, by way of Russia. Sir James traversed at least 230 miles of ice, the bergs of which were frightful, much more so than any of the experienced Arctic voyagers had seen before. Sir James and his party penetrated as far as the wreck of the Fury, where he found the old tent standing, and everything about it in a state of the best preservation. At this point Sir James deposited a large quantity of provisions, and also the screw-launch of the Enterprise. The march of Sir James across the boundless regions of ice is truly stated as a most unparalleled feat in exploration. We are sorry to find, however, that it was in no way successful. The captain, officers, and ship's company have worked together most harmoniously,—a spirit of emulation having animated every one in the great philanthropic task of endeavouring to carry help and succour to their long-lost friends. In the whole course of his researches it is said Sir James Ross never met with a single Esquimaux. Sir James speaks most highly of all those who have been connected and associated with him. He is fully satisfied that all has been done that could be done by the Admiralty in the appropriation of the vessel, the selection of the crew, and the extensive equipment of each vessel, in stores, provisions, &c. The Admiralty have ordered a couple of steamers from Woolwich to the North Sea, to tow up the Enterprise and Investigator to Woolwich to be paid off; and their Lordships have also ordered up from Kirkcaldy the master of the whaler Advice, about which so much has been said.

—Standard

8 November 1849

Sit down, my dearest love,

Absolute and complete horror: Sir James Ross is back, *empty-handed*. How can this be? He landed at Scarborough on 3 November after only half his allotted time away, with *no accounts of you whatsoever*. He found nothing! I find it unbelievable. He was supposed to be out another year, and meet up with Richardson, and drag you home from your post, but so far as I can tell, the minute that unflattering polar wind buffeted his hair, he simply turned around and came home, clutching his wife's lace handkerchief to his nose all the while and fabricating some nonsense about the state of the ice in order to avoid a court martial for rescinding on his promise. Again: how can this be? He had a severe voyage. Oh goodness, did he? The storm that he successfully weathered across the north Atlantic will be *nothing* compared to the time I want with him, alone. He found *nothing*! No notes, no evidence of an encampment, no British cairns under which you explorer types like to hide your treasures—where can you be, my love, and why can we not find you? What kind of game are you playing?

At the same time, in the same paper (!!) is a report of your safety: that an American whaler received word of two ships "all well" in Prince Regent's Inlet—is that you? Is that not where Sir James himself was—and if so, why did he not find you? The report came after Ross and his men would have already left—could you have been so close and missed each other? The thought is incredible, and terrifying. Did we have you in our grasp, and failed to make the final push? Ross will have so much to answer for.

Ross is hatefully triumphant even in his failure: he is, according to *The Times*, "rather the worse for his perilous voyage, but animated with his characteristic energy." I bet he is. What hardship was he forced to endure beyond a season not searching out his own glory? Was he filled with regret for having turned down the opportunity in the first place? Did he exact his revenge by simply saying it couldn't be done? Then he can go home with a clear conscience, his wife won't feel as if she had kept him from any glory that should have been his. But where does that leave us? Oh all the good gods, it leaves us in a terrible mess. He still professes his confident opinions about everything; he's still the expert, but he has become even more than the rest of them the armchair navigator extraordinaire. He has not come to see me. He has no idea where you have gone, found no meaningful trace of your path, and will never, ever, go north again. I hope against hope that his obvious trepidation doesn't infect the other polar captains still willing to see something through. He cannot be our best and last.

I will write again when I have news. For all our sakes, I hope that will be soon.

Your Jane

Times *05 December 1849* p5
NAVAL INTELLIGENCE

PORTSMOUTH, *Tuesday*

Another expedition to search for Sir John Franklin having been for some days talked about as in contemplation by the Government, the opinion most prevalent in naval circles at this port is decidedly against any further waste of money and sacrifice of life and comfort in such an adventure, which, it is believed, will yield nothing but repeated disappointment. If another expedition is fitted out, however, it is hoped Rear-Admiral Beaufort (the Admiralty hydrographer, who is reported to be at the head of the new expedition movement) will be commissioned to take the command of it.

5 December 1849

My poor, dear love,

I have started to wonder whether I should be writing to you anymore; the news I have to tell is too depressing, and you need to keep your spirits up. We are each other's helpmeet, though, and a burden shared is a burden lessened. I have you on my shoulders, so once in a while you must also bear me along a little bit.

There is more absolute fatalistic vitriol from *The Times*, allegedly from Portsmouth, but I know better, for it's not one man in a hundred there who doesn't instantly snap to attention and volunteer his services for another expedition when a trip to the pole is mentioned. Here is the rubbish, so you can see what I mean: "the opinion most prevalent in naval circles at this point is decidedly against any further waste of money and sacrifice of life and comfort in such an adventure, which, it is believed, will yield nothing but repeated disappointment." Ironically, in the midst of all this doom and gloom, they put forward the name of your old (and I use the word advisedly) friend Beaufort as a potential commander! That is just laughable: *you* in your advanced age of 59 were a source of worry and doubt a full *four years ago*, and now they want to send out someone decidedly older than yourself! It is laughable—laughable if it weren't so awful. What has happened to the strong leadership of our youth? It has melted away into the desks and drawing rooms of the nation. Sir Francis wants you found: the message is, well, then he shall do it himself. There is no more dignity in old age, no respect for the generation that has gone before. We simply fall off the end of the earth, and no more thought is given to our passing. If Beaufort goes, I will endeavour to go with him. Someone needs to show a sense of duty.

Yours for better or for worse,
Jane

15 December 1849

My dearest love,

Captain Collinson will head a two-ship expedition to the western Arctic, to proceed through Behring's Straits east in the *Enterprise* and *Investigator*. These were Sir James Ross's ships. I can only hope that the taint of his timorousness was scrubbed away by their time in Woolwich dockyard, and that the copper cladding of Collinson himself is as solid as the plating on his ships. McClure to be his second. I know little about him. This is something to cling to as 1850 approaches.

Your Jane

1850

Times *01 January 1850* p7

WOOLWICH, *Dec. 31*

The Hon. Miss Courtenay Boyle, Mrs. Brodie, and the Misses Boddington, Spring-gardens, near relations of Captain Sir John Franklin, visited Woolwich Dockyard to-day, accompanied by Commander Codrington Forsyth, who conducted them to the Enterprise, where they were received by Captain Collinson, C.B., and shown all the preparations making on board that vessel preparatory to proceeding on a searching expedition to Behring's Straits. The Hon. Miss Courtenay Boyle and party were then conducted to the Investigator, where they were received by Commander McClure, and, after going over the vessels and witnessing the ample preparations made for the relief of the missing voyagers, and the quantities of preserved meats and potatoes which have been shipped, they left Woolwich highly gratified with their visit. Lady Franklin intended visiting the vessels to-day with the relatives of Sir John Franklin, but was detained in town in correspondence with some of the naval authorities.

22 January 1850

A happy belated New Year's wish to you, my dearest love.

1849 is one year I am most happy to see the back of. Too many ups and downs, hopes half-filled and even little dreams destroyed. Your Eleanor married, Sophy with me now, no more Bedford Place. I spent time at Christmas working—Sophy left to spend December with her mother in Guernsey, and I dallied with maps and instructions, and forgot all about the season. I attended dinner, of course, at Bedford Place, and the light snow that fell in Russell Square made the garden look a picture, but I was mostly blue and couldn't cheer at the festivities. Mary fretted overmuch, and Frank scowled. My paper hat was askew, and there was no-one to right it for me. I doubt anyone missed my singing.

But if I've lost some ground in the family line, much has been gained in the Arctic one: the *Enterprise* and *Investigator* are away— round the Horn, up the west coast, and into the waiting jaws of the north. To find you, yes, but as always *The Times* fails utterly to couch its stories in terms of kindness, delivering blows with every sentence. It is, after all, not just you the new explorers are after, but the "well-merited promotion" they will receive once they haul you home by hook or by crook. Human decency isn't powerful enough an incentive any more. I feel too old to carry this fight much further. We no longer hold the same values as the rest of the warriors on the battlefield. I am doing my best to ignore everything but what moves us forward, but it is a Sisyphusian challenge. Ah me—I feel too old for this game, but too old to give it up!

> *Old ladies by the garden gate do wait*
> *Upon their erstwhile lovers' news—*
> *Refusing to release them to their fate.*
>
> *To wait and list, they cannot help but choose;*
> *Compelled, they stay early and late—*
> *To turn away is their own hearts to lose.*

As I said, I was stuck in London over Christmas—there was just so much to do to insinuate myself into the plans of Captain Collinson. He was ever a gracious host, and listened to my suggestions and even took notes—especially when I pointed to the paper in front of him and raised my eyebrows at his pen. But between our meetings, it meant that I had some time to myself, without even Sophy, who has been with me constantly since Eleanor left. I must admit I felt an unaccustomed lightness in my step when I closed her carriage door, though she herself didn't look entirely pleased at the hour of her departure, and sent me abject letters nearly every day. And what did I do with my time? I'm a bit embarrassed, really: I read a novel! I have just finished reading it, and it made me think of you, my love. It was an unusual choice for me, as you know, but I saw Sophy unable to put it down and was intrigued—there was interest rather than passion in her expression as she read it. Much of it was ghastly, but what made me think of you was how I knew that its feisty little protagonist would have found herself tucked under your protective wing from the first page, even though you would have been offended by the book's passionate intensity. Still, like me, you too would have finished it in order to see it through, to see your young charge safely delivered on the other side of adulthood. It is *Jane Eyre* by a Mr. Currer Bell, and the literati here at home have been in an absolute froth about it. Blasphemous! they cry. Grotesque! Mr. Bell, they moan, has drawn a shameful portrait of an ungrateful little girl who wants more than her allotted due from the universe (!!), and strives to better her life—for shame! With such an unorthodox approach to duty, I guarantee that it shall never make it into the Royal Navy library!

I admit, there are parts of the novel that make me turn up my nose – the shuffling creature in the attic, and all the passages about Mr. Rochester's granite features and massive chest (these would be the passages Sophy lingered over, I'm sure)—but little Jane is a girl after our own hearts. (And how can she not be with a name like that!) You would love her and care for her (and the book would then never have to be written), and for my own part, I feel a slightly shameful kindred energy with her. She doesn't want fame, or fortune, or fancy clothes, or glittering parties: she wants knowledge, and love, and freedom, and uses her formidable intellect to secure these on her own terms. The passages in the book in which she describes her desires, and how she chafes under her considerable social restraints, make me shift uncomfortably in my chair: they seem too true to be the work of simple imagination. This leads me to a secret conclusion: "Mr. Bell" must be a woman. She, too, knows what it is to have considerable energy and to be unable to show it, or to have her fire continually damped by the duller lights around her simply because they wear trousers.

It makes me wonder, too, in the few idle moments I've stolen in Sophy's absence, what I might have produced if I had decided to put pen to paper. I never wanted to write a book, though I've almost constantly written journals and letters—and I know I've written more than enough pages about *your* recent adventures to fill more than one triple decker—but it was never an ambition of mine to see my name in print. My travelling mementoes, which I sold to finance the first expedition that never happened (I gave the money to the captain of the *Truelove* and ended up with nothing in return), fetched a tidy sum, but they were objects to sell, not words: things you could put your hands on, see, touch, and smell. I fear my ideas would be considered paltry things and not worth the effort of sharing, or paying for. Besides, there is already a glut in the market for "lady adventuresses," and I couldn't bear to be known as simply one more woman on a camel. So—here is my impasse, feeling empathy for a misunderstood little girl who longs to break free of her social constraints, and yet unwilling to do so myself. These days it is dangerous to look in a mirror, for fear I might start my own little war.

Your troubled Amazon,
Jane

Times *31 January 1850* p4
THE POLAR REGIONS

Whatever depends upon human zeal and ingenuity has now been attempted in order to convey assistance to the missing expedition to the Arctic Seas. The Admiralty, acting in obedience to the general wish, has a second time despatched the Enterprise and Investigator in quest of Sir John Franklin and his companions. This time these exploring ships will take another direction, and from a westerly point enter the inhospitable region in which Sir John Franklin may yet be expecting the assistance of his countrymen. In the sailing orders directed from the Admiralty to Captain Collinson his path has been chalked out for him until the first of August, when, according to calculation, he will have passed through Behring's Straits, and struck the ice. A brief recapitulation of the precautions taken may serve to show that nothing has been neglected to secure a favourable result. The orders given to Captain Collinson are to the effect that he shall take the command of the Enterprise and consider the Investigator under his orders. The ships are furnished with provisions for three years as well as with a quantity of extra stores, and have been fortified in every respect against the dangers and inclemencies of the Arctic seas. Captain Collinson is to proceed to Cape Virgins, where he will find a steamer in waiting to tow him through the straits of Magellan and the Wellington Channel, and so on to Valparaiso. From this port the two ships are to proceed to the Sandwich Islands, where they will receive despatches from home, and meanwhile, if possible, effect a junction with the Herald and Plover. In case he should join company with these vessels, Captain Collinson is directed to add Commander Moore and the Plover to his expedition, and make all despatch so as to reach Behring's Straits in July and actually to strike the ice by the first of August.

The necessary limits to which we are confined forbid us from enlarging upon the many precautions devised by the Admiralty to carry their purpose to a successful conclusion. But they appear in this respect to be dictated by sound discretion, that they are all directed to placing Captain Collinson in possession of every facility for carrying on his operations; but what these operations shall specifically be is left mainly to his own judgment as soon as he shall have reached the scene of action. Once arrived at the ice, for three years Captain Collinson is left to himself, subject only to some general directions as to winter quarters. For three years he will be sedulously engaged in despatching parties of men in such directions as may seem the most likely to produce favourable results, in organizing boat expeditions to search every nook and cranny of the Arctic shores, if yet any trace of Franklin and his companions may be found. As we look at the map of the Polar regions with that anxiety which all must feel for the fate of our gallant countrymen, we cannot but think that what has as yet been done has been merely to arrive on the westerly and easterly edges of the region in which the crews of the Erebus and Terror may yet be expecting relief in lingering misery. The expedition of Sir JAMES ROSS was unfortunate from the premature and unwonted severity with which the bad weather set in; and the westerly course, by way of Melville's Island, into the heart of the Arctic region was hopelessly blocked up. So with regard to the more recent advance of the boats of the Herald and Plover, steering east, which reached the mouth of the Mackenzie River. It is scarcely possible that Sir John Franklin and his party, if their ships be lost, as seems probable, should have arrived so far west. Thus, by an unfortunate conjunction of circumstances, the researches of the parties on either side have just stopped at those points where they were likely to become most useful. With regard to the boat expedition from the Herald and Plover, it may fairly be supposed that, had our missing countrymen been able at all to strike the northern coast of America, they would rather have made for the interior than have directed their steps along the shores in an easterly direction. The distance was too great, the impracticability of finding means to eke out their own failing stores too absolute, the risk of not meeting an expedition which probably might be sent to their relief, too awful for Sir John Franklin to take upon himself the responsibility of such a step. It is possible that our countrymen may have been imprisoned in the ice in the endeavour to pass westerly from Bathurst and Melville Islands, and may still be there; it is possible they may have struck some still more northerly land not known to previous Arctic navigators. Either of these suppositions would tally with what we know of their position when last heard of, and with the reports we have received of the great accumulations of ice in those high latitudes during the last three years. It is possible that Sir John Franklin may have been hopelessly involved in the ice in one or other of these directions, and that he may be still lying where his course was stopped. But when we take into account the enterprising character and the Arctic experience of that officer, we cannot think that if life be yet spared to him and to his companions he would be contented to wait inactive until relief should reach him. The natural direction he would take would be either for the whaling ships by Barrow's Straits or for the northern coast of America, in order to reach one of the settlements of the Hudson's Bay Company.

As we understand the matter, the reason why the Enterprise and Investigator are now despatched by way of Behring's instead of Barrow's Straits does not depend upon any expectation of picking up the lost party near the point where Captain Collinson is directed to enter upon his operations, but is contained in the first paragraph of the Admiralty instructions:—"Whereas the efforts that have been made for the last two years to relieve the Erebus and Terror have failed, and all access to the Parry Islands has been prevented by the accumulation of ice in the upper part of Barrow's Straits; and whereas it is possible that the same severity of weather may not prevail at the same time in both the eastern and western entrances to the Arctic Sea, we have determined," &c. Common sense would have dictated the propriety of following on Sir John Franklin's track, as Sir JAMES ROSS recently endeavoured to do, had it been within the bounds of possibility to accomplish the task. It is only through despair of carrying such a purpose into effect that Captain Collinson has been despatched to reach, by a more circuitous route, the spot where Sir John Franklin must be if he be in the Arctic Seas at all and yet alive. If such be the real opinion of the Admiralty, we trust that no countenance will be shown to a further expedition which it is proposed shall explore the coasts of an island which was discovered last summer by the Herald and Plover. We trust the Admiralty will entirely discountenance any such projects, to be carried out by means of a fresh expedition. In the instructions given to Captain Collinson, we find it very properly set down that he is to remember that his operations are not to be directed to any object of a merely scientific character—he is sent out on account of Sir John Franklin, and Sir John Franklin alone. If it be necessary that a search should be instituted in the direction proposed, surely Captain COLLINSON has already sufficient means at his disposal to effect such an investigation without the necessity for equipping and despatching any fresh expedition.

We yield to none in our strong and earnest sympathy for Sir John Franklin and his companions, yet we cannot but feel that the effort to be now made by Captain Collinson is a last effort. By Barrow's Straits it is impossible to get through the ice. Whatever practical benefit might be expected from a land expedition is amply secured by the exertions and vigilance of the hunters in the employment of the Hudson's Bay Company. What remains? Simply such an investigation of the Polar Seas from the westward as may enable us to feel that we have done all that lay in human power for the relief of our gallant countrymen. Of what avail is it to continue a search when it has become absolutely impossible that it should be attended with any effect, or to direct expeditions to points which the crews of the Erebus and Terror could by no possibility have reached?

3 February 1850

My dearest, poor love,

I am left to my own devices, and am forced to find you myself. Without a doubt I am the sole intended audience for this scurrilous article, which casts your sense of duty in a suspicious light and makes me out as a harpy devoid of common sense. *The Times* is nothing more than an anonymous band of libelous grubbers who hide behind their first-person plurals to deal out acid like candy. It is true: I am disappointed. It is true: I believe the Admiralty should do more. How can it be otherwise? But how, with so little area left to search, can an expedition heading in the wrong direction be reasonably considered the "last"? If the Admiralty is no help, nor *The Times*, nor the Americans, I will try a new path, just as you would have done. You are simply somewhere in the unknown, and there are precious few of those places left. When all the remaining blank spaces are filled, and only then, I say, will "we have done all that lay in human power" to be done. We will find our way back to each other.

Your Jane

Times *04 February 1850* p7
NAVAL INTELLIGENCE

According to present arrangements a Conservative member of the House of Commons will on an early day move for a grant for another expedition to proceed in the direction of Davis's Straits, Lancaster Sound, and Barrow's Straits, in search of Captain Sir John Franklin. The hon. member will be supported in his application by members of both sides of the House, but the Admiralty will take no part for or against the proposal; at the same time their Lordships will most cordially aid in carrying out such recommendations as may be adopted by a majority of the House of Commons, when the propriety of another north-west expedition is brought before them. Lady Franklin has at her own private expense retained the service of Mr. Penny, late master of the Advice whaler, and he will proceed with the expedition in the event of its being approved of by the Legislature, to render his assistance in the Arctic regions, with which he is so well acquainted. Several officers of the Royal Navy have also volunteered their services on this occasion, some of them having formerly served under Sir John Franklin, and being most anxious for his safety and that of his gallant companions.

---

15 February 1850

The Times is wrong—what delicious words to string into a sentence. No "last" expedition about Captain Collinson—indeed, his two-ship command is to be the smaller of the two expeditions now being arranged by Whitehall. Huzzah! Four ships are to come to you by the East—to really, really follow your path. They will meet in the middle, and cradle you between them in their collective embrace. I hardly know more than the bare skeleton of the story, but as flesh gathers to its bones, I will draw the contours lovingly, like a map.

Jane

24 February 1850

My dearest love,

What would you say if I told you that someone knows exactly where you are? What would you say if I told you that such a person was in

England? What if I told you that such a person was a three-year-old girl named Louisa, and that she was dead? Now don't lift a finger in protest, nor clear your throat in stupefied disbelief. (You see? I know you! Now, stop that!) I would not have believed it myself, really, but sometimes the truth arrives in mysterious packages.

A stranger, a Captain Coppin, came to Spring Gardens Monday last. He bore a message from Louisa, his little daughter who had died but who has been visiting her family as a spirit, especially her sister. The two have conversations! I admit that this is highly unorthodox, but there is a growing science behind the study of spirit communication that is gaining ground in these modern times, and actual physical proof of the information she provides. As he related it to me, Captain Coppin has seen the writing his daughter's spirit puts on the wall herself, with the letters "P.R.I." and the words "Victory" and "Victoria" in answer to her sister's questions as to your whereabouts. (Children are asking the dead about you! Your fame reaches even beyond earthly experience!) The last woman we saw with the same reputed talent, a Mrs. Dawson, was frankly untrustworthy, and Sophy kept her busy with questions about Crozier's heartstrings—but this is different. Mrs. D. was a simple charlatan with a few teeth missing and a cheap Indian shawl, but this little girl and her communication have some basis in fact. I am inclined to believe the young sisters (both of them; the living and the dead)— *we* did not consult *them*: *they* have given this information freely, and how can a three-year-old girl know such details of the Arctic map? "Victory"—Victory Point—I take a practical perspective on the information, that she points not to the end result, but to the place where you might be found. I am obsessed with the possibility, but find I can tell no-one, alas! Whom would I tell? *Who* in the stone grey walls of Whitehall would listen to this story? Not Barrow Junior, old before his time, not adolescent Hamilton. Beaufort?

I feel for Captain Coppin, who evidently misses his youngest daughter terribly. Her occasional visitations, especially to his elder child, give the illusion that she remains, somehow, with them. How could I reject his offering of communication from the beyond, when I am constantly seeking the same thing from you? Here I am, writing you letters that never get sent, willing you to receive them through some means other than the penny post, *willing* somehow that the feelings and thoughts I send your way will cross the abyss of uncertainty between us and land safely on your heart, one direct leap from mine to yours. The look in his eyes was not just *for me*; it *was* me. I believe him because I have to, for not to do so is to wreck the entire house of cards I have already built around myself, each card with your image engraved on both sides.

After my visits with Captain Coppin I stuck an arctic map to the wall of my sitting room, on one side of the room where the morning sun hits, and with far too much blank between, on the other end of the wall I stuck a map of England. Each morning since, I have had my new ritual: I find "Victory" Point on the map with my finger and trace it slowly through that impossible blank space you were meant to fill in, right through Prince Regent Inlet ("P.R.I."), right off the map, through the Atlantic (with the occasional loop-the-loop for authenticity, though you are a master navigator, of course), and safe to the shores of Scotland, England, London, and home. The more I do this, the easier it seems. I trace your way home with my fingers— could it be so straightforward with a ship?

Your Jane

10 March 1850

My dearest love,

The Lords and Captains of your precious Admiralty have got hold of the Louisa Coppin story, and are in a terrible pile of humbug about it. Captain Coppin wrote to the Lords himself, though I expressly asked him not to. I have no idea if he mentioned my name in his letter, but as they know I have been pushing for a ship to go to Prince Regent Inlet, undoubtedly they have made the connection. This is the death-knell for my hopes in that quarter. Because of good Captain Coppin himself, they will not send a ship to Victory Point—the planning of their huge expeditions to the East and the West is already underway and no additional ones will be considered—even the little victualling and support transports will not veer off their chosen routes to try the possibility for a single season. You'd think the ships—and the Admiralty itself—were trains on tracks, so difficult it is for them to change course once their steam is up, in spite of the fact that they float on *water*, still are subject to the winds, and routes are infinitely variable. But this is just as I suspected. I am *persona non grata* at Whitehall these days because of it, though I do not blame Captain Coppin for his insistence on telling the Lords the source of his information. I suspect they would have been as likely to listen to him as they would his dead daughter—he, a mere shipbuilder, with practical information on a Navy man? Impossible! Almost as impossible, one might say, as them listening to a woman.

Still, I show myself there with regularity in order to make them remember that someone is watching them, but with their thick files of memos and secret letters, they brush me off like a fly. I'll tell you what: I will organize my own expedition and send it straight to Victory Point and show them all.

Your Jane

Times *13 March 1850* p4
FROM THE LONDON GAZETTE

ADMIRALTY, *March 7*

£20,000 REWARD will be given by Her Majesty's Government to any party or parties, of any country, who shall render efficient assistance to the crews of the discovery ships, under the command of Sir John Franklin:—

To any party or parties who, in the judgment of the Board of Admiralty, shall discover and effectually relieve the crews of Her Majesty's ships Erebus and Terror, the sum of £20,000. Or,

To any party or parties who, in the judgment of the Board of Admiralty, shall discover and effectually relieve any of the crews of Her Majesty's ships Erebus and Terror, or shall convey such intelligence as shall lead to the relief of such crews or any of them, the sum of £10,000. Or,

To any party or parties who, in the judgment of the Board of Admiralty, shall, by virtue of his or their efforts, first succeed in ascertaining their fate, £10,000.

W.A.B. Hamilton
Secretary of the Admiralty

[Editor's note: n.d.]

This is good news: £20,000 offered for the men brave enough to follow you. Is it a coincidence that such a reward be offered on the eve of the Admiralty's own biggest, most concerted push to find you—6 ships in all? Perhaps not, but lest I be accused of cynicism, I shall hold my tongue. As means to an end, I care not. They are doing what must be done.

25 March 1850

My dearest love,

Once again your rebel wife has broken down the barricades of convention and smashed the stained-glass windows of decorum! What, you ask, has that beastly but irresistible woman done? This time she has bought herself a ship, filled it with supplies, manned it with the best, and sent it off with all possible despatch to find you. In spite of her misgivings about appealing to powers other than those sitting on an earthly throne, she has wished "godspeed" to her sailors and received their hearty cheers. Fancying herself quite regal, she has taken ownership of her own *Prince Albert*, a hardy tub of 89 tons. At the helm is Captain Charles Codrington Forsyth, a young man she especially trusts to follow her instructions as well as his heart, which seems to be in the right place—viz., more interested in finding you than the glory and purse that still accrue to new latitudes. Though initially determined not to ask the Admiralty Board for help, your errant bride has successfully negotiated stores of pemmican, Burberry waterproofs, and counted time for Captain Forsyth and his little crew, and now patiently sits and waits (!) for news. She trusts that, as in all like circumstances in which she has overstepped herself in your behalf, you will shake your head, draw her close, kiss her gently on the forehead, and forgive her.

Her

Times *16 April 1850* p8
THE ARCTIC EXPEDITION

ABERDEEN, *Saturday*

The Lady Franklin, Captain Penny, and the Sophia, Captain Stewart, sailed from this port to-day for the Arctic regions, in search of Sir John Franklin. The two vessels were hauled out of the docks at 2 o'clock, and left the harbour amid the cheers of some thousands of spectators. The Lady Franklin is a first class clipper brig, built at Aberdeen, and the Sophia is equally strong, though less sharp in her model, and was built at Dundee. The Expedition is under the command of Captain Penny, who volunteered his services, and in recommending him to the Admiralty Sir Francis Beaufort says—

"The daring but prudent conduct that Mr. Penny is said to have evinced on many occasions, together with the large experience that he must have gained during a whole life among the ice, as well as the ambition he expresses to distinguish himself in this noble enterprise, on which all eyes are turned, lead me to think that it would be wise to let loose his energy, and to give him the opportunity for which he begs. I may add that I believe this would sensibly gratify Lady Franklin."

Captain Penny has been to the Arctic regions almost every year for the last 20 years. He went to Davis's Straits first as an apprentice seaman, and had the experience of his father, who had then been long known as a captain of one or other of the Aberdeen whalers, and soon after his apprenticeship was completed he became first mate, and then a master himself. When commanding one of the Aberdeen whalers in 1839, he gathered some information from an Esquimaux, which led him to believe there was an unexplored region in the Straits abounding with whales; and having got the young native to come to Scotland, he managed to educate him so as to be able to line out a chart of the unknown bay, and to give such an account of its geographical bearings as enabled him next season to explore it, and to open up a new source of supply when whales failed in the ordinary fishing-ground. In this way, and in various other ways, Captain Penny gained an acquaintance with almost every inlet and sound of Davis's Straits; and it is well known that he has been able to add considerably to our stock of knowledge of the icy regions of the North. He has a most perfect conviction that Sir John Franklin is yet alive, and is to pursue his search in the first instance in Admiralty Jones's Sound and the Wellington Channel.

The Lady Franklin and Sophia have 25 men each, including officers, and are provisioned for three years. They have each a full supply of coals, but are to receive additional coals from the Pacific, of this port, which vessel took out a large quantity when she sailed the other day for Davis's Straits. All the appointments of the vessels are of the most simple and practical description. They have boats similar to those of the ordinary whaler; ice anchors, ice saws, warping apparatus, and every sort of machinery necessary to enable them to make way through the ice. There is also a full and complete assortment of geographical and astronomical apparatus, and, what is of no small value in this important expedition, a large amount of discretionary power conferred on the commander.

---

15 May 1850

My dearest love,

Everyone is away in your behalf, and I am spending my days in hopeful expectation of something good. It's May, and 1850 still feels full of hope. With the spring, my spirit has returned to the garden, as always, and the days have been beautiful in Russell Square. You would love it so, this year! In among all the anxious thoughts and worries, like the little buds of campion pushing their way through the solid canopies of holly and boxwood, some pleasant moments actually intrude on my days. I have actually *met* the mysterious Mr. Rowe, and while I was smugly thinking I knew all there was to know about him, it turns out that *he* has some idea of who I am, too. At first I found it disconcerting, but eventually—even in our first conversation—I decided it was like meeting someone I already knew. In these days of official visits, so many strangers, and Byzantine naval protocol, a conversation about flowers was apparently just what I needed.

It happened a week or so ago, on my usual constitutional. I suppose I can't expect not to be noticed if I make myself such a creature of habit. But I actually had my back to the path; I was looking closely at the variegations in the cinquefoil leaves in one of the corner beds, trying to discern a common pattern, when I heard the distinct crunch of adult footsteps on the gravel nearby. I didn't know they were for me, so steadfastly ignored them, but they hovered around my vicinity and stopped right at my side. When I finally turned, I saw with some surprise it was Mr. Rowe himself; I had seen him from afar, but never up close. It was a warm day, so he had his jacket off, and his shirtsleeves rolled, but his waistcoat was buttoned and his collar and neckerchief were clean. His hat he had pushed back on his head—it is a large, straw affair that looks French, but I can't place it—but he took it off when I looked at him by way of starting his introduction. In his other hand, he held a sprig of rose campion from the neighbouring bed, whose blooms were on the verge of opening, so their bright pink tongues were just barely visible. He held it out to me with a smile. I think he is slightly younger than I am, but as I have looked at men so seldom over the last few years, it's difficult to tell.

I accepted the campion, because it was totally irresistible, but even as I did so I felt one eyebrow raise, unsure how to respond. Was I being complimented, or singled out as the culprit who spread the renegade seeds in the other beds? I couldn't be sure. I was prepared to be insulted by his familiarity, but the novelty of being approached and looked at frankly was too much to resist. Here was one person in London who did not appear to think me tragic, or frightening, or formidable, or sad. I knew who he was, but had no other idea for an opening salvo: "And you are, sir?"

"The Gardener, madam. Mr. Benjamin Rowe, currently in the employ of the Russell Square Horticultural Interest." He swung his hat like a musketeer, offered a little bow and, while he was bent forward, turned slightly and reached with his left hand to deadhead an early blown rose. In the gesture I realised that I had often seen him crouched before the rose when I would stop on my rounds at the cinquefoil. The slightly frizzled top of his head—as I suppose my crouched bonnet top did to him—looked familiar; I must have passed him more frequently than I thought, noticing only his hunched form half lost in whatever perennial he was tending. He spends most of his time digging around in the garden's underskirts. "With your permission," he continued, "I notice you here some times, madam, and welcome you as a visitor to the flowers of the little park. You know the flowers here like they're your own, and they seem to know you too."

Well! Here was space for conversation, for observation, for delight. Never in all my many years have I had such a welcome, or such a compliment, especially from a stranger, perhaps not even from the Duke himself. I have come to this park as on a pilgrimage ever since Father moved us to Bedford Place, and whenever we were back from our travels: it felt like my real home, more than the house itself. After all our time away, my love—in the Mediterranean, in Van Diemen's Land—I didn't know if anything would really feel like home, especially without you by my side. But coming back to Russell Square *has* been a real homecoming, and it was deeply gratifying to learn that someone besides me and his Bronze Ploughship not only recognizes my own affection for the park, but sees how absolutely special this little piece of paradise is in the middle of London. With Mr. Rowe constantly rising from underneath the plants themselves, it's as if he, too, is grown here; he just transplants himself regularly to whichever bed needs tending. The Russell Square Horticultural Interest have certainly done themselves an immense service in retaining him.

Of course I told him who I was, and of course he listened politely and pretended that I hadn't been pointed out to him by others in the park—I'd even see them do it, on more than one occasion—people looking and pointing at the sad woman in black, who hangs like a shadow in the Square—or the mad woman who talks to the Duke of Bedford's statue on her way in, and *then* hangs like a shadow in the Square. (When did I get so eccentric? How could you have let me?) In my turn, I did my best to pretend that his own history was new to me, though women are better at hiding what they know than men are, so I think my performance of surprise was more convincing. As we talked, we walked, and at one point he handed me his secateurs and waved his left hand over a holly bush that had got leggy. I took the secateurs and trimmed the new growth into shape, and his look of approval at my sense of proportion was as gratifying as the knowledge that the holly would grow stronger under my ministrations.

All in all, it was a most pleasant morning. We agreed to meet again, perhaps once a month, for the Admiralty and the newspapers often dictate my schedule, and we will continue our conversation about perennials, urban gardens, and the soil of southern England. No more will I feel like a haunting, like a darkened interloper amongst the rolling hoops, perambulators and little dogs. Mr. Rowe—and the flowers who tend to both of us—give me my right to be there.

Your Jane

Times *27 May 1850* p4
AMERICA

BY ELECTRIC TELEGRAPH
The Advance and Rescue, the vessels com-prising the American expedition in search of Sir John Franklin, are all ready and transferred to the Government. A large number of seamen have volunteered.

---

27 May 1850

My dearest love,

Trala! Not to do violence to hackneyed expressions, but the Americans are back on track, full steam ahead, and hitching the wagons. Practice your "howdy." The Government has accepted the kind generosity of a private philanthropist, a new money man, Mr. Henry Grinnell—a business man with the heart of an explorer. Our own Government may yet learn how to say "yes please" and "thank you" when receiving similar suggestions; but it is an ongoing lesson and will take some time. 10 ships to find you so far this season!

Your Jane

1 June 1850

My dearest love,

We always knew Prince Albert was a powerful ally in your behalf, and now he seeks you out himself, trala! My own modest boat, the *Prince Albert*, is on the verge of sailing under the tidy captaincy of Commander Charles Forsyth, a man who inspires calm confidence and whom we knew in Van Diemen's Land, who is all fired up to head north in your name. He has no polar experience, but is a fine sailor, and I trust him. She is victualled for two years, and is heading to Victory Point—and victory, I am sure of it! I don't care what Commander Forsyth may think of my instructions or where I got them (I know he has heard of Louisa Coppin's story): it's my ship and he will follow them. I send him, literally, with a dream—even two: Louisa's own tale, written on her sister's wall, and the vision of a Mr. Parker Snow, not a navy man, and admittedly prone to inspirations other than your whereabouts, but a resourceful one who has grown up in the Australian bush and who, according to most of his visions, also can see where you are. His second sight is consistent with Louisa's, and so he and she will both keep Commander Forsyth on track. To Victory, my love, and victory!

And in case you don't yet know, there is more: in April, and then in May, the grand Admiralty expeditions sailed: the first, two ships under the whaling captain of my own selection, a rough but well-meaning man who will do his utmost to find you—Captain

Penny—and the second comprising four vessels under a man you knew in his youth: Captain Horatio Thomas Austin, who has turned into a capable captain with moral as well as martial control over his four navy ships headed north. His lieutenants were unusually quiet during the official send-off—Austin appears to be a strong taskmaster—but I have no doubt the collective energy will keep all on an even keel once they arrive. Penny is a man you can lean against. I only hope his perception of his inferior status—he is not "true Navy"—does not blind him to the benefits of collaboration with Captain Austin. These ships with men aboard! How many troubles they cause! If only we could launch the ships with only instructions and no-one aboard, to push them with sticks like the young boys do in the pond in Green Park, how easy this search would be. As soon as men board, though, it's all hotheadedness and wrong impressions, as bad as a Jane Austen novel or one of those dreadfuls that Sophy leaves lying about.

Captain Penny was *my* choice, and he was off first in the whimsically named *Lady Franklin* and the *Sophia*. Sophy was quite pink on the dock when she saw the ship, finally, named for her—it is a lesser vessel than the *Lady Franklin*, to be sure, but it will hopefully be as faithful a companion as its namesake is to me. Then Austin in four ships—two steam, two sail—to trail behind and pick up Penny's droppings. Ha! If Penny were to find the trick, it would give me no end of satisfaction. To that end, I feel a poem coming on:

Not Ross, not Parry, but Penny!
Comparisons? There can't be any!
He'll bravely go forth
And conquer the north
His discoveries: they will be many!
To Franklin, John Franklin, he sails!
Against him, the Admiralty rails!
With "LF" and "S"
He'll pass the dire test,
And learn of our heroes' travails!

Of course, if truth be told, one thing *could* give me more satisfaction than having Captain Penny find you, and that would be for my own little *Prince Albert* to sail on by them all, pushing its inconspicuous way to Victory Point and coming back with whatever prize there is for us to find. Haha! What a piquant victory that would be. But I hold out no ambition for any particular one of these captains, my love, and will willingly give all I have left to the one who brings you home.

Your waiting, loving Jane

15 July 1850

My dearest love,

Another blow! President Zachary Taylor is dead! I can hardly believe it. Our greatest ally and advocate on the international stage, who has already done so much to help us but who has yet to make good his promise of government aid—dead. With the political upheaval now playing itself out, I am forced to retrench and turn my attention once more to Whitehall. We will get no help from the Americans. I am too despondent to write more. I can only hope there is good news from the *Prince Albert*, Captain Penny, and Captain Austin.

3 September 1850

My dearest love,

I've had nothing to write, so have written nothing. We are simply playing the waiting game now. Today, however, was a pure pleasure worth sharing, even though I feel somewhat guilty having enjoyed a late summer day without you. Another lovely morning, courtesy of the Russell Square Horticultural Interest, but today the prize for the

moment that most enlivened this tired heart came from dear old
Thomas. I rarely write of him, but I am sure you know that he is still
a frequent presence in our lives, even since Sophy and I have left
Bedford Place. Mary's concession—likely the product of her terrible
guilt for not really wanting us there—was that once a week at the
appointed time (Monday mornings, without fail), Thomas would
come round with the carriage and drive me and Sophy wherever
we needed to go. Being without regular transport was initially a
blow, when we moved to Spring Gardens, even though Whitehall
was right across the way. Though its motivation was wrong-head-
ed, I do appreciate the gesture and take full advantage of Thomas's
time when I have him. Mostly, we go to Russell Square. He rarely talks—I think I wouldn't even recognize his voice if I heard it
behind me—but his presence is calming, and I trust him utterly.
Today I have further evidence of why. We went to Russell Square
as usual this morning, though this time without Sophy, who had
some transcriptions she needed to complete. It was a blustery but
fine day, and as I descended from the carriage with Thomas's help,
the wind came up and my shawl was caught by one of the horse's
buckles as I moved past him. With a gesture as natural and gentle as
Mr. Rowe with his secateurs, without thinking, Thomas unhooked
me and smoothed the shawl back over my shoulder, making sure
the corner draped exactly over my right shoulder blade at the back,
and even pinching the point. It occurred to me that I am one of his
many helpless beasts who find themselves burdened by the troubles
of the modern world, which he soothes by instinct with his rough,
dark hands. Oh my love, it has been so very long since I have seen
your hands, and felt their gentle pressure. Thomas's unexpected
touch gave me pause, but not for etiquette's sake—for memory's. It
was you who used to arrange my shawl, you who shielded me from
the blasts, even in summer. I could not look at him for choking on
the thought, and had to cough out a thank you with a hand on my
throat as I lurched my way to the Duke. Thomas sees all, though,
and when I returned from my sojourn in the garden, he inspected
the placement of my shawl as if he had personally ordered the wind

to stop blowing in order that it stayed on. It did, and I was grateful.

Come home, will you?
Your Jane

Times *30 September 1850* p6
**RETURN OF THE
NORTH STAR FROM
THE ARCTIC REGIONS**

PORTSMOUTH, *Saturday, Sept. 28*
Her Majesty's ship North Star, Mas-
ter-Commander J. Saunders, which went
out in May, 1849, with provisions for Sir
John Franklin and the Arctic expedition,
arrived at Spithead at 10:40 this morning.
We wish that we could report any tidings
of Sir John Franklin, but unhappily upon
this important subject the North Star's log
is an entire blank.

---

13 October 1850

My dearest love,

All is lost from the *Prince Albert*: *Lieutenant* Forsyth has come back after *one* season—not even one season!—with nothing to tell. Not only did they find nothing, they didn't even start on their path down Prince Regent Inlet; he must have seen it off the bow, ticked it off his list and turned around. I am appalled. On our reunion he acknowledged the "dismay" I must be feeling at his premature return. It was all I could do to tell him that "dismay doesn't even begin to touch how I am feeling at this moment." Men aboard their stupid ships! Except that this ship was *not* his to turn around, it was *mine*, and he has turned around with *no* reason that I can see but his own brutish incompetence. Mr. Snow's visions remain only visions—no landscape reared up before him that fit his dreams of where you were—and of course not, since Lt. Forsyth didn't sail far enough west for any of those visions to come true.

I cannot write more. There is no more to tell.

I only know I am still,
Your Jane

12 November 1850

Today I helped Mr. Rowe put Russell Square to bed for the season—
heaping up leaves, cutting stalks that may break, keeping some
"winter interest" as he calls it—tucking the beetles and earthworms,
ants and London hedgehogs into their nests. What we lack in au-
rora borealis in this grey old city we make up in this little corner of
London: streaks of red dogwood, a canopy of vines like the veins
in a human body, glistening holly. Mr. Rowe had two small baskets
of dried poppy and campion heads prepared—one for each of us—
and we took opposite sides of the park to sow them wildly along
the outer beds. The exercise made me buzz inside, and we drank a
cup of tea together in his garden shed before Thomas returned with
Sophy from wherever they were. I felt deliciously rebellious, and the
sleeping seeds are a shared secret we get to keep until spring.

18 December 1850

My dearest love,

This winter the north is crowded, though, alas, without the *Prince*
Albert: Austin's four ships, so *The Times* tells us, are within hailing
distance of Penny's two, while Sir John Ross's *sturm und drang* have
got his two little ships no further than the rest of them. The masts
in Lancaster Sound must look as busy as the chimney pots outside
my window here at Spring Garden—which is where they might as
well all be, for all the good I foresee them doing you where they
are. I hope against hope that you and your men will stumble upon
the party and join it, since that seems more likely than them ever
discovering *you*.

Oh, I imagine that it's one big season of leapfrog on the ice and Her Majesty's Arctic Vaudeville, double pay and extra plum duff. I've no doubt that all the officers are clamouring for the chance to wear a bustle and a wig in the latest version of *Miss in her Teens* or what have you. The theatricals are top rate, the sailors' newspapers expertly edited and illustrated, and all aboard are happy and snug. They always are, aren't they? That is, of course, until they're not, and then it goes so calamitously wrong that they are given up for dead, slandered as cannibals and turned from even in the moment of their greatest need.

You know, I am glad that mad, bad Sir John Ross is back in the Arctic looking for you. Of all the men who have taken up the challenge, he alone is sincere, because he alone knows what it is to starve out there on the frozen wastes, to feel what it is to fall back on the resources of your own body and still see your mission through. If one man can find you and bring you home, it will be him.

Once again I am in no mood for Christmas.

Your humbug,
Jane

1851

My dearest love,

I apologize for the delay in writing to you, and for the dearth of bad poetry that usually comes your way. (Yes, I know it is bad.) I know you feel its absence mightily. But the new year in my head is as dark as that outside my dirty London window—Christmas was all strained dinners at Bedford Place, some of which I attended, and Russell Square a sad collection of tiny evergreen heads bowed under an especially heavy frost. Mr. Rowe leaves for the season. Is it as cold where you are? I hardly think so. I am despondent. Lieutenant Forsyth did nothing; I hold out no hope for Captain Collinson or Austin, Ross, or even good Captain Penny, who, I am sure, will be rubbing himself raw against the navy protocol he knows nothing about. Four more disparate characters stuck together in the ice I cannot imagine, and this does not include the burgeoning ambitions of the many junior officers, intent on making names for themselves in spite of naval tradition.

The one light still shining is Louisa Coppin's vision, and in Lt. Forsyth's failure it remains untried. I have decided to make do without the Admiralty altogether, and have chosen a Mr. Kennedy as the *Prince Albert's* new captain. He is a Canadian Métis trader who remembers you from his childhood—do you remember him? He received your help when he was a young boy and has held you in the highest regard since. He is pious and earnest, even a teetotaller, and while not a trained navigator, I don't count this as a mark against him. What has formal navy training done for us so far? Nothing! So I have thrown the whole lot away and am polishing this "diamond in the rough" to show the world what can be done if one simply has the courage to step outside of stuffy tradition.

I did not want to tell you, but I was very poorly, for some time, after Lt. Forsyth came back. It was all I could do to survive, my love, and the fight I have been continuing here in your behalf went unfought for some time. Over a series of months I have been more or less bedridden, and so I missed most of the family Simpkinson gatherings that occur at the tail end of every year. Father sent me flowers, of course. No one came to visit, not even Mary. I had only Sophy for company—I asked that she stay with me and she happily complied—and I spent most of the time simply watching her read some stupid book. I am grateful she did not share them with me; she offered to read to me a few times—the Bible, *The Times*, her book—I declined them all. (I never told her that I had read *Jane Eyre*; there have been no more "Currer Bell" books hanging about.) I know you would want me to find solace in the Book, but the Bible wants me to be content with my lot and I cannot be; *The Times* reminds me that I am *not* content; and Sophy's books have no content whatsoever! So there we were, at an absolute impasse, and I sat and watched her read. The doctor demanded no writing or reading of me; such injunctions were as torturous as the pain in my throat that kept me in bed. To watch, to listen, and do nothing: it is the hardest thing I have ever done, apart from wondering about you. To be alone with myself these days is simply dreadful.

So Captain Kennedy will sail the *Prince Albert* later in the Spring, and we shall try again. He will call upon Captain Coppin before he leaves to hear again the tale of Louisa Coppin's visitation, and this will once again be our guide. If little "Weasey" can see you, and Captain Kennedy can follow her, this may be the best plan yet.

I would thumb my nose at the Admiralty Lords, if only it did not hurt so much to stick out my tongue. Oh my love, one of the saddest losses in all of this is my sense of humour. How you used to make me laugh. These days I can hardly bear my own company. Nothing is funny anymore.

Your sad Jane

21 May 1851

My dearest love,

With Spring comes all the familiar feelings of optimism, new life, and love. My health is improving, though I keep a shawl about me at all times, and Captain Kennedy is learning how to be a good naval captain. I now have a charming young Frenchman, Lt. Joseph-Réné Bellot, ever by my side. He has taken leave from his own honourable post in the French Imperial Navy, and dedicated the next period of his life to serving you. I call him my "French son" and he responds most enthusiastically to the call: he is a young hero who was raised exactly as I would have raised him, who adores you for your bravery, and is willing to tilt his lance at whatever iceberg stands in his way. Bravo! This is a time when heroes are becoming rarer than golden eggs: the polar "experts" have melted back into the woodwork now that another expedition is being planned. Oh yes, everyone has opinions when not asked to step forward and take charge, but as soon as there is work to be done, you could hear a dog's fart echo through Whitehall. I have asked as always for materiel support, but each time I ask the response lags further and further behind. Even *The Times* is pulling back the carpet and closing the door, as you remember. I have nearly given up reading papers myself, and leave this task to Sophy, who duly cuts out each relevant article and puts it within easy reaching distance of my chair. There has been little of import: Austin, Penny, Collinson are all silent. As they should be, because they were sent out for two and three years, so we should not hear from them until 1852—unlike other little boats that simply return early due to inclement weather, these ships are at least attempting to do their duty. I digress, and these thoughts anger me too much to dwell on.

I have begun visiting Russell Square again, but give the Duke nothing but a silent wave as I enter, since speaking is still so painful these days—and I have even on occasion entered from behind him, off Montague Place, sneaking up on the poor man when he least suspects it. In the absence of talking, it's the only way to get a reaction out of him. He's a tough audience. You, my dear, were always so easy—I could always get a laugh out of you. But my plans for the Duke have had some unexpected results. The first time I snuck up on him I was caught crouching in the boxwood by none other than Mr. Rowe, who must have come over the grass with his clippers, for I did not hear him approach. He seems to be nowhere and everywhere in the garden, and I can never predict where he might turn up. And another time—I blush even as I mention it, it was so humiliating! Picture the scene: I was behind the plinth of the Duke, reaching slowly up to knock on his ankle and then crouch down, a "knock knock ginger," if you will, of prominent London statuary. My hand reached his ankle, and with my gloved knuckles I rapped softly on the back of his lower leg. Imagine my surprise when, instead of the soft "thump" of my own fingers on the bronze, a series of loud and echoing "clangs" rang out, startling the pigeon on his shoulder and giving the dog walkers pause! I looked at my knuckles in wonder, and back at the Duke himself—and then noticed Mr. Rowe "trimming" the high boxwood hedge, his clippers decidedly higher than strictly necessary, preparing to knock against the good Duke again and startle me half out of my wits. He played a terrible prank! His face registered nothing but serene innocence—indeed, he was so intent on the boxwood shaping he hardly saw me at all —but his clippers were too at the ready for me to believe his ruse. With a pointed glance through hooded eyes, I began my constitutional. As I passed him I noticed the merest trace of a smile on his face. I would say it matched mine.

Your Jane, who smiled

18 June 1851

My dearest love,

Things are looking—if not up, at least steady. Steady as she goes! My
health has gradually and steadily improved, and Sophy and I have
settled down to a familiar routine: read the papers over toast and
jam, look at the maps over tea, clear the breakfast things and spend
the morning writing and copying correspondence and organizing
papers. Sometimes it pushes into the afternoon, but we have managed to carve out perhaps one hour each day to ourselves—which
we often spend apart. On good days I can take myself to Russell
Square; on bad, I try to look through the stone walls of Whitehall
and imagine what those men are doing in there, knocking around
in those huge offices, busily sending each other memos, and smok-
ing. Did you ever notice how dirty their nails always were? The papers they interminably shuffle must be greasy with coal.

It is for the most part a pleasant passage of time, but of late
Sophy has taken to whistling tunelessly, which is both infuriating
and compelling; she seems constantly on the verge of bringing it
round to an organized melody, and so my ear picks it up and wills
her to complete the sequence, but invariably she veers it off into
some cacophonic, impossible hybrid between a vaudeville tune and
a dirge. She is no Mr. Rowe in the whistling department, and she
wastes a fine gift. I wouldn't mind it so much if it didn't distract me
from what I was doing, and if it weren't so obviously an attempt at
forced cheerfulness: she begins it when she enters our map room,
waggling her eyebrows at me and practically snapping her fingers.
I told her yesterday that the whistling would give her wrinkles, and
I told her the day before that she sounded like a milkmaid, but she

has not yet given it over. I don't mean to sound ungrateful, but such superficial optimism seems a waste of time when we have so much to do in front of us. The only thing that I have found that works to distract us sufficiently to be happy, for her and for me, is more work, and so we work and work and work.

Although, in my complaint, I must admit I tell a small lie: for me, there is happiness in my *very own* rose campions, little chaotic tunes of colour against the dreary London view. They were a gift I should tell you about, for you might see them before the season is out. As you know, I now go to Russell Square less frequently—it's not merely a short walk anymore, and I usually confine myself to visits when Thomas can take me, unless things are dire and I need the solace. I suppose Mr. Rowe noticed me descending from the carriage one day, and understanding that I no longer lived in the immediate vicinity, he gave me a lovely memento of my favourite place. After I had completed my constitutional winding way through the lime tree bower, I passed him underneath one of the sage bushes. Without a word, he simply held out to me a folded page torn from a book: I looked up to him for clarification, but he simply waved me away and went back to his trimming. I tucked it into my bag and wandered home—when I finally opened it, I saw it was a page from a copy of his own book, and it contained some small dried flower heads and black seeds, those dainty frilled parasols that could only be campion—the leavings from the very plants he was trimming the dead stems from and that must have overwintered there, protected by the sage. Now, growing exuberantly in the sun, the flowers bloom in boxes in the windows of Spring Gardens, and the Gardens are truly Spring with them: how lovely to have this little pocket of snappy Russell Square pushing against all that dreadful Whitehall grey. So I should let Sophy have her whistling, shouldn't I? Since perhaps that is her rose campion.

Your Jane

15 September 1851

My dearest love,

One, two, One, two. This was as high as I could count today. You plus me; your ships that have gone missing; the beat of my feet on the London streets. I just counted my footsteps, as my mind needed to give itself over to utter physical exhaustion. I slipped away from the letters and maps spread across the tables, and Sophy diligently reconciling Lieutenant McClintock's and Lt. Osborn's reports with what we know on the charts. Austin, Penny, et al are back, and the results of Captain Austin's expedition are as terrible as *The Times* predicted, with arguments erupting between ships among both junior and senior officers, Captain Penny and Captain Austin's working relationship almost immediately devolving into an utter mess of misunderstanding and cold naval protocol. Sir John Ross, who has not yet returned, will be the only one clever enough not to get involved, but he must have been laughing all winter long, listening to those two bicker. The Admiralty is trying to sort out the anger and the confusing stories of who refused what, when and where, but I predict right now that Captain Penny will be the ultimate loser in that debate. He lacks the naval suavity of Captain Austin, in spite of the fact that I am sure he is a superior captain and sailor. The Lords are most likely giving each other significant looks as he speaks to the council in his rough brogue, relieved he didn't send their two ships or all their men to a watery grave. A whaler! In an Admiralty ship! And Captain Austin will do his utmost to exonerate himself, and let fall what will on his junior officers. Failure is failure, though, and I am learning the hard way about how captains get treated when their missions don't go quite according to plan. It's a remarkably easier task for the men who are here to defend themselves: in your continued absence, *you* are certainly identified as the principal target for criticism, whereas Captain Austin places the fault on the weather, on the ships, on the men. Lieutenants Osborn and McClintock—and even Lieutenant Inglefield, who only saw the six ships together in the summer season—tell a much different story than that of the "Happy Austin family" that Captain Austin tries so strenuously to put forward.

So I escaped these oppressive tasks and headed outside. The air wasn't actually better out there, but at least it was different. London smells so bad; I really can't remember such a stench, even from Egypt. My black dress made me invisible in the crowds—another widow on the move down one of London's busy streets, ignored by omnibuses and children, men and horses alike. Without knowing why or how I found myself halfway to Bedford Place, my body having taken itself to the end of Spring Gardens, away from the face of my enemy, straight up the Charing-cross-road and across to Montague Place all the way to Russell Square, where my hands instinctively brushed the leaves of the arbour and nature made the same sound as my dress brushing the gravel. But it turned out that even Russell Square was not my destination. Even against my own heart, and in full sight of a beckoning empty bench, my feet propelled me onwards, out of the gates and back to Russell Street, where I found myself looking down the length of Bedford Place. My mind protested, but it had given itself over utterly to my feet, and was powerless. I had no wish to be there, to see Mary or Frank or even Father; I needed to go back to Spring Gardens, to my battle with the Admiralty, to my maps, to the men who believe in you. I had imagined my heart to be on my side, but no—it joined with my feet and pushed me away from everything that reminded me of you, and took me all the way back home, to the place I knew *before* there was you. With its eyes closed my body can find its own way home. I stared at the door, at the bell, at the windows covered with lace, and was frozen with fear. I was so close to home, at the threshold, and had no wish to enter. My husband, are you truly unable to find your way home, or is your mind appalled by it, as mine is? Are you this close to returning, but are hiding, from fear of what you might find if you do come back? In spite of myself, I can find my way home. Why can't you?

Your Jane, if you'll have me

Times *29 September 1851* p6
**REAR-ADMIRAL SIR JOHN
ROSS'S ARCTIC EXPEDITION**

Sir John Ross arrived in town this morning from Stranraer, having arrived at that
port yesterday. We understand that the information he brings tends to confirm the
report received from the Esquimaux last
autumn, to the effect that Sir John Franklin's ships had been lost somewhere at the
top of Baffin's Bay in the autumn of 1846,
and that a portion of the crew had been
murdered by a hostile tribe of natives, said
to be resident in those parts. Sir John Ross
is entirely of opinion that Sir John Franklin never went up Wellington Channel,
but was returning home and met with the
disaster. The Esquimaux interpreter was
sworn before a magistrate, at Godhaven,
when he reiterated his former statement.
The Esquimaux document, written by
him, has been brought home by Sir John
Ross to be translated. Sir John Ross would
not now have returned, but have renewed
his search at the top of Baffin's Bay, had he
had provisions for another winter.
—Nautical Standard, *Saturday*

12 December 1851

My dearest love,

Nothing good, and not much indifferent: Sophy has gone and has
already commenced her campaign of miserable correspondence
from the country. The Americans found nothing, no trace of you
that the British have not already crossed. I am doing my best to refuse invitations to dinner with Frank and Mary. No invitations have
been forthcoming from Marylebone. Our curate must be busy this
time of year. You have two grandchildren.

Captain Penny, who is right to encourage another look in Wellington Channel, seems actually to have won the fight at Whitehall.
Austin says Jones's Sound, and speaks more loudly and with more
brass on his buttons, but with your instructions, and the promise of
an open channel, 1852 will see British tars approaching Wellington
Channel with I hope what it takes to burst through. The debate has
played out in a series of awful, biting letters that *The Times* prints
with relish. There is another expedition to come in 1852 from the
Admiralty. I watch, because I am not invited to speak. The Americans—not the Government, but the men and ships sponsored by

the kind man, Mr. Henry Grinnell—have pushed their way north, and have been pushed back. He and I have much in common: not only do we admire you immensely, but we have grown weary of waiting for our governments to do what they can so easily, and have taken the burden on ourselves.

I am steadfastly picturing you surrounded by your officers and men, each one of you with a double ration of rum in your bellies and before a platter of hot plum duff ready to be devoured. The alternative is simply too terrible to contemplate.

Merry Christmas, my love.

Your Jane

1852

Times *3 January 1852* p7

THE PRESERVED MEAT OF THE NAVY

A board of examination, consisting of Mr. John Davies, R.N., master-attendant of the Royal Clarence Victualling Establishment, Gosport; Mr. Joseph Pinhorn, R.N., storekeeper; and Dr. Alexander McKechnie, surgeon and medical storekeeper of the Royal Naval Hospital, Haslar, has been employed since Tuesday last in examining the cases of preserved meats supplied by contract to the Navy, the Admiralty having cause to suspect their purity. The examination has disclosed some horrible facts. The canisters containing the meat are upon the average about 10lb. canisters. On Tuesday 643 of them were opened, out of which number no fewer than 573 were condemned, their contents being masses of putrefaction. On Wednesday 779 canisters were opened, out of which number 734 were condemned. On Thursday 791 canisters were opened, out of which number 744 were condemned. On Friday (this day) 494 canisters were opened, out of which 459 were condemned. Thus, out of 2,707 canisters of meat opened, only 197 have proved fit for human food, those condemned for the most part containing such substances as pieces of heart, roots of tongue, pieces of palates, pieces of tongues, coagulated blood, pieces of liver, ligaments of the throat, pieces of intestines—in short, garbage and putridity in a horrible state, the stench arising from which is most sickening and the sight revolting. The examining board and party were compelled to use profusely Sir W. Burnett's disinfecting fluid to keep off, or in the hope of keeping off, pestilence. To-day, however, they deemed it prudent to desist from further exposure for a time, to guard against danger, and will consequently not proceed with the examination until next week, the greater part of which will be taken up with the filthy investigation, as there were upwards of 6,000 canisters to examine at the commencement. This stuff was supplied to the Admiralty and delivered into store at the Clarence yard last November twelvemonth, warranted equal to sample and to keep sound and consumable for five years. We are informed it came from Galatz, in Moldavia. The few canisters containing meat fit for human beings to eat have been distributed, under the direction of Captain Superintendent Parry, to the deserving poor of the neighbourhood, and those containing the putrid stock have been conveyed to Spithead in lighters and thrown overboard. The consequences of such frauds as this cannot be too seriously estimated. Suppose, for instance, Franklin and his party to have been supplied with such food as that condemned, and relying upon it as their mainstay in time of need, the very means furnished for saving their lives may have bred a pestilence or famine among them and been their destruction.

3 January 1852

Oh my poor, dear love: this little bit of poison in *The Times* isn't about you, and yet you are at the centre of all its most horrid implications. All the good gods! *The Times* talks of and delivers poison, and reveals it as given you by the very people who were responsible for keeping you safe! What in England's good name has the Admiralty done to you? We knew already that the steam engines in the ships were good for nothing but rusting ballast—you knew that even before you had crossed the Atlantic—but to have your *food* be taken away from you—food that you promised you could *spin out seven years*—the mind absolutely sickens at the thought of where that might lead. No more idle sketches of icebergs, or looking at those frozen wastes for their natural beauty alone; now, they need to hold food, and you need to find it. You have plenty of ammunition, but what if there is no game? You were supposed to be victualled until Fall 1848—it is already well past that date, but what if everything ran out years before? Perhaps we have always been looking for ghosts—this is such a terrible thought. And at the bottom of all this is a base niggardly instinct, isn't it? The biggest, the best, all the innovations on the *Erebus* and *Terror* were meant to push you to triumph with the greatest dispatch—and the Admiralty purchased discount cans *from Moldavia* in order to save a few pounds. You have been betrayed by your own people, and by a pocket book. God help us all.

Your Jane

21 February 1852

My dearest love,

I have been in Russell Square, picking the remains of dried herbs that Mr. Rowe never cut back from last Autumn: rosemary, lavender, some lemon balm—and am adding them to my cups of hot water. The ends of the leaves are a little black, but it's nothing that a little hot stock won't soften. I hunt and gather in the wilds of Russell Square and tell myself I'm gathering "tripe de roche," the lichen you told me about from your first captaincy. I imagine I am with you there, back in 1820, surviving alongside you! Sophy wonders why I am continually requesting hot water, since she sees my tea chest goes untouched from day to day. I imagine I am slowly wasting away in my easy chair; I wait for the cramps of hunger each afternoon, and then the cramps of the poison to take over as I drink from my cup... and, always, I succumb to the lure of the tea cake that comes with the hot water, a little slice of light sweetness on the side of my saucer that reminds me that I am a woman, that I am in London, and that, awful as the rest of my miserable life might be at the moment, teatime is still the most wonderful time to be English. I remember you confiding that the cramps were so bad from the soup you made in 1820 that it was a blessing that poor Lt. Hood was simply shot—I wonder from my easy chair: have you begun to long for the tripe de roche, and the brief respite from slow starvation that it brings, before the cramps set in? Is it really better than nothing? I long for the feeling of the poison in my gut—to feel what you felt, to have my stomach clutch at the knife's edge, to love the stabbing pain even as it tears me apart. I do not want to know what it is to starve, but I long for this feeling in my stomach because I am so very, very tired of feeling it in my heart.

Jane

Times *10 April 1852* p4
THE ARCTIC EXPEDITIONS

TO THE EDITOR OF THE TIMES

Sir,—It is with unfeigned concern I see that, in an article dated 29th March, Captain Penny attempted, through your leading and universally read journal, to lead the public to believe that he above all others is the person who is able to conduct an expedition for the further search of Sir John Franklin, and we should have had much satisfaction in permitting him to enjoy the good opinion he appears to have formed of his superior abilities and acquirements undisturbed among his family and friends at Aberdeen, were it not that his statements and misrepresentations in this last endeavour to gull the public act seriously against the solution of the great question, inasmuch as, with other disingenuous assertions, it has tended to prevent a search being made where my gallant friend Sir John Franklin is most likely to be found; and, as an officer who has proved that he is sincere in his desire to do what is best in the sacred cause of humanity, I trust you will not deny the following observations a place in your powerful journal, in explanation of Captain Penny's letter to you, in order that the public may be disabused.

1. Captain Penny says, "I had the privilege of solving the Esquimaux story," and, as we have fully exposed this discommendable proceeding in the pages of that respectable weekly journal the *Nautical Standard*, in which we first saw Captain Penny's ill advised letter to the Admiralty, we need only add that it is the belief of the Greenland authorities as well as our own, that the "Esquimaux story" is true, and that the ships under the command of Sir John Franklin have been lost where Adam Beck has sworn they were wrecked in 1846.

2. We believe that had not Captain Pen-ny given a copy of the printed Admiralty orders to land the provisions at Disco to Mr. Saunders, he would have returned to land the provisions from the North Star, according to his original orders.

3. The discovery of the winter quarters of the Erebus and Terror is due to Captain Phillips and Mr. Abernethy, of the Felix, and who, by finding the graves, established the fact, and Captain Penny has no right to that discovery which he has claimed.

4. The intelligence communicated to Captain Ommanney was of very little consequence, but it is due to the Americans, we believe.

5&6. The absurdity of "drawing lots," especially with Captain Ommanney, who was under Captain Austin's orders, is beyond all comment, and is no excuse for Captain Penny's not remaining in the Wellington Channel if he chose, or really thought Sir John Franklin had gone up that channel.

7. We cannot contradict that there was no person in the sick list on board the Lady Franklin, but, as we know that several of his men were frostbitten, we think they ought, and would have been on the sick list, if any such list was kept.

8. Captain Penny does not state that he travelled this enormous distance (2,470 miles) continually in his carriage (dog-sledge) with his friend Peterson, who were both in the habit of taking excellent care of themselves; nor does he mention the fact of his boat being hauled up during most of the time he was said to be "contending against winds and tides."

9. Captain Penny says his men and himself went 2,470 miles, and saw 80 miles of open water. If, however, we may judge from the accuracy of the reports he gave us at the time, we think one-half will be nearer the truth.

Captain Penny then attacks Admiral Berkeley; with this we have nothing to do; the Admiral is quite able to defend himself. But we have strong reasons to think that Captain Penny himself does not believe that Sir John Franklin ever went up the Wellington Channel, because he told us, before witnesses, that as it was probable Sir John Franklin's expedition was lost on the west coast of Baffin's Bay, he (having an interpreter) would minutely examine the coast between Pond's Bay and Cumberland Strait, a distance of 600 miles. In consequence of this communication, the day before we parted company (August 11, 1851) I sent no despatches by him; but, instead of performing this service, he pushed home, confident, before we arrived, he would have been off to enjoy himself in some snug harbour in Danish Greenland, to the tune of 800*l.* a year; for he must have known it would have been quite impossible for him to reach the Wellington Channel that season. We regret that Captain Penny appears to think he has been badgered; that his evidence has been cooked, &c., to which he cannot accuse us of being a party; and, recollecting that we passed 11 months together in cordiality and friendship, we regret still more that circumstances have obliged us to change our opinion of a person with whom we were mutually employed in the sacred cause of humanity; but Captain Penny's motives are obvious, and until we find him serving (as we have done) without fee or reward, we cannot place implicit confidence in the purity of Captain Penny's proceedings.

I am yours, &c.,
John Ross, Rear-Admiral

---

12 April 1852

My love,

The fight still rages these days in *The Times* between Captain Penny and Captain Austin, and even Sir John Ross is finally entering the fray. In spite of being correct, poor Captain Penny doesn't stand a chance, now that the Lords (and all their minions) have closed ranks: I can see the naval broadsides arrayed against poor Penny, and yet he continues to stand in front of them. The disgruntled Lieutenants rush to his aid, but they are knocked aside quite easily by their captains, who pull rank and take the credit. I believe Captain Penny that Austin *did* abandon the chase, in spite of ample provisions and open water, but he and I together—a whaling captain and a woman—don't generate much noise. He will never sail under the R.N. flag again, and may even be lucky to get his old whaling captaincy back, so complete has been his public degradation.

Why it is so impossible for such men to work together is completely beyond me. Is there not a common goal here? If you and your bravery are the impetus to send these men out in the first place, should they not also be using your own conciliatory character as inspiration for their leadership? But instead we have epauletted pugilists bashing each other bloody in *The Times*, vying for approval as some "true leader" within a group of men who, collectively, accomplished almost nothing at all (even poor Penny, it must be said). They think universally that the more gold braid on one's arm, the harder one's swing—and the problem is that nearly everyone else feels the same. It means that one of the only men with vision, and real dedication to finding you, gets pushed out of the ring without being allowed to take a swing at all. We have lost Penny, and even young Goodsir. The three Lieutenants who sided with Penny—Inglefield, and Osborn and McClintock—are back in the fold, and this is upsetting but understandable: they still have their careers ahead of them. I can't blame them, really, but wish they would stand up *in public* to what they tell me privately is pure injustice. *You, you* my love, are the ideal of all that is good in naval leadership—and you are missing. It is no coincidence that the men here are all in a humbug over how to behave. No-one knows how to be a hero anymore.

Your maiden in distress,
Jane

Times *14 April 1852* p5
THE ARCTIC EXPEDITION

EXTRAORDINARY STATEMENT

It having lately been stated by a merchant captain at Tynemouth, in conversation with an officer of one of Her Majesty's ships, that two three-masted vessels had been seen on an iceberg off Newfoundland in April, 1851, by the brig Renovation, of North Shields, when on her passage to Quebec, and this statement being accompanied with a surmise as to the possibility of their being Sir John Franklin's ships, the Lords of the Admiralty, notwithstanding the improbability attaching to the circumstances of a story of such interest remaining so long unrevealed, have thought proper to institute the most rigid inquiry.

Letters have been written to the collectors of Customs at all the whaling ports in England and Scotland, in order to ascertain if any whalers answering to the description given were missing in 1850 or 1851. The master of the Renovation will be closely interrogated on his arrival at Venice.

14 April 1852

My dearest, patient love,

Could it be true? Were there really two ships attached to an iceberg off the coast of Newfoundland? Were they yours? And where, *where* on earth are you now?! They were sighted an *entire year ago* and the news only just came to light—what has happened to those poor ships, and those poor men, in the interim? A whaler apparently sailed right by—saw you in the distance and never bothered to come closer to make sure—just toddled its greasy way back to its American harbour, and its captain probably traded the story for a piece of mutton and a watery pint at a dockside public house. The Admiralty are following up with letters and questions and reports, but with all the time between your sighting and the current discussion, I despair that nothing will come of it. We have always, at every turn, been too late for you. The fact that the Admiralty, and even *The Times* consider this trail worth following gives me some hope, but like every clue we have found as to your whereabouts, this trail too is old. John Barrow was right—even in 1848 he warned me that we would get no help from the whalers. With this story so late—too late in coming, I fear he is right. I hope in spite of all.

Your Jane

15 April 1852

My dearest love,

The result of all those careful enquiries: what the captain and crews of the *Renovation* saw was most likely the reflection of their own ship against different angles of an iceberg. Not you. Pah! Now, though I was angry that the news was a year late, I wish I had never known it at all. Every mention of your name now is inexpressively painful. Like the doubled ships of the *Renovation*, all we can see here is the expanding reflections of our own despair.

Your Jane

21 May 1852

My dearest love,

So it is Commodore Belcher who is chosen this time to throw himself against the north: his sailing instructions were published in *The Times* today. A more puffed and arrogant man has never been sent on such a mission, but he is going nonetheless. The icebergs will be no match for his rigid countenance, upright stance, and icy glare! But enough of this woman's jealousy: I should be thankful that anyone is going at all. His arrogance, I suppose, is understandable: this time it is five ships they are sending, victualled for three entire years—an immense undertaking. That said, the good Commodore is already talking of his expedition as the "last" search for you, as if he will both fill in the arctic map and bring you home with a snap of his fingers. Still, if one begins as one would like to conclude, I suppose it's the right attitude. If it was expressed without such a puffed chest and rumbling of the throat, it might be a little easier to accept. The usual lieutenants are also signed on: Osborn, McClintock—the ones who agitate on your behalf in all they say, write, and do—at least in private, and sometimes even in public. If Sir Edward Belcher is the head of such an expedition, Osborn and McClintock might make a very effective neck, who can turn the body of all five ships where they need to go.

And the instructions! How the world has changed for the timid: no more pushing into blank spaces, or trusting to your instincts—now, it's "prudence" and "care." Belcher is *ordered* to turn back when his "stock of provisions shall have been reduced to twelve months' full allowance." Yours, you calculated—and we expected nothing less of you—could spin out for double its allotted time. Your instructions were to find the Northwest Passage, and try whatever means at your disposal; Belcher's, "the safe return of your party to this country." Why they even bother going becomes the question to be answered. If the instructions of the men sent to find you are different *in kind* from the ones you yourself were given, what chance do they have?

But there is a further unreal, tragic quality about the expedition even on the eve of its going—I could not read Belcher's instructions, published today in *The Times*, without weeping for all the hope that has been lost since 1848. What is Sir Edward Belcher's mission? To "recover the traces of Sir John Franklin." They are not even looking for *you* any longer, my love, but your "traces"—those things you left behind on your way to who knows where—what anyone has already found: nothing but piles of empty cans, and garbage, and graves.

Your Jane

5 June 1852

Father is dead, and there is no money left for me, or us. Young Frank Simpkinson has received the lot, much to his own father's delight, I'm sure. The will had remained unchanged until the very last months—when a codicil was added in Father's own hand, changing the direction of a lifetime of affection, from the prodigal daughter to a layabout grandson. I suppose Father decided, perhaps under pressure, perhaps not, I had had enough of the family funds. It is no matter—I already have a ship, and plan to use it.

In fact, perhaps this is the single bright spot in the sea of darkness—my *Isabel* has found a good captain. I have not mentioned this little ship before: she is a yacht I was compelled to purchase after the dreams of one idealistic young landlubber were dashed. A Mr. Beatson wanted nothing more than to sail it in search of you, and solicited my help—I was, I admit now, fully gulled by his enthusiasm. Suddenly short of cash, he abandoned the experiment and forced the *Isabel* on me. Because of my promises of support, I paid him out, and offered the ship to the Admiralty, but with no luck. Yes—I can begin to see my own Father's worry about the future of the family finances, when these errors in judgment are strung together in such quick succession. But this is not my fault! It is execrable in Mr. Beatson to have taken advantage of me in this way, but short of having him arrested, which I would never do, I could think of no other way of getting rid of him. So: even if the Admiralty did not take me up on my offer, it is no matter, for the young, dashing Captain Inglefield has accepted the schooner as a personal gift in lieu of pay, and the Admiralty has granted him leave in order to wend his way north for the summer, once again under my flag. He is taking more food than he needs, and will put it at various points along the coast, for whomever needs it most—in my heart it is earmarked for you, but the thought of *any* man caught in the north without food or shelter thrills me with horror, and so I bequeath it to the north itself: the tides and winds and ice will determine who will find the caches, and may they be received as the treasures they are intended to be. When Inglefield first sailed for me in the *Prince Albert*, he brought back the happy news of your first traces on Beechey Island; may he be so lucky on this modest little run, too.

Your freshening Jane

3 August 1852

My dearest love,

You will not credit it, I know, but this old shoe can indeed learn a new dance. I am embarrassed to say, at this shamefully late stage, that I am learning to be patient. Wait—let me amend that statement; I am learning the unexpected pleasure of patience, like waiting for a drop of cold honey to fall on one's tea-warmed tongue.

It is, I must tell you, as much because of Mr. Rowe and Russell Square as you—read on and become terribly, violently jealous (please!). Domestic, familiar, and yes, strikingly handsome—I can't deny my attraction to the gardener, and it makes me laugh, at my age. He is younger than I—no Lt. Bellot, to be sure, but he has enough of the nephew about him that makes his familiarity unthreatening. He has that combination I have ever found irresistible, and which first attracted me to you all those years ago: a properly tied cravat, a perfectly fitted waistcoat, strong hands, and dirt on his boots—Homo Practicalus! His proximity doesn't hurt either, since you asked, but not to worry: the secateurs are ever between us, ready to slice through social awkwardness or lop off any renegade limb that strays too close for comfort! My pleasure in seeing him fills me with horror even as I indulge my secret heart; in taking delight in a new companion, I feel I am betraying you a little each time, consigning you to a death that is in many ways far worse than all the reported starvation or scurvy or drowning—in my heart, I fear that you are slowly being—and must be—relinquished.

But it is not quite how I have described it. Mr. Rowe and I *do* have a mutual love: Russell Square. It carries no risk of loss, or absence, inequity or betrayal; the flowers and shrubs accept our attentions and give back, every day, in every season, their colours and scents as an expression of our own value in the world, for it is we who help to bring them forth, we who appreciate them even to their very roots. It is sensual and colourful and pungent and passionate, and we revel in it with abandon, touching, smelling, staring into the heart of things and even, in moments of high summer, tasting. It is of course innocent enough on the surface, but my beating heart cautions me to suspect something more. On sunny days or cloudy, windy or benign, we have our Mondays: Mr. Rowe and I wander through Russell Square garden discussing the lives of the plants, watching bees enter and suck fragrant blooms. Each week on my constitutional this summer he has had me sample another plant from the garden with one of my senses; first it was pinching a young rosemary sprig between my teeth, then it was cracking a lime leaf against the inside of my wrist; most recently he plucked two pink rose petals from the bush on the north-east corner of the garden, the colour of English youth (perhaps my cheek once looked as lovely?), and took two small lumps of sugar from his pocket. I watched him as he carefully wrapped each lump of sugar in a rose petal, the shadow of his eyelashes making a pattern like the edge of a rose leaf on his clean-shaven cheek. I stood still, the sound of my dress blending with the slight rustle of the leaves on the warm afternoon. He noticed a spot of yellow pollen on the edge of one of the petals; I watched as it left a slight cloudy streak on his left thigh as he brushed it absently against his trouser leg. He held one rose petal envelope up in each hand, extending his left one, the one he had brushed against his thigh, toward me. Gingerly, so the package would not unwrap itself, I took the gift from him with my bare hand. My nails were dirty. His eyes holding mine, he slowly raised his own rose petal package to his mouth, shaking his hand slightly and nodding to encourage me to do the same. I was mesmerised, utterly hypnotised, and unable even to question what I was doing with this man, a virtual stranger, in the public garden of my youth, but as my eyes took in his actions, I raised my own hand to my lips, closed my mouth around the ersatz sweet, and pressed the rose petal against my tongue. As I had opened my own mouth I caught a glimpse of the inside of his: he was missing a left molar, and one of his bottom front teeth was askew. His tongue was pink. I blushed to see it—and blush, to my private embarrassment, to think of it now, that small, moist, intimate part of him I'm sure he rarely thinks about but about which I have found I now often wonder—a part he takes with him, that gives him pleasure in its use, which vibrates to the sound of his voice, and moves when he swallows. I wonder often what flavours it has tasted during his travels. So there we were, two people, one old, the other not quite so much, standing in the dappled shade of Russell Square, on the path next to the rose bush from whence he had plucked the petals, our eyes on each other's, and sucking our lumps of sugar through our rose petals, together. If I were condemned to die, and were given one last meal, this is what I would choose: a tree-ripened peach from a Mortimer orchard, cooled in the cellar of Bedford Place, and a single lump of sugar folded within a petal of a Russell Square rose.

Still, your Jane

Times *11 October 1852* p5
THE ARCTIC EXPEDITION
(From our own correspondent)

ABERDEEN, *Thursday Evening*
The Prince Albert has just arrived from
the Arctic Regions, bringing no accounts
of Sir John Franklin.

11 October 1852

Mr Kennedy has returned in the *Prince Albert,* with no news. Nothing changes. All is grey here, inside and out. May it not fade to black, not yet. I live in a world of dissolving views, all morbid.

Times *03 November 1852* p2
ADMIRALTY, *Oct. 29*

Capt. Sir John Franklin, Knt., K.C.H., to
Rear-Admiral of the Blue.

3 November 1852

Come back to receive your promotion, you silly man.

12 November 1852

My dearest love,

Captain Inglefield is back in the *Isabel.* He searched, literally, high and low—and, like everyone else, discovered several places where you have not been. It narrows the field of search, certainly, but is a needlessly aggressive positive interpretation of the negative which he has actually produced. If that doesn't make sense to you, neither does it to me! This appears to be the particular talent of polar heroes everywhere—each one has a knack for turning disaster into triumph with the flick of a pen. You did, too, though back then we called you stoic. Now, the actual truth—no news—seems to get lost in the joyous announcements that obscure the dearth of information: that ships avoided gales, managed to deliver letters, turned for England. Triumph! My cynicism is weighing me down. I am losing the stomach for this fight, my love.

Your Jane, but hardly herself, anymore

1853

1 February 1853

My dearest love, let us begin with a poem, shall we?

> *Eighteen hundred and fifty-three—*
> *A year for growing dreams:*
> *For setting them upon the banks*
> *Of rushing arctic streams.*
> *Eighteen hundred and fifty-three—*
> *A Navy man's delight!*
> *Whose wife tirelessly labours on*
> *To bring him home all right.*

This year will be the year of decision; I feel it in my bones, in my throat, the way it feels, for the first time in months, open and new. I have given Mr. Kennedy the command of the *Isabel*, though I had given the whole ship, stores and all, to good Captain Inglefield last year for agreeing to follow my orders. Up into Smith's Sound it went, and though it found a vast expanse of open water, no *Erebus* or *Terror* bobbing happily or otherwise on the waves. Capt. Inglefield, who had outfitted it largely at his own expense, graciously returned the gift for future use in the polar search. This time, Mr. Kennedy will take the *Isabel* around to the West and in through

Behring's Straits. Lt. Bellot has chivalrously agreed to accompany him. They work well together: Kennedy's rough-and-tumble hardihood is smoothed by Lt. Bellot's easy grace. They speak French to each other, but with such vastly different accents, it is a source of wonder that they understand each other at all. Once again, the Navy is supplying goods and men along with Inglefield's leftovers. The Lords are silent in their acquiescence to my requests, but they acquiesce nonetheless. I am grateful for what little they supply.

Other than this, I am doing my best to expect little from this year: Sir Edward Belcher is just beginning his second season, and Captains Collinson and McClure are still in the West—everything seems to be right where it should be—with the exception of you. Sophy and I will spend time in Brighton, I think, and then once more to Mortimer, where the bridge table is open and the conversation flows. Sophy does well with Joseph, you know; they walk together and leave me, Sadie, and Crispin to our own designs. Sadie's sculptures are marvellous, and her drawings of Italy so evocative. In clay, she did a series inspired by you—of arctic bears and foxes. They were brought down to manageable size: not menacing, but beckoning, with an ingenuous invitation to their expressions I think we all, who do not know the north, imagine. February is no time to go to the seaside, but it will be empty and free for the long walks I need. It will do us good to get away for a little while, and visit the sea in its benign, holiday place, instead of thinking only about its deadly force, and the havoc it wreaks on ships and men.

Your Jane

Times *07 February 1853* p8
NEW ARCTIC EXPEDITIONS

Lady Franklin, the devoted wife of Sir John Franklin, still entertains the fond hope that her long absent husband will again be restored to her, and her whole energies at the present time are directed to the sending out the Isabel screw steam vessel of 16 nominal horse power, but, being on the high pressure principle, capable of working to a much higher power. Mr. Kennedy, who commanded the Prince Albert in her recent voyage to the Arctic regions, visited the Isabel at Woolwich on Thursday last, and made a minute inspection of her, as, if it is finally decided that she will proceed to Behring Straits, he will have the command, and be accompanied by Monsieur Bellot, the Frenchman who was with him during the last voyage, and who has again volunteered his services most generously and gratuitously in any farther service Mr. Kennedy may enter upon, in compliance with the wishes of Lady Franklin, in search of Sir John Franklin.

1 August 1853

My dearest love,

We never went to Brighton, but perched at Mortimer Hill for all of Spring, and have returned to London, like all explorers these days, with little news. Nothing progressed between Sophy and Joseph, though they spent some lovely afternoons mounting dried ferns and sketching. Sadie tried to teach me—again—how to knit, but it's no use. My fingers simply won't pull the wool with any consistency through the needles, and squares turn to triangles before my very eyes—how impressed Pythagoras would have been! How was I ever born a woman? It was weeks and weeks we were away, and Spring Gardens holds some charm again, with its window boxes and views of the streets below. Thomas has resumed his routines with us, taking me to tread my rounds in the garden and Sophy to who knows where, hither and thither. I have no idea what she does in those times, I really don't.

On the home front, though, I report disaster: someone is killing the rose campion in Russell Square. Not just killing; I mean tearing up and destroying, stomping and slashing the tender, silver stalks and grinding the blood of the fuchsia blooms into the gravel. How can this be? Sophy and Thomas set me down in Russell Square Monday last for my first constitutional there in months, and again today, and both mornings I found new corpses littering the ring path. You won't be surprised to learn that the Duke has nothing to say in the matter; he has always let his underlings fight it out amongst themselves, but I shook my fist at him and told him I would win no matter the cost. I have so many battles to fight, my love, what's one more? Fighting the destruction of rose campion seems, actually, like one fight I might possibly win. Perhaps one triumph will lead to another. You, of course, are the big prize, but it seems too much to hope for in these dark days. Unsurprisingly, though, perhaps luckily, we've heard nothing from Sir Edward Belcher. Even if he were here, we'd likely hear nothing from him unless we were prepared to pay—but I shan't complain about character failings when someone is off being a hero, and he is doing what is right and good in looking for you. I miss you very much.

Back to the rose campion. Last week I couldn't even write, I was so despondent—all the petals I came across were absolutely crushed, some even torn from the stamen by the grinding action of the boot they had suffered. I couldn't help it and perhaps I shouldn't tell you but I became possessed by the thought that the flowers were you and your men, the high pink of your ears in the cold and the down I like so much to stroke at the back of your neck—those little flowers were men to me, stalked by a wicked, invisible monster and helpless under its attack. I was counting them, too, and it was no coincidence that I came to 133, the original number of men you took with you. How can I not take it as a sign? I think I did not speak from grief, from Monday until Thursday, but only Sophy can say for sure. My throat has been so painful for the last year that a few days of silence go almost unnoticed these days.

This morning during my walk, though, I came across one stalk that had not been completely destroyed. It had been ripped from its parent (thank goodness with no root ball, so the plant will likely grow back) and thrown like the rest, but had caught on a boxwood and thus escaped stomping. I had already criss-crossed the park looking for one salvageable flower and was on the verge of despair when I spied it. It was actually waving to me, gently, in the breeze. I nearly wept when I gathered it from its hiding place, the last tiny pink flower in the park. I carried it to Mr. Rowe, who was on a ladder tending to the lime bower's undercarriage, and asked him for the use of his secateurs. With them, I trimmed the ragged edge of the stalk and placed the remainder in my button hole, giving it a pat to ensure its security and declare my satisfaction. I looked at Mr. Rowe carefully during this performance, to gauge his reaction—he surprised me by offering an apology. He climbed down from his ladder and said, "Madam, I can't sleep in the park, and so have not yet found the perpetrator." Just like you when you have one of your clever tricks coming, I found myself winking and laying a finger on the side of my nose—and truthfully, my darling, this made me feel much better. "Never you mind," I chided, "we'll find him yet." If to say is to do, then Mr. Rowe and I will most certainly triumph. And one triumph will lead to another: if I can criss-cross the Square, so replete with shrubbery and overflowing with fronds, and find a tiny pink flower in need of rescuing, surely five (seven!) ships can steam or sail to the last blank space on the map and find you and your pink ears waving gently in the breeze? Just you wait. They're coming, and I am waiting, and until you are back I will carry you in my button hole and keep you safe.

Your gardener,
Jane

Times *8 October 1853* p10
THE ARCTIC EXPEDITIONS

Important news was yesterday received at the Admiralty with reference to the Arctic Expedition. Commander Inglefield, of Her Majesty's ship Phoenix, has arrived in town, and announced to their Lordships the gratifying fact of the safety of Her Majesty's ship Investigator, Captain McClure, about which great anxiety began to be felt. Commander Inglefield also brings tidings of the discovery of the long sought for North-west Passage. He is the bearer of despatches from Sir Edward Belcher, Captain McClure, and Captain Kellett. No trace has been discovered of Sir John Franklin's expedition, and Captain Inglefield announces the loss of the Breadalbane, the consort ship of the Phoenix, and the death by drowning of a gallant officer of the French Imperial Navy, Lieutenant Bellot.

9 October 1853

Oh my dearest love,

I can't tell *which* devastating item in the little article is the most "important," as *The Times* terms it—is it that Capt McClure is safe? Or that the Northwest Passage is no longer a grail to be searched for? Or that Lt. Bellot is dead? Or that Captain Inglefield saw *everyone else* in the Arctic except for you? All of these are devastating in the extreme, and in their own way: McClure was rescued in timely fashion, sailing where *you* were, too, and *you* found no succour. With the Northwest Passage put down on the map, I can already anticipate Admiralty interest evaporating in the project to find you— if it was ever the purpose of sending all the ships north—perhaps it was just an excuse? The mind revolts at such a suggestion, and I was appalled even at the moment it occurred to me, but once the idea took root, it has proven difficult to shake. And then what of the hundreds of other men still up there: Sir Edward Belcher's and Captain Collinson's, and even Capt McClure's? Are they bobbing around together, passing messages by hand, all of which say "all well," and then packing up and heading home with a pat on the back for a job well done? And poor, poor Lt. Bellot—only he has had the courage to travel beyond the arctic we all know already. He may have unraveled the final mystery, but there is no-one there to listen to his tale. If only he had gone with Mr. Kennedy, all might still be well. Scratch a young man in search of glory, and you'll find a dead one.

Your Jane, who has lost the best men she has loved to the north

---

Times *17 October 1853* p12
NAVAL INTELLIGENCE

PROMOTIONS

Commander Robert John Le Mesurier McClure (1849), in command of the Investigator discovery ship since December 18, 1849, to the rank of Captain for services performed in the Arctic Regions in search of Rear Admiral Sir John Franklin and the officers and crews of the Erebus and Terror discovery ships, and the discovery of the certainty of a north-west passage.

Commander Edward Augustus Ingle-field (1845), in command of the Phoenix screw steam sloop, to the rank of Captain for services performed in that vessel in conveying stores for the relief of Sir Edward Belcher's expedition, and depositing them at Beechey Island, and returning the same season, bringing to this country Lieutenant Cresswell, of the Investigator, with the intelligence of the discovery of the north-west passage; and for his previous exertions, at his own expense, during his voyage in the Isabel screw steamer up Smith's Sound to the open water of the Polar basin.

---

17 October 1853

My dearest love,

Come back to keep your post: soon you will be matched and then perhaps even surpassed by the men sent out to find you. If only their ships and bodies were as efficient as their ambitions.

Come back, come back to
Your Jane

Times *29 October 1853* p4
SIR JOHN FRANKLIN'S FAMILY

TO THE EDITOR OF THE TIMES

Sir,—While the public interest is so justly alive to the claims of those who have suffered, directly or indirectly, from the anxiety of the Polar Expeditions, I could wish that you would direct attention to one whose connexion with them is the nearest and dearest of all—I mean the only daughter of Sir John Franklin himself.

Her husband, the Rev. John Philip Gell, now curate of St. Mary's, Marylebone, was nominated at a very early age to Sir John Franklin (when Governor of Van Diemen's Land), by the late Dr. Arnold, of Rugby, as Warden of Christ's College, Hobart Town. He carried on for several years an earnest struggle with colonial faction, in the endeavour to make that institution all that Sir John Franklin designed it to be as the centre of enlightenment to the colony.

Since his return to England, and his marriage, he has been discharging the duties of a London curate, with how much efficiency, zeal, and ability may be readily ascertained by inquiry among his parishioners.

Is there no one among those who deplore Sir John Franklin, and appreciate his services to the country, who will testify this feeling by bestowing preferment upon his excellent and distinguished son-in-law?

It was understood at one time that Mr. Gell was nominated to a colonial bishopric in the Canterbury Settlement in New Zealand. But the state of that colony appears to have postponed this appointment indefinitely. Cannot something more suitable to his talents and wishes be found for him in England?

I remain, Sir, your obedient servant,
Deeds, Not Words
Oct. 28

---

3 November 1853

My dearest love,

News from Valparaiso, my love, and it is inexpressibly sad: while there, Mr. Kennedy has been unable to re-provision our little *Isabel*, and the expedition I have sent under him to Behring's Straits is abandoned. There was apparently a disagreement among the officers—I suspect it was Mr. Kennedy's teetotalling ways that may have prompted it—and once disembarked, the navy crew simply refused to re-board. There are just so many ways for disaster to strike, and we seem to be finding all of them. Sophy and I are trying to get a new crew, but it is not hopeful; the Admiralty do not even respond to our appeals. Mr. Kennedy and his erstwhile men will find their own way back, and I doubt that any of the men will see the least punishment. In the engineer's journal, there is nothing but catastrophic predictions on the safety of the little steamer; he never trusted that it would make it across the Atlantic, let alone up the west coast and into Behring's Strait. And the Admiralty, in spite of the ratings being navy men, will do nothing to correct their rebellion, for Mr. Kennedy is an outsider. The mutiny of the sailors is merely the latest manifestation of what the Lords have been doing to me all along: saying no, but this time with a clarity and direction which the Lords themselves are incapable of expressing.

Something is afoot with the Gell: an anonymous well-wisher hoping to secure for your son-in-law some more gainful employment than his Marylebone curacy is stirring things up in *The Times*. I can make hide nor hair of it, but wait for developments. I have not seen Eleanor since her marriage, but hear of her through Mary.

I read, too, in *The Times* a characteristically weak defence of you as a good captain: you were 59 rather than 60 when you went out, and therefore we are urged to use caution when "casting the pall of death over our unfortunate countrymen." It was written by Mr Weld, the Secretary, and is so crushingly typical of Admiralty ways: with one hand they bang the drum of hope, while with the other they tune for the funeral dirge.

Caught in the middle, I say nothing at all, but am still,
Your Jane

Times *7 November 1853* p10
THE FAMILY OF FRANKLIN

TO THE EDITOR OF THE TIMES

Sir,—I cannot admit the justice of the appeal made to us on behalf of Mr. Gell. As the son-in-law of Sir John Franklin, and his *protégé* through life, the rev. gentleman is, of course, an object of interest; but, before we bestow our sympathy, let us be sure that it is not thrown away.

The heroism of Lady Franklin, to whose untiring exertions and sacrifices your correspondents appear to be indifferent or blind (for they ignore her as the representative of her husband), commands the respect and sympathy of every one of us, and will surely be one day acknowledged by our Government in a shape suitable to the occasion. But what are the claims of Mr. Gell?

Has he in any way promoted or encouraged the honourable endeavours of those engaged for so many years in the search for Sir John Franklin?

Has he not, on the contrary, done all he can to discourage their ardour?

Is it, or is it not, true that for the last two or three years Lady Franklin has been menaced with legal proceeding at his instance, to compel her to produce and prove Sir John Franklin's will at Doctors' Commons—in other words, to admit his death and put an end to all further search?

When these questions are answered, it will be time enough to parade the impecuniosity of Mr. Gell before us. Yet, even then, I would pray his friends to consider that Lady Franklin, in favour of the search, has reduced her once ample income to the scanty yearly allowance of 300*l.* for several years past—that is to say, to one-half the amount of the income which he enjoys, and they find insufficient.

Anxious for the success of the good cause, and not willing to see it endangered by these attempts to mislead us from the true point to which our sympathies should be directed, I request the insertion of this letter, and am,

Your obedient servant,
One of the Public
Nov. 6

Times *8 November 1853* p9
THE FAMILY OF SIR J. FRANKLIN

TO THE EDITOR OF THE TIMES.

Sir,—My attention has been directed to a letter in your paper of to-day, containing an anonymous attack upon my character, which leads me to regret more than ever the well-meant endeavours of unknown friends to turn aside to my wife, or myself, any portion of the public interest which ought to be exclusively devoted to ascertaining Sir John Franklin's fate, and to securing the safety of those gallant men who are still endeavouring to discover his track.

I will only refer to Admirals Parry and Beaufort; to Sir James Ross, the leader of the first search; Austin, the leader of the second; to Captain Inglefield, and to the faithful and indefatigable Kellett, when he comes back, as the witnesses how far I deserve the imputation of selfish indifference conveyed in the first inquiry of your correspondent.

I do not name the leaders of private expeditions—first, because I was not admitted by Lady Franklin into her plans; and, secondly, because (had I approved them) I was not in circumstances to assist them with an adequate subscription. Lady Franklin was then, and is now, in full control of Sir John Franklin's private property, including the settled estate of Sir John Franklin's first wife, Mrs. Gell's mother. The insinuation is simply untrue that I have menaced Lady Franklin with legal proceedings to compel her to produce and prove her husband's will; but, as falsehood has generally some fact to build on, I suppose the present arises from some hearsay account of the extreme displeasure which I felt and expressed two years ago, upon hearing that Lady Franklin had caused Sir John's presumed will to be opened, contrary to my advice some time previously, and secretly to me and my wife. Lady Franklin then made herself mistress of its contents, and nothing, in my opinion, could justify such conduct, since Sir John did not entrust his will to her care. If I have spoken strongly on this unhappy subject to her or to others, it is because I feel it was treating him as if he were dead before his time, and that, too, against the known wishes of his daughter.

The comparison of our respective incomes is simply untrue, as might be expected from "One of the Public" entering into the domestic affairs of a private family; but my "impecuniosity" sits lightly upon me, and I am content to know, that though I did leave Van Diemen's Land poorer than I went there, it was no disparagement in Sir John Franklin's eyes, when I solicited from him the hand of his only child. My wife and children are his child and grandchildren, and I trust his wife will learn some day that they are hers also, when the fever of excitement is past, and she sees that our counsel and advice would have been more valuable to her than the wild schemes of needy and sometimes unprincipled adventurers who have made their account in practicing upon her passions and feelings.

I am, your obedient servant,
John Philip Gell
Nov. 7

Times *10 November 1853* p12

TO THE EDITOR OF THE TIMES
Sir,—With reference to a letter which appeared in your paper yesterday from Mr. Gell, giving his explanation of certain circumstances connected with Sir J. Franklin's family, I am desirous, as a relative of Sir J. Franklin, to be allowed to make a few observations on Mr. Gell's letter, independently of a statement which I believe will be forwarded to you for publication, emanating from Sir J. Franklin's sole executor.

The explanation given by the latter was made at the time in the fullest manner to Mr. Gell, who, however, informed Lady Franklin that if she drew any portion of her husband's pay she would have to re-

fund it! The intercourse between the families did not, however, suffer interruption, and it was therefore with great surprise and concern that about six months after, on the occasion of Lady Franklin's father's death, and of an invitation which she sent to Mr. Gell to attend the funeral, which he accepted, Mr. Gell was found to seize that solemn moment, before Lady Franklin's father was as yet in his grave, to call upon his executor to prevent Lady Franklin getting the will into her own keeping, as he affirmed she had already endeavoured to do, adding an observation which insinuated that it was not safe in her custody!

When this insult and untruth, in spite of the indignant contradiction it received from the executor, was repeated, all intercourse necessarily ceased, though Lady

Franklin, it is right to state, has frequently made it known to Mr. Gell that nothing more is necessary to a renewal of amicable relations than the simple expression of a desire to withdraw the letters containing those offensive aspersions.

So far from this, Mr. Gell has thought proper to hold forth to Lady Franklin threats of exposure.

It seems scarcely necessary to remark that Mr. Gell was not admitted into Lady Franklin's confidence respecting the private searching expeditions, as, from the first, he did all in his power to thwart and oppose their organization.

With reference to the entire control which Lady Franklin enjoys over her husband's income, including "the settled estate of his first wife," I think it but right it should be known that the latter was the main source of Sir John Franklin's income. But Mr. Gell has omitted to tell the public that, in order to enable him to marry Sir John Franklin's daughter, Lady Franklin voluntarily resigned to them, on their marriage, above one-half of the income arising from this property, which they enjoy to this day, and will continue to receive as long as the rental remains at Lady Franklin's disposal.

Before concluding, I cannot help deploring Mr. Gell's great want of good feeling in stamping the names of honourable, gallant, and good men by the titles of "needy, and sometimes unprincipled adventurers."

The adventurers thus darkly alluded to can be no others than Forsyth, Kennedy, Inglefield, and, lastly, poor Bellot, who is now mourned by two nations—all of whom organized and commanded Lady Franklin's private expeditions, and, to their honour be it recorded, gave their services gratuitously.

I am, Sir, your humble servant,
A Relative of Sir John Franklin
Nov. 8

Times *10 November 1853* p10
THE FAMILY OF SIR JOHN FRANKLIN

TO THE EDITOR OF THE TIMES.

Sir,—When attacked in the highway of public life by a masked individual, under the name of "One of the Public," with weapons borrowed from a familiar source, and with a challenge to "stand and deliver" (not my purse, indeed, but) my good name, I obeyed the first instincts of self-defence, in demolishing falsehood and substituting the truth; and a moment's reflection will, I hope, convince any one that it was absurdity, or worse, to accuse me of endeavouring to make Lady Franklin produce a will which I knew she had not got. "One of the Public" says my story is of my own making, but a "Relative of Sir John Franklin," on the contrary, virtually admits the fact, by seeming to know who Sir John Franklin's sole executor is, which was certainly not known to any one before his will was opened. If the one is a true witness, the other must be a false one on this point. Imaginary accusations are always easy to produce, and not always easily repelled.

I must be permitted to let what I have already said stand as a specimen of the way in which I am prepared, if I will, to answer anything else which may be insinuated; but I have no intention of amusing the thoughtless public, and distressing our friends, with any further discussion of domestic matters in your columns. My character is not worth having if it will not take care of itself; and, so long as Sir John Franklin's relatives and best friends, and Lady Franklin's own relations also, continue to approve me, I shall still venture to hope that I have not missed the line which true wisdom and affection dictate in the difficult task of dealing with her.

I am, Sir, your obedient servant,
John Philip Gell
Nov. 9

---

13 November 1853

Oh my poor, dear love,
(how often do I address you thus these days!)

How poisonous is the atmosphere here these days, not from the coal fires or the ditches or the Thames, but the spleen coming from identified and unidentified quarters and swirling around your poor family. There have been letters from the last few weeks, that, taken one at a time, seemed unimportant—anonymous letters asking for some kind of patronage for the Gell—nothing out of the ordinary, but a consideration that your fame and his marriage to your only daughter should be reason enough to promote him beyond his humble station as a curate in Marylebone. And why not? Perhaps he does his job well; perhaps his parishioners think him worthy. Such letters were worth a glance over breakfast, but nothing more. As I told you, I already settled £500 per annum on them from your interest upon their marriage in 1849, and until I know otherwise, the Porden estate is still yours to keep. But what has appeared in the papers over the last few days is appalling in the extreme—I find myself drawn into a scandal in which I have no place, and no defence. The argument has erupted over Mr. Gell's right to promotion within the Church. What does it matter to *me* if he receives a promotion? Is it in any way invidious to me or my efforts to find you? No—my name was never mentioned, and indeed you were only tangentially, as the father of his bride, and as someone who believed in his talents in Van Diemen's Land. But what this "One of the Public" has done is to pit Gell against me as one more deserving of the public sympathy. I'm not in line for a curacy or a bishopric in New Zealand, or whatever, and simply *don't care* what happens to Gell. But in these letters, for better or worse, Gell is vilified, embarrassed, called out, humiliated, and it's only natural he should fight back—though in the absence of a known enemy, he sets his sights on the only named target: me.

I see Sophy's hand behind all this, and despair because of it. She thinks she is helping, but in the details in her "anonymous" letters she reveals herself and damns us both. Gell obviously discerns our shadows behind the letters, and points his arrows directly at me in his responses, and those poor saps who have "the difficult task," as he puts it, of dealing with me.

As a corollary to this sad turn, I am ashamed but compelled to tell you that Eleanor and I are all but irreconcilable now. She chose irrevocably to throw in her moral lot with her avaricious Gell—the letters weren't inaccurate in his quest for a more generous income, though he continues to deny it—perhaps having been thwarted in the family inheritance line, he's gone back to the Church. They are both *wary* of their *inheritance*, and I am *weary* of *them*. They want no more of our money to be spent on anything connected to you or the polar regions. I and the nation are to give you over, because Eleanor, dear her, wants a new pianoforte!

You may forgive her her youth, but I do not. What Eleanor fails to understand, in spite of my repeated efforts to compel her to do so, is the importance of memory; the legacy she seems to prefer these days is written on a pound note, and Gell is just the same. I know you will tell me, as you continually used to, to be more generous of spirit when judging the motivations of others, but here I tell you I cannot. You are her father, and there can be no consideration for the fickleness of youth, for the petty ambitions of a spoilt girl. Do not deny it: I know that you always saw this in Eleanor, and yet I also know you loved her nonetheless and for this I love you all the more. Through this whole humiliating spectacle of a public family spat I have come to realise that it is not that you didn't see it in her; you rather turned your loving eye away from that shadow lurking in her girlish simplicity. Well, she is a girl no longer, Gell has nurtured her into what she has become, and the vulture is fully grown. I'm sorry for this, for her, for us all. We have all become ugly, haggard, and torn.

All is given to you from what is left of
Your Jane

Times *19 November 1853* p10

THE GEOGRAPHICAL SOCIETY ON ARCTIC EXPEDITIONS

TO THE EDITOR OF THE TIMES

Sir,—It is stated in this day's *Times* that "it was unanimously agreed at the meeting of the members of the Geographical Society on Monday night last that the chairman, Sir Roderick Murchison, should solicit the Admiralty to send out another expedition to the Arctic regions in the summer of 1854."

As this statement is calculated to convey an erroneous impression to the public, I beg you will allow me, as one of the members present, to make a few observations on the subject.

No proposition of the kind was put to the meeting, which, being chiefly composed of ladies and strangers, was quite unsuited for discussing the grave question whether the Geographical Society should recommend the Government to send out another Arctic expedition; and, so far from the opinion of the members of the Geographical Society being unanimous on the subject, I heard many persons near me express their satisfaction that the completion of the north-west passage by Captain McClure left no further excuse for sending out fresh expeditions.

And among those who expressed this opinion I think I could name a distinguished Admiral who has had peculiar facilities for testing the value of the various theories which have been promulgated relative to the Polar basin and the fate of Sir John Franklin.

Not one of our experienced Arctic navigators, except Captain Beechey, appeared on the occasion; but that scientific officer, from his personal knowledge of the shores of Spitzbergen, was enabled to refute the vague speculations of Captain Inglefield, by a short and simple statement of his observations on the state of the ice and the climate of that part of the Arctic regions.

Whether the Admiralty intend sending out another expedition, I cannot tell; but, should such be their intention, it will not be in consequence of the "unanimous" opinion of the Royal Geographical Society.

I am, Sir, your obedient servant,
F.R.G.S.
Nov. 18

19 November 1853

My dearest love,

More frimmery from *The Times*. I am thinking that I might kill myself. I think Sophy knows this and is colluding with Thomas to watch over me wherever I go.

1 December 1853

My dearest love,

Don't worry, I'm still here, such as I am. There's still too much to see for me to throw this shabby life away. And who knows—you might come back, and then where would I be!

Saturday morning, I had an unexpected visit from your nephew the poet, Lord Tennyson, who married your niece—the last time we both saw him you had very low expectations of his success in the world, I recall. You would be highly amused by his transformation! He still smokes his cheroots, but doesn't lounge on the settees in quite such a dissolute way—marriage to your niece seems to have improved him, at least in manners. He was very considerate on the whole during the shortish visit, and wanted particularly to learn any news of you, and also to know how I was bearing up under the pressure of public scrutiny. From one celebrity to another, I suppose! I was both flattered and embarrassed by his questioning, as it implied that he had been following us both in the papers. His visit may have been prompted by those absolutely ghastly letters in *The Times*—the concentric rings of family lap once again against the shore of scandal. Did Sophy contact him, thinking he might break me out of my funk? Though perhaps not: this is not the first time we have had unexpected visits from extended family, eager to feed off the aura of tragedy we emit from time to time.

For better or worse, I must admit I spoke frankly: so few people ask *me* as plain Jane Franklin how I myself am coping, I probably frightened him with my response. No doubt when observing me he sees an old crone; I saw both the shock and shame of recognition when I described myself as such, an aged crone managing state affairs, stalking the beaches of home hoping to recognize the signature wake of my husband's missing ship. How am I different from a fisherman's wife? Because I am not invisible. But, as I revealed to him over more cups of tea than I could count, I am both more and less than this—an old woman left behind in old age, but also no longer a person at all, a legend of fidelity, a symbol of—what? Ironically, dignity in age, of glory in sunset—all through you, of course, but in explaining my desire to find you again, I may have waxed a little poetic. I suspect what Alfred failed to understand, in his relative youth (for all his bushy beard and swinging cane), is the fragility of the older public figure, and most difficult to explain, the roughness, the rudeness, of the savage crowd who point at me, look at me, speak of me as if I am not passing right by them, or approach me with an upsetting familiarity even in the high street, asking questions, demanding news of what has lodged so close to my heart that each word cuts my throat as it comes out. Sophy works her magic on this savage race, placing herself between me and them, and in doing this she doesn't see my face, or see what I fear is an expression of gratitude, for protecting me.

He actually had a mission, a gift to deliver, though *un cadeau empoisonné* it most certainly is—it was a rolled up, hand-written scroll of one of his own poems, *Ulysses*. I enclose it for you to read, though I hope you don't appreciate it[2]—it's much more flattering to you than to me, your "aged wife." But if he brought it to give me strength to bear your absence, it has had unexpected consequences: it has made me powerfully angry. I tell you why: the poem, which is, I think, supposed to be about heroes "following knowledge like a sinking star" and all that claptrap that sends men off the ends of

---

[2] Editor's note: this poem was not included in the collection.

the earth, is *really* about the incessant, thankless labour of all of us poor saps left behind. The best he can say about the rest of us? We are "blameless." The rest of us, who stay and live and pay tribute to your household gods, and pick and unpick countless tapestries to remember, we are there too, but woven only into the pale background of every hero's selfish tale.

Your Penelope, but angry

8 December 1853

My dearest love,

Another back and forth as fresh and lively as if we were sitting to tea in 1848: Captain Inglefield, who keeps bringing the big news back, urges another expedition, to the north and west—where he saw open water, and where he contends you may yet be. Captain Beechey, in spite of his *book* that states to the contrary, dismisses the idea of sailing in that direction as an outrageous dream that will do more harm than any good. Indeed, he says, even the *suggestion* of such an expedition is "wounding unnecessarily the feelings of those whose happiness may be wrapped up in the fate of their missing friends, for it can only have the effect of uselessly reviving feelings which time and resignation may have begun to alloy and temper down to a tender recollection of the past; and at a time when the mind may have begun to experience consolation from the bright hope of at length meeting in those bright regions of eternal happiness where the weary spirit shall be at rest and where the mourner's grief shall be for ever stayed." Where has this man been for the last eight years? He certainly hasn't been at *this* house, where no "resignation" exists and where there is certainly no expectation of the world to come: *here*, you are still in *this* world, still out there for us to find, still most definitely worth the candle. Let it be *us* who decide how wounded we are prepared to be, not some blasted administrator! And besides, so many Captains are still on your trail: Collinson, McClure, and even Sir Edward Belcher!

Young Inglefield has his work cut out for him, and I wonder if Capt Beechey, as a man who sits these days in Whitehall, has another agenda behind him. I am afraid for you, yes, because of what may be coming. There are storm-clouds ahead, my love, and we must brace ourselves. Rest assured—on *this* side of existence—that I will be with you no matter what comes.

Ever your Jane

1854

My own John,

Forgive me; it has been some time since I last picked up my pen for you, and for your cause. We often argued (lovingly, as I recall) of the different effects to be had through gunboat or treaty diplomacy—I remember fondly our sometimes heated talks over sherry after a good supper. You, a navy man wed first to the service, knew as well as I did that paper and signatures only won half the battle; you learned that in more than one place. I write to you now with a devastating lesson to the contrary: the Admiralty has proven once and for all that the pen is mightier than the sword, for with the stroke of a single pen they have killed you, my darling. This, so you know the full story, is what appeared within the pages of your beloved *Gazette*:

> *"Notice Respecting the Officers and Crews of Her Majesty's Ships Erebus and Terror."*
>
> *Notice is hereby given, that if intelligence be not received before the 31st of March next of the officers and crews of Her Majesty's ships Erebus and Terror being alive, the names of the officers will be removed from the Navy List, and they and the crews of those*

ships will be considered as having died in Her Majesty's service.
The pay and wages of the officers and crews of those ships will
cease on the 31st day of March next; and all persons legally enti-
tled, and qualifying themselves to claim the pay and wages then
due, will be paid the same on application to the Accountant-Gen-
eral of Her Majesty's Navy.

By command of the Lords Commissioners for the Admiralty,
W.A.B. Hamilton, Secretary.

Last week I was too blind with bad news to write—too much re-
reading of Sir James Graham's letter of apology to me (at least that
letter was private) for killing you off at the end of the financial year,
too much (too late) revising of my response—and needed solitude,
even from you. Even now that Sophy and I are within waving distance of elegant Green Park, the Embankment, and I can easily lose
myself in Hyde Park, my feet and fingers still favour the quietude of
old Russell Square, with its lime tree bower and modest perennial
beds, even in this bitter season. It's not crowded enough to hear
the whispers, and that is where I have been spending my time. The
weather and the hunkering beds match my mood. Sir James originally set your death date as 5 April next, but then robbed me of a
further five days in an efficient post-script; he could not even spend
the time to rewrite his letter. I am sure those five days will save the
Admiralty at least £50. Well done.

And what am I now? I believe, now, that I am a monstrosity,
one of those women passersby instinctively pretend they don't notice as they slide on past into the anonymous crowd. I was simply
one more hero's wife, but now I'm a symbol of something much
worse. In protest over the Death Notice in the "Gazette" this week
I've transformed myself from the grieving widow into the jubilant
wife, much to the horror of your Eleanor, and I suspect, even Sophy. I admit, as I smooth my hands over the silk purchased in Paris
with Eleanor in 1846, a naive, hopeful year, it's nice to wear colour
again—my green and pink gowns haven't been out of their paper

for far too long—but the confection of my appearance doesn't sit with the darkness of my mood. My dress blooms while I shrivel inside. People now think me mad. Do you?

And yet, even with this terrible blow, I cannot deny there remains within it a shred of hope—*if* you be not heard of, you will only be *considered* as having died; the gentlemen in blue seem still unready to consign you unequivocally to history. Still, the shade of widowhood, at least officially, looms dangerously close, and I ward it off with ridiculous pinks, flaunting the death that follows me just beyond my sight. With my health troubles over the years I have always felt close to death—but, my husband, I always thought it was my own. I fear this one, yours, so much more, since I must be the one to bear it.

Do forgive these thoughts of mine; you must know all my mind, or none of it. I write to you such lines to assure you of my continued faith in your existence, and in your admirable, brave, and loving self. Here is a poem for you, asking for what I feel, at the base, I have a right to receive:

> *It troubles me to have grown old—*
> *The world's continued turning;*
> *In spite of hand and hope grown cold,*
> *My love for you's still burning.*
> *Where you now lie, we only guess:*
> *I beg of you, let me know!*
> *Please, do this so my heart can rest—*
> *Speak clearly, and then let go.*

Come home to claim
Your Jane

Times *03 April 1854* p12
NAVAL INTELLIGENCE

PORTSMOUTH, *April 2*

In the official *Navy List,* published yesterday, Rear-Admiral Sir John Franklin's name, together with those of all the officers, retain their places.

6 April 1854

My dearest, enduring love,

There is a delay in execution: *The Times* announces the continuation of your name on the Navy List. Perhaps we still have some friends in Whitehall—or they're searching out a new editor.

The Times has things to say about me, too: I have become the "Penelope of England." At this I have a private chuckle—I see Sophy looking at me quizzically when the laugh rises in my throat, but I don't explain it to her. Everything now comes with endless explanation, justification, qualification, but this laugh I have just for myself. If I am Penelope, where are my suitors? If they be the men by whom I am beset, I certainly don't rebuff them at every opportunity, for they are the ones who refuse to give me what I want. Instead of a tapestry I endlessly weave and unweave, I carpet the desks of the Admiralty with letters rich in rhetoric and complex in pattern—I am constantly completing my tapestry and throwing it in their faces: take it, take it, in the name of human mercy, take it. No, I am not quite Penelope, for while I hate these men and want to crush them (and what would I crush them with? The mark of my own weakness: love), I pursue them, too—they are not just the Lords High Commissioners of the Admiralty; they are the Lords over Life and Death. They are paper-pushing judges on high, wiping a man's life away with the scratch of a pen. They turn me from wife to widow in one short letter, citing fiscal constraints and "the end of the financial year" as the most convenient time to clear the Naval Lists. I am disgusted by these penny-pinching pantry-dwellers: you sailed away to the end of the earth; your track will be visible as a long black line on the world's map; you penetrate the darkness, and everything that follows you is bright; your name is part of history, embedded forever on the land and in the chronicles of England's heroes; and with the signature of one miserly clerk in the Department of Seaman's Wills, your heart simply ceases to beat. How can I not rage? I refused the widow's pension—you must understand that I could not accept it—and have renewed the campaign to count you among the living. Increasingly I stand alone in this, but continued life is continued honour, and I cannot abandon you now. So I court these horrid men, and am rebuffed, and their coldness matches my desperation.

If the suitors are the flashing young heroes who continue to believe in you—gentle McClintock, vivacious Osborn—they court you as much as they do me, old leather that we both are. I merely represent you, and am happy to be in your shadow. Where you stand, so stand I.

All this to say, again, that I have refused my widow's pension. It would have done me good, perhaps, but eventually it would all go to the Gells, and I am in no mood to encourage contact with them over money. For them to know I have refused it is reward enough for losing the income. A suitable alternative, of course, is to draw on your accumulated pay—the wage of living men, not the compensatory vestiges dangled before their sad relicts.

Your wife, not your widow,
Jane

15 June 1854

My dearest love,

This letter is not for you; it is for me. It is the whole story of what happened the last day I went to Russell Square.

Something happened that day beyond my grief. Beyond the grim and desperate round of letters I can't bear to write anymore, and the equally horrific glimpses I get of myself in the windows of shops and carriages, a fragile connection was made, and I was frightened by it.

The inestimable Sophy had accompanied me as usual in the carriage to my old and favourite haunt; the drive was full of the old rituals we have both come to rely on: she holding on to her bonnet, I with my face to the side like a tern facing into the wind, eyes mostly closed—I always check the breeze for a whiff of the arctic, but there was none that day. I left Sophy at the top of Bedford Place with a book in her hand, and Thomas sitting as still as a statue on the box. On entering I had of course given The Duke of Bedford my truncated salute—"Your plough, my Lord Duke"—something so normal about the day, thank goodness—and was standing in front of a drift of rose campion in the South East corner, willing my dress to burn a brighter shade of pink, when Mr. Rowe appeared before me.

"You're welcome here, madam," he said, with no formal approach or particular sign of humility, as if I'd been away for some time, though I was right on schedule according to my weekly routine—it was he who had been absent, or at least unseen of late. His sudden presence confused me. I had not heard him approach on the gravel path.

"I beg your pardon, sir?" I pulled my hands to my side, lest I inadvertently snapped a bud from the campion in my surprise.

"The flowers, madam. They welcome your presence today."

He paused. He shuffled his secateurs to his other hand, cast his eyes over the bed in front of us, and inhaled. "It's a nice surprise to see you in colour." I felt pressed by the sudden understanding of his presence; he knew, of everything.

"I have a husband, sir." This line, unconsidered before delivered, was spoken with a terrible conviction; I stood straighter and stared into the middle distance. I could smell the roses to his left, and the freshening mock orange behind us. I watched Mr. Rowe from the corner of my eye. I had resisted touching the campion blooms for fear I would transfer my fears to their beautiful delicacies, but Mr. Rowe seemed to draw strength from them, instinctively reaching for their stalks, and running the underside of their leaves across the backs of his hands. Following his lead, I edged closer to the campion, but my shadow darkened its shades. The stalks looked bruised, the flowers angry.

"And how have you the right to speak to me today, Mr. Rowe, if I may?" I needed to deflect, refract, offer an ice blink, force an abrupt tack. This is how the ice traps unwitting sailors; it can be my escape. Though I knew my question was impertinent, I was armed to wound.

Mr. Rowe paused again; I heard a quick clearing of his throat and knew he felt the barb; the former warmth of our horticultural friendship was perhaps at an end. To his surprising credit, he picked up my hasty gauntlet and returned it to me as a gentleman. "Some time ago, the life I once led was suddenly no longer open to me. It is the kindness of these gardens here that brought me back to life."

Do you remember the life *we* had together before the Northwest Passage changed it all? You were captain of the happy *Rainbow*, and I had a shiny new ring on my finger, a freshly minted Lady Franklin a world away, just like Mr. Rowe had his family in May Street. Now Mr. Rowe pushes his tragic, broken-hearted hands through the familiar earth of Russell Square, and I wander here like a haunting. I never told him how I sleuthed out his story; I hoped my eyes didn't give me away at his first allusion to it in all our conversations. I snorted lightly, knowing the sorry state of the garden before his arrival. I felt the velvet of the campion leaves brush the back of my wrist. "They brought *you* back to life?"

"Yes, madam. A rose in particular can be quite exacting in its wishes for attention, and requires an active presence even on the easiest days. On cloudy days, when the dew is heavy, after a cool night—I always approach with caution, and address them with respect. It's my duty to be good to them, and they in turn give *me* their kindness." Mr. Rowe's face received a flash of sunlight, as his eyes were caught by the roses in front of him. At the same time, a light gust of wind seemed to draw the roses higher, settling the bush and its blooms slightly closer to Mr. Rowe's outstretched hand. His fingers gently cupped a perfect bloom, which nestled in his palm like a young bird. In spite of my scoffing, I thought I saw in this unconscious moment proof of their mutual affection. A word, something caught in my throat, and I understood in that fleeting gesture years of solitude, yes, but also of loneliness kept at bay by the lovely gardens of my own youth. I knew then why he had come to me; he had seen the same look in my eyes as he had once, I am sure, felt in his. The path, from my own present to his, was suddenly terrifyingly clear to me, and I wrenched my hand again from the flowers, cracking a campion stem in my panic. My feet crunched the gravel and I stood back in the path, rubbing the memory of the leaves' softness from my skin and looking past Mr. Rowe to the Montague Place exit of the garden. The pink dress looked ridiculous, and the paleness that I know was on my face made me ghastly.

Mr. Rowe took his small pair of secateurs from his waistcoat pocket, and clipped off a single bud of the pale pink rose he had been tending. "This is what you need, Lady Franklin. A softer shade." He held it out to me. I hesitated, and took it with one hand. The pale pink faded almost to white at the edges of the bud. Against its quiet beauty, the rage of my dress began to falter, and my heart, too. I began slowly to back away, moving around him and towards the coffee stand at the corner of Montague Place. Without raising his voice, he invited me back. "Don't forget that you're welcome anytime, madam. The flowers enjoy your company."

He had said this as I turned from him, and I paused at his words. I wanted to say something, anything, that would release me from the dread of what lay before me, what had been revealed in Mr. Rowe's hands on the rose. I could only repeat, "I have a husband."

"Of course you do, Lady Franklin. And a very lucky man he is." I heard him turn back to his work, crouching under the small overhang of roses to inspect their thorny underskirt.

As I left the garden I furtively glanced back at Mr. Rowe—he was standing now before the rose campion, one hand propping up my cracked flower stalk so the flowers looked trustingly right into his face, while the other gently eased the secateurs around the stem.

Please tell me that I am right in my declarations, my love. Even better: show me.

1 July 1854

My dearest love,

We have decided not to go away, despite the oppressive heat here in London; it's just so wonderful to have the streets to ourselves. London is empty. Sophy has now hidden all the scissors, but it doesn't matter: I've done all the cutting I need to do to those awful dresses save one. Do you remember the Egyptian mats we sat on aboard the *Rainbow*, woven from papyrus reeds? Especially that hot afternoon when all you wanted to do was eat olives in the shade, and endless lieutenants and aides de camps and who-have-yous kept coming to you with documents to sign... Those mats were all that kept you sane! I loved laughing at you all that day, and you accepted all the teasing with your usual good grace. I ate all the olives and enjoyed the mats. Well, in sleep the other night, I remembered the weave pattern as if I were looking at the mats right in front of me, and reconstructed a small one in my bedroom from the remains of the mourning dresses I cut apart before Sophy got the upper hand. They were rebuking me from the wardrobe; every time I opened the doors their dreadful blackness would burst through and press out all the other colours, and it was becoming too much effort to stuff them back in. So I cut them up! What else could I have done with them? The prospect of giving them away and seeing one walking towards me on some London street one day was simply too much to bear. I feel forced to admit, too, that it comes as some satisfaction to cut them up even as Eleanor starts her own girlish performance of grief that I doubt she really feels. That girl will be the death of me, as much as you, my love. Sophy does her best to keep me busy, or at least occupied.

The mat I managed to put together was smaller than the ones we sat on, but it only needed to float me and my dress, and perhaps a small picnic. I tried it out beside the bed and it was not quite on the square—I am still learning the craft—but it felt a little buoyant, a little forgiving to my aging frame, and there was ample room— perhaps for even the idea of you to join me. I kept it rolled under the bed so Sophy would simply think the rag ends were thrown away, and packed it in a carpet bag yesterday and took it to Russell Square.

Yesterday Sophy left me to my own devices, so Thomas, who asks no questions, ferried me and my cargo there under cover of perfect secrecy. I lugged it out of the cab and gave the Duke a quick wink. He knew what I was up to; I am sure he's kept up on the gossip, just as everyone has, but he knows that I am still alright, and that my heart is true. I circled to the left to get to the lime tree bower without passing the tourists at the cafe. You would love it; it has filled in most beautifully this season. This is where I placed us: just behind the curve to the left of the bower, off the path, but in its shade, where we could see the vista through the park, catch the breeze through the stiff lime leaves, and smell the roses blossoming behind. I brought olives, a book, and a carte de visite of you in all your finery, employed handily as a bookmark so that I might have you with me wherever I go. I know how you love to be useful! I read poetry (that Tennyson again, but well beyond *Ulysses*) while you enjoyed the view. Once again, I ate all the olives.

At the end of the day, I tucked you between Tennyson's pages, packed up our mat, and headed back to Spring Gardens, Sophy none the wiser, though she definitely suspects something. It may be the feeling of calm that has improved my mood this evening, or the subtle smell of grass and sage that clings to my skirts, an unmistakable sign that I have dallied in the Square. But she has not found the carpet bag, and our little raft remains safe from raiders who would climb aboard and overturn our tender bark. We will go again, my love.

Your first mate,
Jane

8 July 1854

My dearest captain,

Our Egyptian mat is gone. I have lost it and we are both lost. I was sure I had carried the carpet bag to the carriage, that Thomas had picked it up and hefted it beside him—but I cannot clearly remember now if this is true. Terrible! You and I were safe on that little raft, and it is lost in the wide, wide sea of London, probably sold to some rag picker and being torn apart by shoeless children even as I write. Sophy watched me silently taking my room apart looking for it yesterday—I had planned to bring it with me again to Russell Square and have a float in our usual spot: she said nothing as I looked repeatedly under the bed without telling her why. I think she thought there was a rat or mouse under the bed, for she started looking askance and angling toward the door, one hand on the knob for a quick getaway. It's not the dresses themselves, or even the mat: it's what it represents that is so painful to lose: a place in all the world just big enough for two, where there is no room for anyone to take you away from me.

Your Jane

15 July 1854

Oh my love, you will never believe what has happened! It is with the sincerest gratitude that I write these lines, to say I did have you with me this morning in Russell Square, and kept you safe on my raft right where you should be. Thomas dropped me off at the usual place and took Sophy shopping, and while I shuffled my despondent, hopeless way around the garden, I happened to glance at the little patch of grass that would have been our place—and there was the mat! All laid out, and with my book of poetry lying on it waiting. Incredible! I had no olives or bread to eat on this trip—I had no thought that I would stop during my walk today—but I was able to buy a warm bun from the little shop and nestled myself down like a bird on the mat to eat it. Oh, what a lovely hour we spent there, you and I. Your postcard was still marking my place, and I propped you up before me while I read, and you looked with your benevolent eyes at the bustling world before you.

When our time was done and Thomas was come once more to collect me, I was unsure of how I would explain the mat to Sophy—she would see clearly that it was made from the remains of my mourning dresses, and she would not approve of my carting it back and forth, and consider me maudlin. What to do? At the last minute, I hit on asking Mr. Rowe to store it for me in his garden shed—and when I arrived at the shed itself, saw nothing less than my very own carpet bag at its entrance, open and waiting to receive its intended contents. Mr. Rowe himself appeared from inside, and wordlessly taking the bag from me, placed it just inside the door. Thomas must have left it at the edge of the park, and Mr. Rowe has been keeping it against my return. He will keep us *both* safe from now on.

Your Jane

31 *August 1854*

My dearest love,

I am casting about with greater desperation, trying to find some meaning behind this ridiculous situation. I have to stop myself from taking your absence personally—did you leave me? Have I been abandoned? Is it really possible that some random convergence of unfortunate circumstances has literally, as Richard King portended, made you the nucleus of an iceberg for the sole reason that you just happened to be there? Can there really be no other message than that you are gone? These days my thoughts are verging on the blasphemous. There is no reason for my feeling this way other than your continued absence, but I awoke this morning filled with a final dread.

I have lately suspected that your disappearance is a punishment for my godlessness. Your death is so much worse than my own, since I would simply be dead, but now I am forced to live through yours, a constant rebuke from the universe that I didn't do enough to save you. If I do not believe in a higher power, we are simply left with chaos, and my own lack of faith has brought this on. I have believed in powers, yes, but the powers of adventure, of imagination, of creativity and love: everything I found in you, and all your kindnesses to me. I continue to believe in you, your gentleness and stoicism, your inner strength and unwavering politesse. These are true pillars of wisdom that make the world a better place. But if I ever did have an inkling that some higher power was governing our paths, it is simultaneously crushed and confirmed by your absence: more than anything I feel punished. You always tried to make me believe, and I did my best for your sake, my love—if I ever disappointed you in one thing, I know it was my poor relationship with God. I am so sorry. But still I look for succour not in a higher power, but in the belief that, whatever terrible hardship you were facing, you faced it with the perfect and unshakeable equanimity of your own beautiful faith. It is nothing that God has ever done for me that will make me believe, but *your* own sense of His plan for us all. If you could face what comes at you with peace, then so must I.

Times *02 October 1854* p9
RETURN OF THE ARCTIC EXPEDITION

Sir Edward Belcher, on his own responsibility, ordered the abandonment of the entire five vessels, which were accordingly left to their fate, and the crews distributed among the store-ships.

9 October 1854

My dearest love,

The unthinkable has happened, and it is not good: Sir Edward Belcher is back, minus four of his five ships, Lieutenant Osborn has spent his last few weeks at sea under arrest, and has ordered a court-martial against Sir Edward for his treatment of him and of the expedition as a whole. The man is absolutely hated through all the ranks, and his decision to run home with a year's provisions still aboard has caused outrage everywhere. The men were packed in every which way—aboard the little seasonal transports and on Belcher's last remaining ship, and each one of them with a hang-dog expression that tells me that no-one is proud of the state of affairs—except Sir Edward, of course, who still holds his head up so high you'd think clouds might form in his nostrils. His arrogance has come home to roost, and I hope he never sails again. Captain McClure, who sailed back with him, is also facing court-martial for abandoning the Investigator, even though he is fêted as "the discoverer of a north-west passage." All is an absolute mess, and no-one will set it right.

War is beginning in the Crimea, and beckons all the young heroes. They would rather die vainly with a lance or a musket ball in their hearts, facing an enemy stinking of rye bread and herrings, than live for any kind of human ideal.

Your Jane

20 October 1854

My Rear Admiral,

Court-martial for Captain McClure, for losing the *Investigator* while finding a north-west passage: fully acquitted. Court-martial for Captain Sir Edward Belcher, for abandoning four out of his five ships to the polar ice and returning home with his tail between his legs, one full year's worth of provisions, and his wig: fully acquitted.

Times *23 October 1854* p7
THE ARCTIC EXPEDITION

Intelligence which may be fairly considered decisive has at last reached this country of the sad fate of Sir John Franklin and his brave companions.

Dr. Rae, whose previous exploits as an Arctic traveller have already so highly distinguished him, landed at Deal yesterday, and immediately proceeded to the Admiralty, and laid before Sir James Graham the melancholy evidence on which his report is founded.

Dr. Rae was not employed in searching for Sir John Franklin, but in completing his survey of the coast of Boothia. He justly thought, however, that the information he had obtained greatly outweighed the importance of his survey, and he has hurried home to satisfy the public anxiety as to the fate of the long-lost expedition, and to prevent the risk of any more lives in a fruitless search. It would seem from his description of the place in which the bodies were found that both Sir James Ross and Captain Bellot must have been within a few miles of the spot to which our unfortunate countrymen had struggled on in their desperate march. A few of the unfortunate men must, he thinks, have survived

until the arrival of the wildfowl about the end of May, 1850, as shots were heard and fresh bones and feathers of geese were noticed near the scene of the sad event.

We subjoin Dr. Rae's report to the Admiralty, and a letter with which he has favoured us:—

The following is Dr. Rae's report to the Secretary of the Admiralty:—

"Repulse Bay, July 29, 1854.

"Sir,—I have the honour to mention, for the information of my Lords Commissioners of the Admiralty, that, during my journey over the ice and snows this spring, with the view of completing the survey of the west shore of Boothia, I met with Esquimaux in Pelly Bay, from one of whom I learnt that a party of 'white men' (Kabloonans) had perished from want of food some distance to the westward, and not far beyond a large river containing many falls and rapids. Subsequently, further particulars were received and a number of articles purchased, which places the fate of a portion, if not of all, of the then survivors of Sir John Franklin's long-lost party beyond a doubt—a fate as terrible as the imagination can conceive.

"The substance of the information obtained at various times and from various sources was as follows:—

"In the spring, four winters past (spring, 1850), a party of 'white men,' amounting to about 40, were seen travelling southward over the ice and dragging a boat with them by some Esquimaux, who were killing seals near the north shore of King William's Land, which is a large island. None of the party could speak the Esquimaux language intelligibly, but by signs the natives were made to understand that their ship, or ships, had been crushed by ice, and that they were now going to where they expected to find deer to shoot. From the appearance of the men, all of whom except one officer looked thin, they were then supposed to be getting short of provisions, and they purchased a small seal from the natives. At a later date the same season, but previously to the breaking up of the ice, the bodies of about 30 persons were discovered on the continent, and five on an island near it, about a long day's journey to the N.W. of a large stream, which can be no other than Back's Great Fish River (named by the Esquimaux Ootko-hi-ca-lik), as its description and that of the low shore in the neighbourhood of Point Ogle and Montreal Island agree exactly with that of Sir George Back. Some of the bodies had been buried (probably those of the first victims of famine); some were in a tent or tents; others under the boat, which had been turned over to form a shelter, and several lay scattered about in different directions. Of those found on the island one was supposed to have been an officer, as he had a telescope strapped over his shoulders and his double-barrelled gun lay underneath him.

"From the mutilated state of many of the corpses and the contents of the kettles, it is evident that our wretched countrymen had been driven to the last resource—cannibalism—as a means of prolonging existence.

"There appeared to have been an abundant stock of ammunition, as the powder was emptied in a heap on the ground by the natives out of the kegs or cases containing it; and a quantity of ball and shot was found below high water mark, having probably been left on the ice close to the beach. There must have been a number of watches, compasses, telescopes, guns (several double-barrelled), &c., all of which appear to have been broken up, as I saw pieces of these different articles with the Esquimaux, and, together with some silver spoons and forks, purchased as many as I could get. A list of the most important of these I enclose, with a rough sketch of the crests and initials on the forks and spoons. The articles themselves shall be handed over to the Secretary of the Hon. Hudson's Bay Company on my arrival in London.

"None of the Esquimaux with whom I conversed had seen the 'whites,' nor had they ever been at the place where the bodies were found, but had their information from those who had been there and who had seen the party when travelling.

"I offer no apology for taking the liberty of addressing you, as I do so from a belief that their Lordships would be desirous of being put in possession at as early a date as possible of any tidings, however meagre and unexpectedly obtained, regarding this painfully interesting subject.

"I may add that, by means of our guns and nets, we obtained an ample supply of provisions last autumn, and my small party passed the winter in snow houses in comparative comfort, the skins of the deer shot affording abundant warm clothing and bedding. My spring journey was a failure in consequence of an accumulation of obstacles, several of which my former experience in Arctic travelling had not taught me to expect. I have, &c.,

"JOHN RAE, C.F.,

"Commanding Hudson's Bay Company's Arctic Expedition."

Dr. Rae adds, that from what he could learn there is no reason to suspect that any violence had been offered to the sufferers by the natives. It seems but too evident that they had perished from hunger, aggravated by the extreme severity of the climate. Some of the corpses had been sadly mutilated, and had been stripped by those who had the misery to survive them, and who were found wrapped in two or three suits of clothes. The articles brought home by Dr. Rae had all been worn as ornaments by the Esquimaux, the coins being pierced with holes, so as to be suspended as medals. A large number of books were also found, but these not being valued by the natives had either been destroyed or neglected. Dr. Rae has no doubt, from the careful habits of these people, that almost every article which the unhappy sufferers had preserved could be recovered, but he thought it better to come home direct with the intelligence he had obtained than to run the risk of having to spend another winter in the snow.

24 October 1854

My dearest love,

Before I tell you what has happened, and you are not to interrupt me, I say that you are still my husband, no matter what! I write to tell you, though, that I am mourning you for the second time, and this time I fear it is real. I can barely see to hold the pen, but you have to be on the other end of this letter for me to tell you what has happened. Oh my love, how can I be the one to tell you that you are finally, really, irrevocably dead?

The way I learned of it had all the hallmarks of an awful gothic novel—if it hadn't been so ghastly, I would have laughed to hear it—a dark and stormy night, two o'clock in the morning, a panicked rider on horseback delivering a soggy note, with news of Dr. John Rae's return from the north with news of you and your men. He is a Hudson's Bay Company man, one who assisted good Sir John Richardson on his unsuccessful overland trek to you in 1848. It is frustratingly ironic: the H.B.C. hardly raise a finger in your behalf—with Sir George Simpson saying in 1847 that nothing can be done—and then at the very end one of their own men discover the tragic truth.

We were visiting the Keables in Mortimer Hill and they found us even there—the house was not so large that, in spite of my bedroom being down one wing and away from the entrance hall, I heard all. Sophy kept the note with our hosts for the night, thinking to save me one last night's sleep before breaking the news—she couldn't possibly have known it was playing out before me through the door just as much as if I were there with her. I kept to my room, though, hoping to compose myself in the intervening hours between that moment and breakfast, where I knew I would have to confront her and start my life as a true widow. I could hear her choked sobs for the remaining hours. At breakfast I refused to meet her eyes, and both Sadie and Crispin had found themselves something to do for the entire morning, so we were alone—do you know what she did? She gathered all the jam to her side of the table, and when I was forced to reach out for a pot, she grabbed my hand and made me look at her. All she said was, "Aunt—" and the look in my eyes told her there was no need for more: that I knew. I didn't know the details at that moment, but even without the evidence of your K.C.B. crest, I knew that whatever Dr. Rae had found in that godforsaken wasteland was true. This was, I thought, the bitterest of blows, but more was yet to come. A scribbled private note is one thing, just to pass on the terrible news, but a public scandal, full of salacious detail and flagrant dreadful speculation is the lowest, worst, ever.

All the bluff and bluster of that monster of efficiency, Sir James Graham, is nothing compared to the cold sterility of Dr. Rae's report as it was printed in *The Times*. My copy is stained from the tea I spilled upon first reading it, and by some of my own tears as I was cutting it out this morning with the small shears from my sewing basket—Sophy has still barred me from using the larger scissors after she caught me cutting up those stupid dresses. Who needs those rags unless to bind our courage to the sticking place? She is perhaps right to have taken them away. The raft is still safe in Russell Square.

Just yesterday, when you were still simply dead (!!), the weather was sunny and unseasonably warm, and Sophy had put my tea by the front window, along with the paper, which she knows I like to read in the sunlight as soon as it comes in. I remember we used to do this together, you and I. I suppose she had some other errand to do, but I can't think what it was—she usually wanders through the paper herself, looking for what Princess Potato was wearing when she called on Prince Roast—who knows what she searches for—all the same, the paper was pristine, and a particular treat that morning, since *I* was the one to unwrap the pages and snap them to attention, and I have learned over these last years that one must gather in small pleasures when one can. Ads, personal messages, trade news, Admiralty news I hardly look for anymore, so untrustworthy each announcement seems to me; those men know nothing, you know, and they still don't. They might as well get their news from the paper just like I do.

But having just remarked on the sound of a bird outside my window—not a dirty pigeon, but a migrating songbird, just for me!—and I tell you I was, for one brief moment, at peace somehow in the world, my eye found Dr. Rae's letter, right on page 7: "THE ARCTIC EXPEDITION." I tell you it was no expedition, my poor husband, but a slaughter. A slaughter! A slaughter of you, of your men, of your dignity, of your memories, of all our hearts and hopes here at home—so many stupid paragraphs that led only to your humiliation—shots heard but no food, so much ammunition but no food, so many men and no food—bodies lying on the beach, their guns underneath them, and no food. Bodies in graves, bodies on the shore, bodies under a boat, bodies in tents, bodies in the kettles—Christ, I tremble to write it! One man only who looks like an officer, lies face down on the shore, mutilated and naked. *Mutilated and naked.* Do you hear me? All books destroyed; coins as playthings; bodies torn up and eaten. Torn up and eaten!!

And to crown all, *Dr. Rae* reports in a postscript that he himself passed a fine winter in a snow house, growing fat on birds and deer, warm to his fat guts in deer hide and meat! The last part of his mission was a "failure," apparently, but what doesn't look like a goddamned triumph if you don't get *eaten* by your companions!? His "failure" is a rebuke to the best of you, who died on some march at the end of the world. *Rae* is "abundant" and "comparative comfort" and "ample"; *you* are "fruitless" and "desperate" and "wretched." Are you truly beyond these words that hurt the living so very much? They haunt me every single second since I read them—I cannot divest myself of the thought of what you witnessed, what those poor boys felt, what they may have done. What else can fate throw at you, at us?

The worst part of it all is that now everyone knows. All this was in the *paper* for ridiculous girls to titter over and clutch at their foppish lovers, for arrogant husbands to curl their mustachios and snap the paper in consternation, glancing over at their sallow unhappy wives being mother over their watery teapots—this is the hateful nation you've left me in, full of people who revel in sick details of your death and smear their faces in melted butter while they do it. I hate them! I hate everyone! I love you and want you so very much to come home my love! Oh, please please come home. Please.

10 November 1854

My dearest love,

You will not credit it, but I saw you! Last week in Spring Gardens, sending myself halfway to Bedlam looking at the polar charts, trying to send my vision like a bloodhound on your trail through unknown mazes, the rain rapped suddenly at the window. I glanced out and was drawn to the sight of a man, an officer, approaching Whitehall through the back way, where we used to wander. He was hunched against the rain just as you hunch in your navy cloak; he had your gait, your pace, that sense of purpose I always admired in your walk. With a lurch of my heart I was literally thrown to the window, and my ring knocked loudly against the glass. Of course I was too high to get his attention, and perhaps it was for the best, for how could it really have been you? Writing this now, I feel silly. Sophy, sitting in the corner putting a border on a sampler, glanced up at my sudden commotion, but silently fell back to her task without even a shake of her head. I suspect she fears a recurrence of the Louisa Coppin episode, and looks for signs of my becoming un-hinged. She has conveniently forgotten her own role in that event. She doesn't speak much these days, at least to me. She writes and sews and wears black, as I have begun doing again.

Still, I feel there was something in that vision: you were in the air, and could touch down at any time, like one of your precious arc-tic balloons. And then you did: not two days later I saw you again —not in body of course, but in your sad, few effects: the *Illustrated London News* published an engraving of relics brought back from King William Island by that horrid shifty Scot, Dr. Rae. And do you know what was included in this invidious collection of Rae's? Your K.C.B. crest. There you were, as proudly displayed against a canvas background, surrounded by your officers and men, as if a lost da-guerreotype of you and your crews had suddenly surfaced. I had not expected to see you again so soon. Just as you were supposed to do upon your triumphant return, your few effects are now going on tour, making their way through crowds more maudlin than origi-nally planned.

And what right had Dr. Rae to display you as part of his travel-ling menagerie? None, of course. Those relics are no more his than they were the Esquimaux from whom he procured them—and how *they* came by them is anyone's guess, though none of the ideas *I* have about how this occurred in any way redound on the native character. I was shaken by the surprise of your presence—especially as this display was intended as a post-script to Rae's salacious tale of you and your party, dead, mangled, and neglected on the shores of King William Island. To join that story with the symbol of your military honour is too incongruent, and I steadfastly refuse it. To write any more about Rae's awful tale is to sink to his level.

But at his travelling display I must protest: your few and scat-tered final effects, and those other shockingly insignificant items belonging to your fellows that Dr. Rae has got his hairy hands on, belong with the families whose memories they would serve so well; hands that touched each discarded yet infinitely precious piece of wood or metal were hands much loved; the tines of a fork that held meat to your lips; the handle of a knife grasped between strong fingers; the face of a watch lovingly wound and cared for, tucked in a pocket and warm against a belly. A portion of a pair of spectacles that had been played with by a child before his father's departure. These objects *must belong* to the families who have lost so very much. It is all we have left!

> *A lone broken relic*
> *Brought home from the ice;*
> *For a heart-broken relict,*
> *This alone must suffice.*

Because I simply could not bear to do it, Sophy wrote to Dr. Rae herself, requesting the return of your crest and flatware, and the return of the other items to the families who could identify the objects in question. I confess the letter was somewhat strongly worded; we determined a bold approach was what was needed, given Dr. Rae's innate taciturnity and tendency simply to disappear in silence—whether into the bush or into his outrageous beard, it's all the same. What else could I do? When navigating, one uses the charts one has, and when in foreign waters, one relies on experience and a sense of the wind to guide the way. Perhaps it is needless to say that Dr. Rae did not respond as we had hoped. I believe we did accuse him of thievery—what else could it be?—a label he refuses to accept, just as he refuses to relinquish the last piece of you we may ever recover. No doubt he has an idea that some reward will be coming his way, and he needs to keep the proof about him to support his case.

I feel another public fight coming; today I had a brief note from Mr. Dickens (I know you didn't enjoy *Oliver Twist*, but really some of his writing is quite good and he adores you), who will be taking Dr. Rae's story to task in his weekly magazine, *Household Words*. He says he has "ample evidence" that Dr. Rae's story is simply an impossibility, and plans to take an historical approach by proving

English fortitude in hardship and extremity. Of course, who better could he have to support this argument than you? You, John, are the ideal representative of that proof, are you not? How can you eat poisonous lichen and your own boots on one voyage and the bodies of your comrades on another? The mind and soul revolt equally at the suggestion. I don't subscribe to his magazine, but I will follow his efforts. Mr. Dickens is not the Admiralty, so perhaps he may do something.

In any case, if I have any say in the matter, Dr. Rae will not see a penny of reward until definitive proof of your fate is discovered. If I have any say in the matter, I will send that man to hell.

Would that be a suitable gift for the season?

All love, ever, from
Your Jane

1855

Times *17 February 1855* p9
PROBABLE FATE OF
SIR JOHN FRANKLIN

An additional gleam of light has been cast over the probable fate of the Franklin expedition by an Esquimaux, named Mastitukwin, who accompanied Dr. Rae's party, and who has been for many years a member of the Wesleyan congregation at Rossville, in Hudson's Bay. Dr. Rae has always considered this native highly efficient and trustworthy. On his return to Rossville the Esquimaux stated that he wintered with his party in a snowhouse, where they had six weeks' constant night. In March last (1854) they started, on the ice, to the north, and were 37 days on their northern journey. They were 100 miles beyond the region inhabited by the Esquimaux, but they still found the tracks of the musk ox. Sir John Franklin and his party are dead; but perhaps one or two of the men may still be alive, and among the Esquimaux. Sir John's watch, all in pieces, with his silver spoons, knives, and forks, were found. The ship was a great godsend to these people, and they now all have good sledges, spears, canoes, &c., of oak wood. Dr. Rae and his party did not see any of the remains of Sir John and his party; but the Esquimaux informed him that Sir John was found dead, with his blanket over him and his gun by his side. The probability is that it is not more than two or three years since the party perished by hunger. Such are the words of Mastitukwin's narrative, as detailed to the Rev. T. Hurlburt, of Rossville Mission, Hudson's Bay. They are entitled to credence because the narrator is a native of the country, acquainted with the language, and could have had no object in making a false statement. The various implements made of oak, which were seen in the Esquimaux encampment, prove that they must have had access to at least one of the ships of the missing expedition.

—Athenaeum

20 February 1855

My dearest and *only* love,

An Esquimaux, a travelling companion to Dr. Rae, says he saw your body—you were covered in a blanket. You and your men died of hunger, perhaps three years past. Your watch was found in pieces, and your ships were made into sledges and tools. Your books were broken up and scattered to the winds by Esquimaux children.

In the days just before you left, you shivered in your sleep on the settee, and I placed the Union Jack I had been working on over you to keep you warm. When you awoke, you threw it off with a shudder, telling me that flags get thrown over corpses. It should have been a blanket in 1845; perhaps what the man saw keeping you warm in the north was the flag that had already learned the contours of your body. I made you a shroud, and fit it to you lovingly. I'm so sorry, John.

Your Jane

1 April 1855

My dearest love,

Are you surprised that I continue to write to you even now that I know that you are dead? Habit, I guess. We were often far from each other in life; this threshold you have stepped over now has taken you no further away from me than your precious *Erebus* or *Rainbow* did. On some days I almost feel that you are closer to me now than you have been in years; I can simply reach into the air and touch you, rather than having to rely on the vagaries of wind, weather, and whalers to send a post. I think of you, and you are here. No more slips of paper filled with silly, hopeless thoughts to bridge the distance.

Would it also surprise you to know that I am still urging a search for you? Well, I am. Again, perhaps it's habit, but I feel with a powerful instinct that I must keep trying for you—and if not for you, then for your memory. I alone fight for this—the Admiralty, the public, and even your own daughter have fallen silent.

So to work once more, on what precious little remains of you, my husband! I have in mind three possibilities; a fourth—your discovery alive, or one of your companions—is too remote even to enumerate here and I feel a shiver just writing the words.

First, with one more expedition, perhaps your final resting place will be found; your grave will be for all the civilized world a shrine to duty, to perseverance, to bravery. The shifting Pole must give way to your grave as the Mecca of the far north for all who pilgrimage there.

Second, perhaps even within your grave, or close to the indescribable site reported by Dr. Rae, or *somewhere* on your mysterious path which is little by little known, may be your own collections of letters, notes; documents that would offer me and all of my fellow watchers and waiters here at home a small but priceless relic of your last days. To know from your own hand what befell your poor expedition is a far cry from hearing the story from your own lips, but if it can only be found, it must suffice.

Third, and barring the other two concrete proofs of your trials, I will urge the reconsideration of your memory. I must return to this, for, in the absence of any concrete evidence, what else do I have? You were and are a hero, my darling, and the world must remember you as such. You were a great captain, a brave explorer, a fine administrator, and a proud representative of your nation. You are a good man! But the collective memory of your lifelong goodness is being forgotten amid the scandal of your son-in-law's grasping hands, the Admiralty's short-sighted budgeteering, and Dr. Rae's horrific Esquimaux gossip. As I told you in letters from more hopeful days, *it is for you I live*. If I want to keep on living, I will keep up the fight. You deserve this. I deserve it. And in spite of all, Eleanor deserves the best memory of her father, too.

I write to the Admiralty once I sign off here. Wish me luck.

With all love,
Your Jane

1 July 1855

My dearest love,

The Arctic Committee is convening. As usual I am the thirteenth fairy, not invited to the table and filled with doom and gloom for the heir apparent. This time, it is not your life, or fate, or dignity at stake, but your whole entire purpose in the north, the value of your sacrifice. Captain McClure has started this latest round of betrayals—he has applied for the prize money *still in play* for the title of "discoverer of the Northwest Passage." £10,000, my love, for himself and his crews—those who remain. They were sick with scurvy, on the verge of starvation, and unable to drag themselves over the last piece of frozen ice. They were rescued at the last extremity, and would not have survived had not they been rescued by sledging parties from the East. And here is McClure, ignoring the scathing report of his men's health that is currently before the Board of Inquiry, brazenly demanding a prize that is yours by right—if not the money, at least the title. The route that Dr. Rae outlined in his terrible story put you crossing a better and closer passage a full two years before Captain McClure literally stumbled across his—and it is only through the timely assistance of others that he has a story to tell at all. I am writing to the Admiralty this week with a rebuttal. Let him have the money, if it makes him feel better, but you and you alone deserve the title. You have sacrificed more than enough to get it.

Your Jane

12 August 1855

My dearest love,

Hudson's Bay Company Factors have taken a canoe to find the truth (!!) of Dr. Rae's Esquimaux tale.

Captain McClure has been given the reward. You can guess where the money came from. My letter appears in the appendix, not part of the proceedings proper. Worthy, unworthy. We are on the outside together.

Your Jane

Times *13 August 1855* p4
SIR JOHN FRANKLIN AND THE ARCTIC EXPEDITION

TO THE EDITOR OF THE TIMES

Sir,—I beg to place in your hands, for publication, the letter addressed by Lady Franklin to the Chairman of the Arctic Committee, to which special allusion has been made, in the report of the committee, printed in the columns of *The Times* of yesterday, and to add that I believe the evidence of some of the principal witnesses heard before the committee amply corroborates the claim made by Lady Franklin on behalf of her husband's expedition.

I am, Sir, your obedient servant,
G. BAL
Aug. 11

"60, Pall-mall, *July 5*

"Sir,—I venture to trespass a few minutes upon your time and that of the committee over which you preside in behalf of the claims of my late husband, Sir John Franklin, and his companions, as connected with the object you have under discussion.

"When it is remembered that these brave and unfortunate men, after years of intense suffering and privation, were found dead of starvation upon a spot which they could not have reached without having first solved that geographical problem which was the object and aim of all these painful efforts; and when it is also remembered that they are beyond the reach of their country's rewards, you will not, I think, refuse them the acknowledgment that is due to their memory.

"It would ill become me, and it is far, indeed, from my wish, to attempt to question the claims of Captain McClure to every honour his country may think proper to award him. That enterprising officer is not the less the discoverer of a north--west passage, or, in other words, of one of those links which was wanted to connect the main channels of navigation already ascertained by previous explorers, because the Erebus and Terror, under my husband, had previously, though unknown to Captain McClure, discovered another and more navigable passage—that passage, in fact, which, if ever ships attempt to push their way from one ocean to the other, will assuredly be the one adopted. And it can never be denied to Captain McClure that he is the first who has by his own skill, and mainly by the timely assistance of the brave men who were in search of him, made his individual way from one ocean to the other. Such a transit, though not the object which has engaged the attention of the civilized world for centuries, is a distinction of which any man may well be proud.

"What I presume to claim for those who can urge nothing for themselves is the first discovery of a navigable passage for ships in that unknown space which lay between the discoveries of former navigators, for to such connecting channel has the solution of the geographical problem for many years past been reduced. My husband was specially warned by his instructions not to seek it in the quarter where the Investigator lies, lest impenetrable ice should, as was anticipated, arrest his progress, and he found it, in conformity to his instructions, by acting on the theoretical convictions which Sir John Richardson has shown he deliberately entertained.

"Convinced, Sir, that it must be your desire, and that of the hon. members of the committee, to do justice to the dead, while you duly and generously honour the living, and believing that these two objects do not clash, but may be harmoniously combined, I have presumed thus to address you. I trust you will pardon the widow and the friend this last effort in behalf of those who have nobly perished.

"I have the honour to be, Sir,

"Your obedient servant,
"Jane Franklin
"To the Chairman of the
Arctic Select Committee."

18 September 1855

There are times I worry that I no longer know who I am, that I am what they call me, the "Penelope of England." I think that at one time I have even called myself this, back when I considered your absence some grand romance. Naive! I suspect the press considers this a compliment, but I'm now terribly wise to its true irony.

First, I am no Penelope: I'm far too old and toothless to be much of a prospect for marriage, and as the press is so fond of reminding me, I've already sunk most of my miserable little fortune under the polar ice.

Second, I am no Penelope: I'm far too scattered in both my heart and mind to be the symbol of fidelity the public takes me for. The image of me, in a coach, in an anteroom awaiting an audience with the Lords Commissioners of the Admiralty, taking tea with the unctuous Sir Roderick Murchison at the Royal Geographical Society, always in black, always deep in conversation concerning my absent husband, is all they see—all they want to see. I must admit that I have been complicit in this ruse, but you would know that it hides my true nature. When I first donned my black stuff gown in your behalf I felt invisible, but now, with my celebrity around my neck like a millstone, I know what true invisibility is. People no longer see me; they see what they think I should be, what they themselves wish me to be. In this sense, my celebrity is not really a millstone; it is a mirror in which my audience simply sees a perfected image of itself. And what is that image? Loyal, soaring above despair on the wings of love, and all the old trite orthodoxies of Coventry Patmore and his ghastly "Angel of the House"—what a horrid poem! If only they could know how I have laughed over that ridiculous poem in its application to our lives—if only you were here now to laugh with me at it and at the farce that is my life. I know that not a day went by when I didn't harp at you about something, and not a day went by when you didn't love me more for it—my siren song, you called it, that kept you from your heroic destiny, at home on our own little happy isle. Well, where are you now? Whose siren song fills your ears?

Third, I am no Penelope, because I know that you are not Ulysses—you are Helen, that saucy beauty whose passion for another launched a thousand ships. Your lovely blue serge, the gold epaulettes of your uniform, your Order of the Bath clasped at your neck, and that look in your eye, waving at me but already looking north, already searching a way through the Passage. How like young Helen you were then, and are still, hiding in Priam's frozen city, refusing to come out. If you are Helen, I suppose I must be Agamemnon, the angry, jilted lover—certainly not the image the press would ever approve, not least because then I have a right to go to war to get you back. I have, however, mustered an army to drag you back, and my men—my men!—have thrown themselves at the fortress which has you still: Inglefield, Forsyth, Kennedy, and poor dear Bellot, drowned under an ice floe. Three expeditions, public dishonour at the hands of an ungrateful son-in-law, a death-bed disinheritance from my Father, and all for nothing. And who is Paris? None other than the godforsaken pole itself. But while you put on your masquerades, and push balloon papers through your printing presses, and imagine your triumphant return, I remain here, matched to an aged husband, and dole out laws unto a savage race, who eat and sleep and feed and know not me. In spite of the anger his poem engendered in me, I thank your nephew Tennyson on a daily basis for giving me the words to express my impossible situation.

The sails of my own vessel are exhibiting signs of catching a wind; I've waited here for you, to the best of my ability, for too long already. I fear you wouldn't know me anymore, I've stayed at home waiting for so long. I, too, want to follow knowledge like that polar star you follow. But I don my black dress, and take tea, and write letters, and move the lace curtain aside to glance out the rain-streaked window that shows me how locked in the bowels of London I truly am. Penelope was mother to a people; I am a bossy, premature widow with a taste for argument.

Sophy is patient, neatening the papers at my desk when she notices I've been standing at the window for more than an hour—the chiming of the clock seems to be her cue to transform my space into one of functionality and order, from the chaos of maps, papers, Blue Books, and cups of tea. She calls it her shake of the head, and it clears my attention for the next round of business, whatever it is. Was ever woman so set upon by worry? Was ever king so betrayed? Was ever explorer so lost? And I turn back into Penelope, don my black dress, and take tea, and write letters, and shuffle the lace curtain back in place, and turn away from the window to begin again.

Ever your Jane

1 November 1855

My dearest love,

I am exceedingly angry with you at the moment. All these years I have lugged your small writing desk around with me, treating it not merely as a piece of (awkward) furniture but nearly as a member of the family—indeed, one of the most accurate representations of you I have about me, one of the few things left that still smells of you—though perhaps *you* smelled of *it*. After all this time, that companion betrayed me, and I'm here to protest my ill treatment at its hands. Today a letter of yours fell out of your desk, as I closed a drawer in search of more ink. I have never made a habit of reading your correspondence, unless expressly invited to do so—we always did each other the courtesy of respecting our private writings—but this one I couldn't help. Really, you weren't there to invite, and I hadn't seen your handwriting in so long, just retrieving the pages from the floor and recognising the sharp letters made my throat ache with longing and my hand shake. My eyes blurry with anticipation, my first, naive consideration was that you had meant me to find it, that it was addressed to me, urging me to take heart and not to worry. I flipped the pages and noted it was long, detailed—like your early letters to me, descriptive of the world we would see together; its long paragraphs promised their own romance to my parched memory. Too excited, I couldn't even begin to read the words until I had settled onto the chaise and my eyes had a chance to focus; I saw immediately that it was written from our old rooms in good old Bedford Place—you felt very close to me at that moment, as if you yourself were standing behind my chair, just beyond my vision. To the salutation with relish—and what slumping of back, what cold-ness of hand, what nauseous disillusionment, when I saw it was to your mistress, Lady Whitehall. I border on blasphemy when I write this, I know, the Admiralty is a national treasure, and *your* partic-ular friend, but as I pushed my way through your fervent words I felt like a Pinkerton on a trail of illicit lovers; your enthusiasm, your unalloyed energy, your irresistible masculinity—in short, all that had made me love you—burst from the page—those pieces of you were meant to be mine, but those words, in which you offered your best self, were never for me. You left me no personal note, but copied the offer of your life to the Royal Navy for me to find, after you were long gone. What I know now, too, is that the Navy isn't your mistress; I am. I came second; the Navy came first. How could I ever have had the arrogance to believe otherwise?

15 November 1855

My dearest love,

See how we fall back into those old habits? I fall into you like donning a shawl, or sipping tea. You are as natural, invisible, and necessary: my rainy English afternoon.

A rainy morning, afternoon and evening with no one I wanted to call on, and no one for company. Sophy has taken herself off to a charity supper for the Foundling's Hospital, and I wish her well. I am reverting to my occasional bouts of adolescent frowziness tonight and don't want company. I've been thinking more on your discovered letter, and how it has utterly transformed my impression of your disappearance. In some respects, really, the discovery is a relief: in my darker moments I have had occasion to call my own self to account for your departure; I sometimes wondered if I pushed you too relentlessly to take the captaincy, and that you were simply acquiescing; a quiet, fluid brook flowing past me, your immoveable object of a wife. Was I too ambitious on your behalf? Did I want too much glory for myself by association? I have more than once considered my role in this unfolding horror. The letter, though, recalled to mind a scene in the drawing room I had already—had willingly, forgotten. I remember it in painful detail now. To remind you of it is to make you share my guilt, for you are complicit in all that has unfolded, too.

After Van Diemen's Land we were both so broken, my love. I can admit that now. For one of the first times in my life, I actually felt content to be back in London in the old place and not rushing off anywhere; a few weeks just to recuperate, some months to settle in, and then the rounds begin again—and then in what seems like the flash of a magician's prestige, it was Fall and you were restless once again. I had spent part of my morning inspecting the gardens in Russell Square, saluting our dear Duke as usual and greeting the cinquefoil with its proud, tiny leaves, dainty as fairies' wings. I'm not sure who was gardening then; before Mr. Rowe, I never paid any attention. I breathed in London, and London breathed in me that morning, and I loved it, every soot-begrimed, cobblestoned inch. Even when it rained after elevenses, I hadn't felt cooped in or trapped, just thankful for a comfortable roof and a worthy partner for chess. I set up the board next the window in the drawing room and went to fetch you for a game. You were not in the study, your usual haunt at that time of the morning; I found you up in the bedroom, looking out the window and absolutely still in the rather uncomfortable armchair you had pulled up as close as you could get to the wall. I couldn't see whatever you were looking at; there seemed to be nothing to see. It was after you had already said "yes" to the Admiralty—or, to be strictly accurate, the Admiralty had already said "yes" to you—and all that was left to do was enjoy each other until you set sail again—nothing to yearn for, and enough time to relish the present. Seeing you in your chair, though, I knew you were already imagining yourself there, in all your woolens, breathing in that sharp polar air. It hurt me very much to see you with your back already turned to our bedroom.

Sliding my arm round the front of your neck from behind and keeping my mouth against your ear, I played the familiar trump card, "can't wait to get going, away from the old shoe?"

You turned round, as the moment had been scripted since its first occurrence on our honeymoon, and caught my hand. Ah! Rising, pulling me towards you, you murmured in my ear, "who's an old shoe, then?" with a firm hand against the small of my back.

"Sir, I am nothing but an old shoe, not even worth a glance," I was confident of my line. I looked at the floor as I felt your breath on my neck.

Sure enough, the promise fulfilled: "I can show you what I do with old shoes…" and away from the window and back into the privacy of the bedroom. You; Me. Dashing, valiant, starving hero, permitted, in the last extremity, to dine and survive; modest, unsung object of everyday utility, raised to a hallowed pedestal of life-giving power. Bravissimo!

But, if truth be told, that is not what happened, is it? In spite of my overpowering desire to remember that afternoon in exactly that way, you and I both know that is not how it turned out. So many of those ribald memories of rainy days so admirably filled obtrude on the reality of that particular day, and I thank them for it, but they must be put aside this time for the truth. Loving you silently, intensely for a moment before I began, I slipped my arm round your neck and whispered the familiar words in your ear, "can't wait to get going, away from the old shoe?"

But instead of turning round, you caught my arm and held it with a pressure that almost hurt, keeping your face turned to the glass and saying nothing. I lurched in alarm around the chair to see you; your face was wet from prolonged and silent weeping—I only realised at that moment that I hadn't seen you since 10 that morning; it was now 1 o'Clock; you could have been here the entire period, watching what you considered the remains of your life wash down the streaking windows and into the London gutters.

I knelt beside you and extricated my arm from your distracted grasp, taking instead your hand in mine and placing them in your lap. I was at a loss, but knew something had to be done; to see you like this was to lose everything. I looked at you, and it was all I could muster to admit the truth: "you are ready to go, aren't you?"

Your gaze finally left the window and settled on me. "I'm sorry," you said. "I'm so sorry."

I have been accused of many things by many people. I can see my judges sitting before me—Admirals, Vice Admirals, women on the street, convicts. They imagine that because they are not me they would not make my decisions, but I tell you they cannot make my decisions because they are not me. I own I am guilty of many of the things of which they accuse me: pride, ambition, melodrama, desire, histrionics, a fiery temper, insubordination. Too often they forget love: I am too rarely accused of loving you. Too often they forget fear: I am too rarely accused of being afraid in your behalf. And one thing I shall never be accused of: avarice. I shall never be accused of avarice, as I will spend what little fortune I have, whatever fortune I can put my hands on, the money of a nation, of two nations, of three nations, of an empire, in order to trace my way to you, to bring you back to me. My life is to find you and I will, my husband, my lost Captain.

> *Right where I have always been, I remain,*
> *Your Jane*

15 December 1855

My dearest love,

A brief note, military style, to say regretfully that the war was waged and, I'm afraid, settled inconclusively amid the pages of *Household Words*. Mr. Dickens's "proof" pointed in strange directions, from undisciplined Spanish crews who *did* eat each other, to the improbability of your own noble character succumbing to such desperation. He was correct in stating of you that "the more disciplined the habits... the more unlikely the last resource becomes" and some turns of argument were well placed, but overall his response to Dr. Rae rested on our continuing belief that (in Mr. Dickens's words) the Esquimaux savage is "lying, treacherous and cruel." He leaves the horrific suggestion of *murder* unspoken, but to imagine you and your disciplined, capable party overrun by a disorganized gaggle of seal hunters is as utterly unconvincing as Dr. Rae's bleak nightmarish tale of cannibalism. I am certainly prepared to believe that the Esquimaux are a race of liars—they have done little but engage in storytelling in this whole ordeal, I am convinced. Perhaps they do have a secret. What needles me, however, is that I am not convinced that *you* would feel this way, and so I doubt the completion of Mr. Dickens's case. Would *you* think the Esquimaux liars and murderers? Your gentleness is legend among the polar set—Sir George Back still trots out the tale of your calm response to the attack by a northern mosquito the size of a child's fist on your arm—that "there is room in the world for the both of you"—so I am doubtful you would endorse this tale of fear and violence. I readily suspect, too, that Mr. Dickens himself is guilty of exaggeration, misdirection, indiscretion, as much as I hate to admit it.

Of course I am grateful to Mr. Dickens, and wrote him a letter accordingly. But I suspect that Dr. Rae's frustratingly cogent response to Mr. Dickens's leaders, which were published in *Household Words* in their turn, leaves the argument far from settled. If Mr. Dickens drew from historical experience to prove that Englishmen were not cannibals and Esquimaux were liars, equally did Dr. Rae draw on *his own* life in the north—just as you did when you made your bid for captain in 1844—to support his position that Esquimaux *can be* relied on and that their story is true. Dr. Rae's mistake is not, I think, believing in Esquimaux, but rather, no longer seeming to believe in Englishmen. Perhaps this is where we will win.

Your lass,
Jane

1856

Times *09 January 1856* p10

SIR JOHN FRANKLIN'S EXPEDITION

LIVERPOOL, *Tuesday*

By the Baltic we have advices announcing the return of the Hudson's Bay Company's Arctic expedition, and the confirmation of Dr. Rae's melancholy report as to the fate of Franklin's party.

It will be recollected that Dr. Rae has been employed by the Hudson's Bay Company for the last four or five years in an effort to discover any traces of the remains or the fate of Sir John Franklin and his party; that he has made two expeditions into the Arctic regions for that purpose, and that he was so successful in the last expedition as to discover evidences of the fact that a party of white men, with ships and boats, had perished in that far-off hyperborean region several years ago, which Dr. Rae concluded to have been the ill-fated expedition he was in search of. Beyond finding some spoons and other trifles among the Esquimaux bearing the name of "Franklin," and the above tidings which he gathered from the inhabitants, his expedition amounted to nothing. It will also be recollected that soon after the

conclusion of his last tour the Hudson's Bay Company sent out another party to elicit still more facts on this point, and that, in pursuance of this design, a messenger was sent from their head-quarters in Montreal to Governor Simpson at the Selkirk settlement to make the necessary arrangements for that purpose. Mr. J.D. Stewart and Mr. Anderson were selected for this duty. The full account of Mr. Stewart's expedition and its sad result sheds little new light on the mystery, but confirms Dr. Rae's discoveries. The Montreal *Herald*, of December 24, sums up the conclusion to this mournful tale:—

"One word in conclusion as to the Franklin Expedition. The two vessels, Erebus and Terror, left England in 1843— were last heard of in 1845. They probably tried several passages, but were baffled by the ice, and finally in 1848 were crushed, probably in Victoria Straits. Many of the crews perished, but one or more boats got off with the survivors, who took all the stores they could collect and travelled southward towards the Arctic coast in the hope of reaching some of the Hudson's Bay Company ports. The season of 1849 was probably spent on this dreary journey, and renewed in 1850, when they reached the coast at the mouth of Fish River, but in so exhausted a state that they could merely run their boat on the beach and crawl ashore to die. This seems all that is certain, and all that we can ever know, of the fate of the Franklin Expedition."

---

9 January 1856

My dearest love,

Factors Anderson and Stewart are back, Hudson's Bay Company men in two frail canoes and no interpreter, sent to verify Dr. Rae's findings. They never succeeded in reaching King William Island, and only visited Montreal Island, where they "spoke" for a few moments with some native women, by signs alone. The women rubbed their stomachs and bit their arms. This debased pantomime on a hostile shore is taken as proof that Dr. Rae's story is true. Then the men turned home. They were there a total of nine days, the quality of their provisions and canoes only allowing them such a truncated expedition. Mr. Anderson has lost his voice.

This is how we ring in the New Year. It is all we will ever know.

Your Jane

Times *23 January 1856* p6
THE RESCUE OF
THE DISCOVERY BARK
RESOLUTE FROM THE ICE

This vessel, which was one of five ships sent out in 1852 in search of Sir John Franklin and party, and which was abandoned in 1853, by Sir Edward Belcher, in Wellington Channel, in about lat.76, long. 94, has been recovered, after drifting 1,000 miles, and taken into New London, United States, by Captain Buddington, of the whaling bark George Henry, belonging to that port.

24 January 1856

My dearest love,

Here, for once, my love, is an incredible piece of luck: 129 men lost in the polar fastnesses, hundreds of men off to search, years, ships, so much involved, no-one can find them, years pass ... and suddenly an unmanned ship *sails itself* out of the arctic and meanders down towards the American coast, virtually unscathed! It is for many a freak of polar weather, but for me, it is proof there is hope yet! If one empty ship can drift its way out of the pack ice, what about hardy British men—however few—who know how to read a compass, who know where food caches wait for them? Some of you may yet be living, and the arctic itself has given us one more chance to find you!

The *Resolute*, one of Commodore Belcher's abandoned ships, made it through all on its own, and was "rescued" by an American whaler, who manned it and brought it into New London harbour. It was announced yesterday! It had had a rough journey, having one side sun and one side ice for months on end, and everything out of its place, but there it was sailing itself south. This is a good omen. *This* is how we ring in the New Year!

Your Jane

Times *05 June 1856* p8
RELIC OF THE FRANKLIN EXPEDITION

A box has been received at the office of the American European Express Company, New York, which contains a portion of the relics of the unfortunate expedition of Sir John Franklin:—one piece snow shoe, marked Mr. Stanley (the name is cut into the wood with a penknife); some pieces of cane and wood; one piece leather, the inside of a backgammon board; one piece metal, the graduated part of a barometer; one piece ivory, part of a mathematical parallel rule; one piece ivory, apparently part of a mathematical instrument.

Forgive me, but here is the article as it should have been written: Relict of the Franklin Expedition.—A woman, all in black, has been received at the office of the British Admiralty, London, which represents the life of the unfortunate Rear Admiral of the Blue, Sir John Franklin. One piece Mediterranean, woven from papyrus; one piece Van Diemen's Land, smelling of burnt paper; part London, decidedly sooty; and one incomplete journal, apparently the remains of an unfinished marriage.

Times *25 June 1856* p6

ADMIRALTY, *June 24*

In reference to the announcement contained in the *London Gazette* of the 22d of January, 1856, that the Lords Commissioners of the Admiralty would proceed within three months from that date to adjudicate upon the claim preferred by Dr. John Rae, under the third paragraph of their proclamation of the 7th of March, 1850, by which the sum of 10,000*l.* was offered to any party or parties, who, in the judgment of the Board of Admiralty, should first succeed in ascertaining the fate of the expedition under the command of Sir John Franklin, and that all persons who by virtue of such proclamation deemed themselves entitled to the whole or any part of the reward in question, must prefer their claim within such time—

The Lords Commissioners of the Admiralty hereby declare that they have duly considered all claims preferred by persons deeming themselves entitled under such proclamation to the said rewards therein specified, and have determined Dr. John Rae to be entitled, on behalf of himself and companions in his expedition, to the reward of 10,000*l.* under the terms of the third paragraph of such proclamation as aforesaid.

---

24 June 1856

My love,

The money is now all gone. Of the original £20,000 the Admiralty offered for your rescue, the last £10,000 have gone, this time to Dr. John Rae for "ascertaining the fate of the lost expedition," according to the hateful third paragraph of the original 1850 reward, which we have all forgotten. Actually, it looks like I was the only one not to pay attention, because in looking at the "Blue Book" printed in behalf of the committee, nearly every captain, lieutenant, rating and cabin boy has put his name forward as deserving of at least some part of the reward. It was your K.C.B. crest that finally decided the First Lords—neither you nor any of your men, they estimate, would have given this treasure of British patronage away unless at the last extremity, and from your cold, lifeless hands it and other small treasures provide the irrefutable evidence that there is no one left. I have done what I could, my darling. What could one woman do? Even Penelope faltered, and in this modern age the beleaguered queen can't fall back on ancient craft. In this modern time, I did simply what I had to: put myself in the path of the oncoming train, only to be pushed unceremoniously aside by the cowcatcher of progress and forced to watch from the gravel side as decisions about your life, death, and memory are made in the dining car, by people who neither know or understand you. We are finally alone, you and I. Don't worry, my love, I am keeping my promise to you.

> *In the absence of all other evidence to the contrary, I am still,*
> *Your wife*

15 July 1856

My dearest love,

Perhaps there are happy days ahead! According to the papers, the American Congress has refit the *Resolute* once again for Arctic service and is having it sailed back to England to begin its work anew! Not since our first hopes with Sir James Ross has there been such an optimistic gesture in our behalf, in your behalf. This is good, very good. Sophy is hard at work sleuthing out the whereabouts of remaining idealistic Captains and Lieutenants, those who might think it worthy of their time to lead one final expedition in your behalf, and I am considering whom to ask first. We've had no word from the Admiralty as to what might happen to the ship—worryingly, no expeditions seem in preparation in the least—but I will be ready with options.

Your resourceful Jane

20 September 1856

My dearest love,

I am sorry for my silence; once again the doctor has forbidden reading and writing, urging only bedrest. He might as well say "torture." I have hibernated through the summer season, but could stay inside no longer, despite the pain. Really, today I felt I must get up or die. It was not so much that I was more terrified of death today than usual, or of growing old—it's too late for that fear to catch hold, I know— but I was suddenly terribly afraid of dying without one last rush of feeling, one last thrill of the heart. Teeth have gone missing, throats closed with sickness, eyes have gone bleary, and hands sometimes shake with palsy, but the heart seems to retain a youthful frenzy, no matter how slowly or feebly it beats. My weeks of bedridden misery had made me desperate for a walk; I still can't talk, I can hardly read, and Sophy now leaves the soup on the table by the window for me to reject in private, rather than show her disappointment at my lack of enthusiasm. But today the clouds outside the window were calling to me, and I saw they were gathered over Russell Square. I wanted to see the flowers in the varied light of an oncoming storm.

While Sophy stoked the fire in the morning room, I pulled myself feebly from the blankets, my legs almost buckling at first from standing for the first time in weeks. I would never have called myself an elegant woman, but this morning I lurched like a wounded soldier to my dressing room, grabbing the back of the chair by the window with one hand for support, the other at my throat, as if to contain its soreness. Sophy heard me; she knocked to warn me of her approach.

"Aunt! You should stay in bed. The day isn't warm—you can't go outside!"

As I turned to respond sharply to her, a dragon sank its teeth into my living throat: swallowing is still agony; speaking impossible. With my chair hand I waved her away, and managed to walk upright into the dressing room, where my most comfortable (and last) black silk dress, with the ruffles around the collar, awaited me. The ruffles have saved it so far from the mourning dress cull—they may look delicate, but they are my secret armour against pain. I donned them like a talisman, a glowing star upon a shield. Sophy is a smart young woman, and she wordlessly helped me dress. She did not look me in the eye. Instead, she returned to the morning room and gathered our shawls, which she had warming by the fire. She gave both to me after fastening my bonnet under my chin, wrapping the first around my shoulders, and the second more tightly around my throat. I looked slyly at her, giving her the benefit of two quickly raised eyebrows. I felt like a highwayman; she rolled her eyes but smiled. She took my arm and led me carefully down the corridor to the front hall. I pulled on her to stop at the entrance table, where I scribbled a few words on a piece of paper. Sophy read it as I handed it to her, unfolded. Her lips pursed slightly, as if she didn't understand, or didn't approve. I pulled on her arm again to get her started.

Somehow, Thomas had anticipated our progress, and was found to be already waiting for us outside in the carriage. I remembered, then, that it was the regular morning for my weekly constitutional—since I've been bedridden, I wonder how often Thomas has sat out front, waiting for us. I have no idea if Sophy took advantage of his services while I was too ill to move. I wonder if he has mentioned to Mary how seldom I've been out of late.

Sophy was right; the day was not warm, but with a bonnet and two shawls, and the anticipation of even a short walk, I was buoyant in spite of the pain. Sophy spoke briefly to Thomas: "Russell Square this morning, please." I saw her touch his shoulder. The wheels rolled, the breeze cooled the skin around my eyes—almost all of me that was visible beyond my cocoon of black wool and silk, and the morning of London unfolded around us. Even Sophy was interested, though she pulled her eyes away from the passing market stalls and omnibuses every now and then to cast her eyes on me. Occasionally she readjusted my shawls, but I suspect she did this more to remind me of her presence than for any practical purpose. I kept my eyes straight ahead, anticipating the next turn, watching beside the horse's head for the telltale dark brown brick of the Bedford Place terraces, our standard approach to the garden.

We turned off Bedford Place and stopped along Montague, and after briefly soothing the horse, whom he loves, Thomas jumped down to offer me his hands. I gratefully took them; he is tender to all mute beasts, and I am happy always to be another in his collection. When he offered his hands to Sophy, I put my hand on his arm. Sophy raised her eyes from Thomas's hands to his eyes—no look of surprise, but a look of knowing within them. She rested back in the seat and returned her gaze to the middle distance. I turned to the garden.

My walk was slow, and it was a mental effort to keep one hand from constantly clutching my throat; the best I could do was an almost rhythmic light touch: step, touch, step, touch. I needed a baton; I could be on parade—Sick Parade, you would have liked that one. But really—what am I thinking? I didn't go there for you. The extremity of my sickness betrayed my heart, and I was there for the selfishness of my own pleasure that could not be denied. My voice no longer works; I've lost all sense of taste, but I see and hear and touch and smell, and all these things I love most when I am here in the garden.

My salute to the Duke was silent, but I sensed his welcome and entered. I headed straight to the fountain, which seemed overly exuberant to my cloistered ears. Some children were playing quietly nearby, and a woman was feeding some pigeons by the bordering trees. I saw through the water that Mr. Rowe had already installed himself on a ladder as usual in the lime tree bower. When you and

I are on our raft, I feel he watches over me like a benevolent care-
taker; I am one more vulnerable shrubbery for him to care for. But
today was not for sitting: it was for movement. He faced me but
didn't see me; his concentrated gaze fell on a supple branch he was
bending into form. I could tell by the movement of his lips he was
talking to it; describing its beauty, convincing it of its larger purpose, loving it in the same way Thomas loves the horse. I stood still
and watched him there, and when he finished and descended, he
stood with his hands on his hips, smiling. Slowly, his gaze fell to
me, a black smudge against the greens and whites and pinks of his
garden, distorted by the fountain and by the doubled shawl at my
throat. He smiled again, and my parade hand moved to my throat,
which flared suddenly with a single surge of heat. I moved to the
left, walking around the fountain on the outside of the bower to
the perennial bed at the corner of Thornaugh Street. It was shadier
there; my dress didn't present such a challenge to the darker trees
and bushes. I'm still small enough that I almost disappeared behind
the taller perennials; between the rose and the holly, I was practically invisible. The path makes a sharp turn to the right; instead
of looking into the trees of the border my gaze turned back to the
garden, toward the lime tree bower, and there at the end of it, with a
branch of fresh-cut rosemary in his hand, was Mr. Rowe.

I kept to the path but took the left turn, which again took me beyond the bower and along the edge of the garden. As I approached
Mr. Rowe, he stepped onto my path and silently extended the rosemary to me, which I took in my free hand, my other continuing
its marching rhythm on my throat. Our eyes met and I gave him
a silent salute, and he nodded very slightly. Like the good Duke at
the entrance with his plough, I sensed his welcome, as well. I did
not pause in my walk, but continued to skirt the edge of the garden, along Bernard Street and behind the bun shop. Once again I
was invisible, though my mind reached over the small building and
tables to imagine the loving hands shaping the bower. As I rounded the corner of the café, I was surprised to meet Mr. Rowe again,
waiting for me at the end of this corner bed, this time with two pur-

ple bachelor buttons, their deep green leaves extending like hands, and cross-hatched buds pushing their way open above them. As he placed them in my hand, his look was the same one he gives to his lime trees; if to Thomas I am a horse, for Mr. Rowe I am a tree—no sapling, surely, but one he nevertheless tends with care. My eyes stung with the recognition of tenderness and I had to look away. If my throat hurts at the best of times, crying would tear it apart. But my throat was not the only part of me in danger of breaking. I moved toward the centre of the park, back to the fountain, and brushed against the far tables of the shop with the skirt of my dress. I could hear soft conversations from the open doors—people were inside to drink their coffee and tea today, keeping out of the breeze. Mr. Rowe had disappeared again behind me, and I continued once more past the fountain and down to the corner bed at Montague Street, from where I could see the back of the Museum looming over the trees. All the world's knowledge in one glossy building, and 129 men missing in a mess of frozen water, one old woman with a sore throat telling the Admiralty of an Empire it's wrong, and one silent gardener making her feel alive, perhaps for the last time in her life. I was suddenly, violently disgusted with the meaninglessness of grand gestures, and turned my eyes to the gravel, where beetles and ants were gathering their prizes—seeds and crumbs left from yesterday's luncheons. It occurred to me then that the most important life happens at the level of the invisible, and wanted to scream with rage at the thought of the futility in all our petty ambitions. I passed between the bed and the bordering trees. This bed has the tallest roses, and as I walked slowly by them the buds nodded their heads to me, giving me absolution for my momentary flash of hatred. I breathed in their scent along with the rosemary, and felt the slight weight of it and the bachelor buttons against my arm. I was back in the present and even saw a break in the cloud cover, and the pale blue background gave the roses an angelic crown. I was still looking back at the roses when I rounded the corner of the bed, and the scrape of gravel at its end surprised me. I looked forward again, to avoid running into playing children or a curious dog, and there, once again, was Mr. Rowe, waiting respectfully at the edge of the path, with four pale pink roses, from the same bush, I am certain, from which he cut my first widow's boutonniere those summers ago. Their blooms were perfect, their stems the exact length of the bachelor buttons. The thorns had been removed. As I moved by, he placed them silently on my arm.

My legs were almost at their limit, but I was determined to navigate the last bed, the one with my favourite flowers in it. It's perhaps the most modest—the flowers are shorter, the spaces between them more distinct—but I have ever been inspired by their hardihood; their littleness is no barrier to their strength. From the corner of my eye I took attendance: lamb's ear, bleeding heart, campion, rosemary, phlox, cosmos. From under the shawl I almost felt a smile emerging, and my heart slowed with the feeling of returning home. When I looked up again to once more round the corner of the bed, Mr. Rowe was there, with his final addition to my bouquet: a single stem of perfect campion, full of burning pink petals and icy grey leaves. I could only look him deeply in the eye as I silently accepted his last gift; we have not spoken in months, and I had not once slowed my progress through his garden today. His gift was a path of passing beauty in a terrible world, and somewhere in the darkness, with danger all around, we two weary travellers had found one another. This fragile raft of Russell Square garden, with its tender lime branches and suckling buds, cannot last forever, but we two will cling to it as long as we can. For the first time since I arrived, just before I walked past the Duke's statue and out again onto Montague Place, I paused and turned to give Mr. Rowe the only thanks I could. One hand was at my throat, while the other moved the flowers toward my heart. He stood still where he was, his hands at his sides. Looking steadily at me, he nodded slightly and turned away.

From some deep recess in his waistcoat, from some long-forgotten trip to the countryside, Thomas had managed to find a grass stalk, and was chewing on it thoughtfully while he waited for me to return. They did not go shopping, but stayed there, not knowing how long I would be. Sophy's anticipation of my wishes had prompted her to bring—and then hide—her own solitary pleasure, and she tucked her yellow-back novel away in her skirt when she noticed my approach. I don't mind so much anymore—there is so little pleasure in the world for women in our position, I have to let her have it. Her eyebrows rose briefly at the bouquet in my hand, but she remained silent, knocking at the back of Thomas's seat to get his attention. Thomas stepped down, ambled around the horse, and guided me safely back into the carriage by the elbow, nickering quietly at me as he made sure I was settled in the seat. Both he and Sophy checked my shawls. He easily swung himself back onto the box, clucked once, and we began the journey home. This time I closed my eyes, and relived my silent walk through the garden of my youth—though this time everything had changed: at the end of each bed, around each corner, was not my girlish ambitions, my wifely plans, my dreams of life beyond London; it was Mr. Rowe, silently waiting with a flower in his hand.

Sophy put me quickly back to bed; I can't quite remember how she manoeuvred me out of my dress and back into my nightgown, but I slept for hours without moving. I can tell this because of a soreness in my hip when I awoke this morning. And it *is* morning again—I must have slept all day: the blinds are ajar, and sunlight now takes a guarded approach through the lace curtains to a small table that has been placed beside the bed. On the table, illuminated by the single drift of light through the otherwise obscure room, a vase of flowers watches over me.

Jane

Times *13 December 1856* p10
THE FRANKLIN EXPEDITION

On Wednesday evening last a public meeting, attended by most of the distinguished Arctic voyagers who have been hitherto engaged in the search after Sir John Franklin, was held at the Russell Institute, to consider whether the probabilities of success in consequence of Dr. Rae's discoveries were such as to justify a new expedition.

25 December 1856

My dearest love,

Forgive me: I am tardy in my writing, but events have moved so thick and fast around me, I can hardly keep up. I didn't want to miss a thing. In November the *Resolute* made her way back to England, under the captaincy of a gracious American, Captain Hartstene, and just last week she was visited by Her Majesty, who is, as even *The Times* is forced to admit, "very anxious for another expedition." On Wednesday last there was a public meeting at the Russell Institute, and attended by all the young men who have made their name in yours, distinguishing themselves in ingenuity and hardihood as well as loyalty to the cause of humanity: Osborn, Inglefield, Mr. Barrow—even Dr. King (though I can't credit that he has any designs that do not have himself at the centre). They were gathered to *you*, my love—to make a powerful public appeal to the Admiralty for *one last expedition*. With the *Resolute* at our fingertips—and another expedition urged by the Queen herself!—we can't lose. Sir Roderick Murchison of the Royal Geographical Society has written, Captain Pim, Captain Collinson, Captain Inglefield—it is all over *The Times* and everywhere once again in people's hearts. There is a banquet for the officers of the *Resolute,* brave and lovely Americans whose captain has offered me his services, to take the ship once again into the frozen world for which she was intended, and make good on the promise that was made when she sailed south to be found. For the first time in so long, it feels like the universe is about to say "yes." I am leaning forward to hear it.

Your Jane

1857

Times *06 January 1857* p12
NAVAL AND MILITARY INTELLIGENCE

The Resolute Arctic discovery ship, which has been towed by the Dragon, 6, paddle-wheel-steamer, Captain W. H. Stewart, from Portsmouth to Chatham, has been lashed alongside the shear-hulk at Chatham Dockyard, where she remains an object of great interest. It is understood to be the intention of the Admiralty to have her stripped and placed in ordinary at Chatham.

8 January 1857

My dearest love,

I cannot rest these days or nights—the wind is terrible, and sounds like my heart beating on the window pane. I can never offer you a decent New Year's wish: every turning from December to January brings with it only despair. At first I thought it was me, but looking back through my letters I see that it's not: terrible things really *do* happen in January!

Let me tell you of something that has frightened me. It is a moment that has repeated itself many times over the last years: I am standing under the lime tree bower—the slow rain has stopped, but I feel the dark broodiness of the clouds on my brow, and feel deliciously invisible in the shadows of the canopy. Mr. Rowe has emerged from his potting shed; I don't want to admit it, but I recognize him with a rush of pleasure—his company is a source of comfort to me that I cannot get from you no matter how often I write. We discuss plants, and the weather—in England, in London, in the little microcosmos that is Russell Square—and I don't think at all, for these brief periods, of my starving heart. Indeed, it was with some little guilt that I realised after my sojourn to the bower last week that in fact his company made me physically improve—it was the closeness to the plants, I'm sure, but I can't deny that his attentiveness made me feel more, even the sensation of my own dress against my skin, after our meetings. Am I disloyal to you? I think not, my love, but I find I have grown tired of being alone, or grown tired of playing the widow, or grown tired of only being known for my associations with you. It is all I do now, and I want another consciousness—not just of my position, but of my own experience. *I* want to follow knowledge like a sinking star—but what is left for me? Only knowledge of my self—every other option is simply scandalous. So I drink in Mr. Rowe's company among the flowers, and imagine another existence amid the blooms of Russell Square, that he and I have grown old together and live in France, where he tends to Paris's public gardens and I run a scientific society for young women, that the Northwest Passage was discovered just past the Croker Mountains by senile Sir John Ross, that Captain Sir John and Lady Eleanor Franklin are living comfortably in a rented Tudor manor somewhere in the West Country, where Sir John breeds sheepdogs and an aging but healthy Eleanor still dabbles in poetry, when she's not caring for her three daughters' many children, whom she adores and who adore her equally. There are times when this is almost real—and my heart is both broken and whole when it feels so, but when the fantasy ends, I am left simply broken.

You know, I could have been somebody different than I am now, somebody bigger; I had a romance once with Peter Mark Roget, who was working on his *Thesaurus* even while we were courting. I did really consider it; he was excessively refined and I thought him very handsome, and generally good company, especially in public. But his constant need for reassurance in private, touching at first, wound so tightly around me I could scarcely breathe. Being with him was like being tied to a wharf post with an incoming tide; there was no escape and the cold waves of his insecurities seeped ever closer, causing slow but inexorable suffocation.

I could also have been somebody smaller; my Italian language master was as much a catch as I was in the early days, and I would have happily spent my youth strolling through piazzas, discussing Renaissance art and coping with a hopeless addiction to coffee. The trouble with that one, was that I was already too much of a nobody to be somebody for him.

One had no room for me to move in; the other too much. You met me right in the middle, and there I must be content to stay whatever the circumstances. I would rather be the widow of a perfect husband, I suppose, than a wife in an unhappy marriage.

Your widow,
Jane

15 January 1857

My dearest love,

A plan has been hatched between Sophy and me: I will ask them for the loan of the *Resolute*, and will man it myself by public subscription. Captain Hartstene will command, and perhaps Osborn and McClintock will assist. At no cost to themselves beyond a few men and the arctic stores now mouldering at Portsmouth, the Lords cannot deny me this—it would rest so heavily on their consciences, not even their somnolent lordships could sleep.

As always, I remain,
Your Jane

Times *24 January 1857* p10
NAVAL AND MILITARY
INTELLIGENCE

The Resolute Arctic exploring ship, stationed at Chatham, has had nearly the
whole of her internal fittings removed,
and yesterday her water tanks were taken
out and placed in the dockyard. The men
belonging to the dockyard are busily engaged dismantling her, and a great part
of her rigging has been removed. She is
lashed alongside the Resistance, but will
be removed to the sheer hulk for the purpose of having her masts taken out.

25 February 1857

My poor, dear love,

There is no predicting the perversity of the Lordships' whims. No
Resolute. First Lord Sir Charles Wood has spoken, and Belcher's
abandoned, rescued, miraculously hopeful gift from the Arctic itself is not to sail again—to you, or to anywhere. While sensible to
the earnest feelings of the Americans, and aware that Great Britain's
own established scientific bodies as well as the public urge one final
expedition to the locale delineated by Dr. Rae, it is not to be. The
Resolute will be stripped of all its materiel and left in Woolwich, and
never to set her cap, as she did in 1852, at you again—nor even to
leave harbour. She will lay on her side in the muck and slowly be
flensed of all her value, like a whale. Some of her will be made into
a keepsake desk, in appreciation of the efforts the American people undertook to furnish and return it to England. The rest of her
will be left to rot. 40,000 American dollars they voted, and spent,
in order to bring her back to us. She will be a desk. I am not much
prone to wishing ill on others, but may the letters the Admiralty
lords write on that desk—and the lords themselves who use it—
carry with them for ever more the stench of guilt, of avarice, of ex-
pediency, of the terrible triumph of bureaucracy over compassion.

As they contend, too much money, too many lives have already
been expended, and they cannot do more. Sir James Graham, in

1854, gave me the courtesy of a private letter when he decided to declare you dead. Today, I read about your final, irrevocable abandonment in the paper. For the rest of the nation, and now for me, it is news to shiver over while crunching on toast.

But I am not quite finished, my love. This is my promise to you. If I cannot *have Resolute*, then I will *be* resolute, and I will not abandon hope no matter the cost. I have already lost so much—what more is there that is worth anything? We are back to Tennyson and his silly poem—which he thought was about heroes, but is really about their poor abandoned families: for you, my husband, I vow to strive, to seek, to find, and not to yield.

> *I am your Ulysses, your Penelope, your Agamemnon,*
> *Your Jane*

Times *15 April 1857* p6

SIR JOHN FRANKLIN'S EXPEDITION

We have for several years past most urgently and consistently opposed any further expedition to the Polar Seas in search of the relics of the Erebus and Terror. We are fully persuaded that many years ago the last survivor of the unfortunate expedition in which Sir John Franklin and his companions were engaged had ceased to exist. We rejoiced in the recent determination of the Admiralty not to throw away good lives after bad, and to refuse absolutely the countenance of the Government to any further explorations in the Polar Seas with the hope of recovering that which had long since perished. When we say thus much it will not be supposed that we are asking for any assistance from the public authorities, or even from the public, towards a new expedition which Lady Franklin has set on foot. This lady, as we

have been given to understand, has embarked the last relics of her fortune in an ultimate expedition, which is to be directed towards that particular spot of the Polar regions where tidings may be expected from the Esquimaux of the lost voyagers. The expedition we believe to be a Quixotic one; but who will venture to speak with disrespect, or even with indifference, of the efforts—ay, of the desperation of Lady Franklin, in such a cause? Looking at the matter as one of plain common sense, we believe that speedier and cheaper access to the region in question might be obtained by overland and smaller excursions from the extreme settlements of the Hudson's Bay Company; but Lady Franklin has resolved upon a final expedition by sea, and therefore we can only say "God speed" to the adventurers in so noble a cause. Public assistance to this bereaved lady might have been given in one way. What if the old Resolute had been handed over to her as a gift from the English public? The sea-battered and ice-worn ship might thus have been turned to some account, and Lady Franklin might possibly have been saved some expense. We can form no favourable expectations as to the results which may be looked for from this last Arctic Expedition; but, as far as Lady Franklin is concerned, she has every right to the sympathy of her fellow-countrymen.

---

25 April 1857

My dearest love,

It is done: the little schooner *Fox* is mine, Captain McClintock has asked for and been granted leave for the period of two years, he is following my instructions, the men are aboard, and I am coming to get you.

  The little *Fox* is just the perfect vessel to find whatever is left of your sad memory and your poor companions—it is a former pleasure craft, one that you and I would have revelled in had we had it for a cruise in the Mediterranean. It was only after many sighs and wistful fingerings of the velvet tapestries in the stateroom that I determined all its refinements had to go—it had to fit a crew of 24 plus all the overwintering gear, hawsers, extra wood, pemmican and shelter—these things the Admiralty have given me outright, along with Captain McClintock, who has been more steadfast than most in believing in you, and in me. He is the only one I trust anymore to complete the task that is before him: if he can't find *you,* then he will find what he needs to secure your memory. To sweep away the rest of the dark shadows, my love: that is all I ask him to do.

Times *30 April 1857* p9
LADY FRANKLIN'S EXPEDITION

Lady Franklin has resolved to send out another and a final Expedition in search of whatever trace may exist of the lost crews of the Erebus and Terror. We have so often and so earnestly come forward to deprecate the renewal of these Expeditions in a public sense, that we cannot now with any reasonable grace advocate the propriety or policy even of this limited attempt. The thing, however, is to be. Already a screw yacht, the Fox, now lying at Aberdeen, has been purchased, and the command is to be given to Captain McClintock, who has already distinguished himself even among the adventurous band of Arctic Navigators. Thus much, however, we may venture to say, that it is impossible not to respect the noble pertinacity of Lady Franklin; and, since another of these desperate ventures is to be made, it would be a pity that the last relics of her little fortune should be sunk under the Polar ice. Others may look at this question from a different point of view, and may still entertain hopes which we have long since resigned. If any such there should be, we would call their attention to the fact that a subscription list has been opened for the purpose of assisting Lady Franklin in this her last effort. We can give no further aid to the cause. We entirely approved the determination at which the Admiralty recently arrived, not to send out any more Arctic Expeditions at the public expense. Year after year they were despatched, and, save the barren honour of having achieved the North-West Passage, we know not what we have gained by these hazardous struggles among the eternal ice. Others, however,—we repeat it—may take a different view of the matter, and, certainly, as far as Lady Franklin's cause is a sacred one, we very heartily wish that we could, in conscience, give it a more hearty support. Sir Roderick Murchison, however, Sir Francis Beaufort, Lord Wrottesley, General Sabine, and many other gentlemen of high scientific eminence, are strenuously exerting themselves to promote the objects of the Expedition, and it may be that the announcement of this fact may induce others to follow their example. The advertisement in which they develop their views will be found in another portion of our impression of yesterday. For one thing, however, we stipulate. Let it be clearly understood by Captain McClintock and his officers and crew that, come weal, come woe, another series of voyages in search of them is not to be commenced. After an infinite series of hairbreadth escapes all the other search Expeditions have safely returned; let us not incur the liability of having to send out half-a-dozen others in search of one from the success even of which very little is to be expected.

8 July 1857

My dearest love,

Sophy and I have seen the *Fox* off in Aberdeen, and now back home we are preparing for our own departure. I can't bear to be in England any longer, let alone in London.

I have even said goodbye to Russell Square; we stopped there just this morning, though it wasn't my usual day. This time I allowed Sophy to accompany me, as the gardens have become as much a part of her life as they have ever been of mine—though her time in the carriage has been her own as she has waited for me over the years. Thomas, ever the silent watcher, helped us both down with no comment, though I saw his eyes meet Sophy's with some silent understanding. I no longer resent them and their secret language of managing me: I don't have the energy. I don't know how much longer any of us will last.

The Duke took my admittedly indifferent address with his usual gentility—he has got used to my mood swings, but I suspect he knows as well as I do that we will not see each other for some time. It is with a heavy heart that I say good bye to two of my favourite men in London—the Duke, of course, and to you—of course you are not here, but everything that surrounds me is suffused with the feeling, the memory, the smell, the purpose of you, and I simply can't bear it any longer. Every piece of paper on my writing desk, every cup and saucer in the cupboard, every new black dress in my wardrobe, every street drowning in the soupy fog of its own coal fires. These either remind me of my own pathetic widowhood, or they remind me of my happier times as your wife, and I truthfully cannot decide which is more terrible. Yes, I am a widow, a widow, a widow. But I am still a wife. You have not come home, but you haven't told me yet that you are not coming, and so I am caught as surely as you are in the fastnesses of ice, between progress and stasis, life and death. Your death, my life: what difference does it make anymore? For so many years—nearly half our marriage—I have waited for you to come home. I must tell you, my lovely husband, that I simply cannot do it anymore. I'm so very tired, my heart is so sick, my throat is so sore, and I'm just too tired. We did not see Mr. Rowe, though we waited.

Sophy and I need some time away from the maps, and from the grief. First we go to the Keables, to wend our way one last afternoon through their dappled orchard, and to sit one last time at the best table in England. We are going to the continent, and will be gone a long while. We may even lose ourselves in anonymity. I do not expect Captain McClintock to return until 1859, and do not think I will survive if I stay, with the expectation of more waiting, or more disappointment if the expedition is unsuccessful. The sweet men left cheering, but in my deepest heart I fear that what they will encounter will be no cause for celebration. Let them find something, anything, to redeem you, my love. You must have left something behind. Let us find it.

I will not be taking this journal with me when I go this time; you will have to get used to my silence.

I will always be,
Your Jane

AFTERWORD

Some have suggested that Lady Franklin never really loved Sir John. I disagree, though the historical record is imperfect in finding proof for either position. As most of her biographers acknowledge, Lady Franklin destroyed or altered so much of her personal correspondence and private writing that it remains largely a matter of speculation. Given her intense, prolonged, excruciating efforts to find Sir John after 1847, I choose to believe in her love for him, and I have written this novel, imagining her unrecorded private life during the years of search, with this in mind. She was herself an extraordinary woman caught up in extraordinary events, and she more than rose to the occasion. Today, I would say that we know who Sir John Franklin is largely because of her.

It is easy to become immersed in stories about the Franklin Expedition. The story itself is deeply compelling: two ships lost in a small blank space on a map; gun shots heard in the distance; boats, books, and bones on a trail leading south. The hunt for the men, and then the hunt for Franklin's two missing ships, the *Erebus* and *Terror*, has gone on basically unabated from 1848 until 2016, when the second of his two ships was found by the Arctic Research Foundation. Though European searchers came and went, since 1848, the narrative trail also remains unbroken, most significantly through Inuit oral history: Louie Kamookak (1960-2018), an Inuit historian, provided Parks Canada and ARF researchers with testimony he remembered from his family and community in order to locate the *Erebus* in 2014. All of this is now public record. Lady Franklin's involvement in the search, too, is a matter of public record: tirelessly, she wrote to newspapers and to politicians in an attempt to move the Government, as well as the English public, to continue the search for Sir John. Sometimes these efforts backfired: as the searches wore on, she received perhaps more than her fair share of criticism. That said, as her son-in-law John Gell admitted in one of his letters published in the *Times*, "dealing with her" was never a job for the timid or the shy. Though through sheer force of will and canny use of her pocketbook, she threw ships, men, and resources at the Arctic as much as she could, nothing more than the Victory Point record, a single piece of paper recording Sir John's death as 11 June 1847, was found in her lifetime. She never stopped looking for him: in 1870, Lady Franklin and Sophy Cracroft travelled to Alaska, where they continued to question people who may have had news of Sir John and his fate. When she died in 1875, her own epitaph read that she had gone, like Tennyson's Ulysses, "to seek and to find" Sir John beyond the sunset. This short dedication acknowledged what has ever been for me the two parts of Lady Franklin that keep me coming back to her life and character: her dedication to Sir John and his name, but also her own unquenchable sense of adventure for the life that had spread out before her, her own blank map waiting to be filled.

THE END

Acknowledgements

First thanks go to those without whom the novel would never even have been imagined: to Professor Mel Wiebe and Dr Mary Millar of the Benjamin Disraeli Project (Queen's University), who first introduced me to Lady Franklin's writing and to the pleasure of reading lives lived in letters. Grateful bows also to Christine Fader and Julia Blackstock, who heard and responded to parts of the narrative in its early stages. A huge thank you, too, to my writing mentor, Helen Humphreys, who offered expert guidance. Final thanks to Julie Yerex and Netta Johnson of Stonehouse Publishing, who helped the book take its exciting final steps.